"Are you ready to go home?" Kirkland asked.

Cassidy stood frozen in the middle of the waiting area. She summed up the situation, without any concept of time, as Kirkland stood at the door waiting. A too-sexy man, eight years her junior, had kissed her and now he had come to check on her daughter at her doctor's appointment. When Cassidy looked at Kirkland she saw a young man who was bold and reckless, hot and spicy. He had a body designed to be a woman's playground. His smile made the most sanctified woman a sinner. Men like Kirkland didn't pay pediatrician doctor bills and buy baby seats.

What were his motives? His sister-in-law had warned her he couldn't be trusted. She'd also heard rumors about his conquests. He had a reputation for being an educated, well-off, ladies' man. Handsome and suave, he had a gift for getting what he wanted, and smiling like an adoring little boy the entire time he took what he needed. Hard to believe this Kirkland was the same man who delivered her baby, looked at her like she was a precious jewel, bonded with Courtney, and kissed her like she was the object of his greatest desire. Too many men wrapped into one. Her life was too complicated for casual sexual encounters, and she couldn't begin to figure out how he would fit into her and Courtney's life in any other way.

She didn't know her own motives when it came to Kirkland Ballantyne. The thoughts she had about him late at night made the steamy romances she drew covers for seem like kiddie picture books. He scrambled her mind and warmed her body. As she watched him standing at the door of the clinic, she realized she needed a man in her life. She wanted a man in her life. A strong man who could rule her body and run her household. A man to raise and protect her baby. Her mother might have been right about a couple of things after all.

# To Love A Ballantyne

# Kimberley White

ARABESQUE

BET BOOKS™

**BET Publications, LLC**
http://www.bet.com
http://www.arabesquebooks.com

ARABESQUE BOOKS are published by

BET Publications, LLC
c/o BET BOOKS
One BET Plaza
1900 W Place NE
Washington, DC 20018-1211

All Kensington Titles, Imprints, and Distributed Lines are available at special quantity discounts for bulk purchases for sales promotions, premiums, fund-raising, and educational or institutional use. Special book excerpts or customized printings can also be created to fit specific needs. For details, write or phone the office of the Kensington special sales manager: Kensington Publishing Corp., 850 Third Avenue, New York, NY 10022, attn: Special Sales Department, Phone: 1-800-221-2647.

First Printing: April 2005
10 9 8 7 6 5 4 3 2 1

Printed in the United States of America

# Prologue

Kirkland Ballantyne's stomach wound up in a tight knot as he stepped across the threshold of his oldest brother's elaborate home. He followed Greyson into the study, doubting his sanity in coming. He had the crazy notion to run. He knew, deep in his gut, that what he was about to do would set off a series of events with long-lasting repercussions. He had just begun to build a solid relationship with Greyson; Greyson's wife, Sutton was another matter entirely, which is why he wanted to turn and run out of the house. He had put it off too long. Today he would come clean.

Greyson closed the door on ripples of feminine laughter.

"What's going on?" Kirkland asked as he took a seat on the sofa.

"Sutton is having some friends over. She's celebrating taking the LSAT."

"She wants to become a lawyer?"

Greyson nodded, beaming with pride, and happy his success as a corporate attorney had influenced his wife's desire to pursue the profession. "Scored high enough to get into the law school of her choice. Mama and her mother raced over to cook a celebratory lunch. The next thing I know, I'm hiring a couple of sitters to play with the kids out back, and we have a full-blown party."

"I should go see Mama."

Greyson stopped him before he could stand. "You can see her after we finish talking. Let me go get Sutton."

"I could come back another time." Kirkland rose, ready to embrace any excuse that would allow him to leave.

"No. She's expecting you." Greyson left him alone in the study with his guilt. It beat down on him, burning like the blazing sun. He wanted to be anywhere but there.

Before he could contemplate an escape, Sutton breezed into the room, all smiles when her husband was near. Greyson sat on the edge of his desk, Sutton on the opposite end of the sofa.

Kirkland's eyes followed the pendulum on Greyson's desk. With every passing second he thought of reasons he should forget his purpose in coming. Greyson and Sutton watched him, waiting for him to disclose the reason for the meeting.

"What is it, Kirkland?" Greyson prodded.

"It's about the old Galloway place."

"What about it?" Greyson's brows always knit together when the Galloways were mentioned.

"The old Galloway place including the acreage north to the freeway and south to the woods," he clarified.

"I heard developers were trying to buy up that land since the paper mill has revitalized Hannaford Valley. They're talking about building condominiums. It's a lot of acreage."

Sutton glanced at her husband, a question clearly written on her face. "Mother Galloway hasn't mentioned selling it."

"Would she discuss it with you?" Greyson asked.

"Probably not."

Greyson brought him back into the conversation. "I can't see the mayor letting it happen. The charm of Hannaford Valley is in it being a small, sleepy town. No one wants it to change. Did you hear something, Kirkland?"

Kirkland couldn't look at his sister-in-law. He didn't want to see the pain when she heard what he had to say. He took a deep breath and spilled the news. "Alex willed it to me."

Sutton's lips parted, her forehead wrinkled. Not pain, but rage twisted her features. "Alex willed it . . . to you?"

Kirkland nodded. "The will stipulated I hold it two years before I do anything with it."

Sutton rose slowly. "You're the owner of the old Galloway place? Alex left the land to *you*? And you've had this land for over a year and never said a word? Not even when Sierra and I were left penniless on the street?"

"You were never on the street," Greyson corrected, his pride wounded.

"Homeless," Sutton challenged.

"Sutton." Greyson reached for her, but she pulled away.

"I can't believe you, Kirkland! You and Alex were two peas in a pod, weren't you?"

"I didn't ask for the land," Kirkland defended himself.

"But you accepted it, and you never said a word."

"Sutton, stop shouting." Greyson eased off the desk and stood between them. "Both of you. Calm down."

"Calm down, Greyson?" Her complexion reddened, and her mouth hardened. Her hands were in tight fists, trembling. "How can you defend him?" She turned on Kirkland, beyond angry. "I know you helped Alex cheat on me. I know you helped find apartments and jobs for his mistresses."

"This isn't helping." Greyson had no control over his wife when she was this wound up.

"This is too much. I won't forgive you for this, Kirkland."

"Like you've forgiven me for any of the mistakes I've made," Kirkland said, stopping her cold. "Alex was my best friend. I loved him like a brother. You've never even tried to understand how I felt when he died."

"This isn't about you." Sutton arched her back like an angry cat. "Get out of my house."

"Hold it," Greyson interjected. "Kirkland is my brother. He's always welcome here. Let's sit down and discuss this calmly."

"You don't expect me to forgive him—again."

"You know what," Kirkland interrupted, becoming defensive. "You don't have to forgive me, Sutton, because I didn't do anything wrong. True, we've always indulged you, but we're grown now, and I don't have to mold my life around you."

"Enough!" Greyson shouted. "You," he pointed at Kirkland, "don't disrespect my wife in her own house. Don't talk to her like that *ever*." He turned to Sutton. "And you *will* work this out with Kirkland because he's my brother. Now, enough shouting and yelling. Let's sit down and discuss this calmly."

"You're right," Sutton said, storming across the room. She yanked the door open. "I've had enough."

Kirkland waited until Sutton marched down the hall before he turned to Greyson. "Do you blame me for this too?"

"I've never understood your friendship with Alex Galloway, but I don't blame you." Greyson closed the door and spoke candidly to his little brother. "You have to get yourself together, Kirkland. You can't live in Alex's shadow anymore. Mama can't keep doting on you like you're still a kid. You're twenty-five years old. You have a good education. Do something with it. Stop blaming everybody for the bad decisions you've made in your life, and clean up your mistakes. You're not a baby and you're not a victim. Get your act together before you look up and your life has passed you by, and you've got nothing to show for it but regrets." To soften the blow of his words, Greyson squeezed his shoulder. "I need to check on Sutton."

Kirkland stood in the den thinking over Greyson's words. Greyson didn't understand. He could never understand what it was like to be one of their pack growing up. How could he compete with Greyson, the oldest Ballantyne brother, the cerebral one who made his way in the world and came back to save the town? Or, Chevy, the one who loved and cherished the land more than he valued his personal life? Alex, who was handsome, rich, and self-confident to the point of arrogance. Alex had it all, and had it all thrown at his feet. Who could forget Sutton? The only girl in Hannaford Valley tough enough to hang with their rowdy crew. The woman who grew up to live a fairy-tale life, shielded from the pain of never being wanted.

Alex was the only one who treated him as an equal, and now he was gone.

No, he couldn't deal with the harsh truth of Greyson's assessment of his life right now. Instead, he pulled his shoulders back and headed for the front door. He'd known it would be a hard, ugly scene when Sutton found out about the land, and he'd been right. He struggled to tamp down the raw, painful emotions fighting their way to the surface.

Lost in his thoughts, rushing to get out of Greyson's house, he never saw the woman in his path. His tall, lean body slammed into her, throwing her off kilter. He grabbed the woman by her shoulders, steadying her after their collision. "Sorry. I wasn't paying attention to where I was going."

The woman looked up at him and her gaze pierced the armor protecting his soul. She wasn't just beautiful. She was poetry. He'd been with a fair share of women, all of them gorgeous, but this woman packed a powerful punch. She was on another level. This woman represented sunsets and beaches. She would cause a man to behave irrationally, igniting his jealousy if another man glanced in her direction. He felt an instant connection with her, as if he had been waiting for her to come into his life for years. No woman had ever affected him this way. With one look, his heart shifted on an angle, making room for her possession. He tried to shake it off, telling himself his emotions were in overdrive because of the scene with Sutton.

"Are you Greyson's brother?"

"Yes."

"This is embarrassing." She smiled, smoothing her skirt. "I'm Cassidy."

The name wasn't familiar. He wished it were.

"Cassidy Payne. Sutton set us up."

Now it made sense. "You have me confused with Chevy, the middle Ballantyne brother. I'm Kirkland, the youngest." And Sutton would never think him good enough to set up with one of her friends.

"Now I'm really embarrassed."

"Cassidy." Sutton appeared from nowhere. There was no indication of her anger as she addressed her friend, but it was clear when she glanced in his direction. "I was looking for you." She swept Cassidy away, not even giving Kirkland a backward glance.

# Chapter 1

*One year later*

The interstate traffic came to an abrupt halt. After five minutes of sitting at a standstill, Kirkland Ballantyne glanced as his watch, put his car in park, and shut the engine off. *Probably an accident up ahead. Or someone hit a deer*, he thought. The bad thing about living in the capital of Charleston was the drive to see his family in Hannaford Valley. One fender bender on the two-lane interstate and traffic could be backed up for over an hour.

After ten more minutes, Kirkland thought to call ahead and notify the construction companies he was to meet with that he'd be late. No cell phone reception this deep in the mountains. He'd send them to lunch and all should be fine. By the time they finished eating, he'd be walking through the door of his office. He hadn't even seen police or fire or emergency service. Someone heading in the opposite direction on the highway would pass the accident and call for help once they reached the bottom of the mountain. He rested back in the seat, prepared to wait until the traffic started moving again.

He rolled down his window and let the summer heat wash over him in humid waves. His thoughts soon trailed off. *Get your act together*, Greyson had told him a year ago. Well, he was doing just that. He had big plans for the land Alex had left him. He'd prove to everyone he wasn't just the young, wild, reckless Ballantyne boy who couldn't get his act together.

People exited their cars, craning their necks to see what was up ahead. His patience was melting in direct proportion to the rising afternoon temperature. They'd been parked on the interstate for twenty minutes now. "Hey," he yelled, stopping a man jogging by, "what's going on up ahead?"

"A bad accident. I'm going to flag down a car to call for help."

He'd never been one to go out of his way to find or avoid trouble, but something whispered on the next heat wave, *Go check it out.* Before he could justify his actions, he was jogging to the scene of the accident. The closer he got to the scene, the more urgent his heart raced. His intuition pushed him into mindless action. He was running, but didn't know how or why. He pulled to a stop at the accident scene. His chest heaved, not from the exhaustion of running, but from painful memories. He had lived this scene before, in his mind . . . the day he received the call telling him his best friend had died in a terrible car crash.

A semi truck had mangled a black Escort. The truck driver was standing in the middle of a crowd, waving his arms, frantically trying to explain how he had fallen asleep behind the wheel. "I didn't see the car. I didn't see it," he cried out.

As Kirkland neared the twisted metal half-rammed beneath the truck, his stomach churned. His body moved in slow motion, but his mind was reeling. Afraid of what he might see, he approached cautiously. The crowd muttered incomprehensible words. *I have to get to Alex.* If he had been there, he could have pulled his friend from the car. He could have rushed him to the hospital. He could have done something and Alex would still be alive. He frantically peeled back the gawkers, pulling a man and woman out of the way, trying to get to the driver.

*Cassidy Payne!*

He could never forget her. Even if he hadn't seen her in a year—since she had announced she was his brother's blind date. He couldn't forget her, even if her beautiful face was contorted with fright—and pain. And even if she was no longer reed thin, but plush and curvaceous—

"Kirkland!" Cassidy reached for him, relief settling on her face.

As if he could save her.

*You couldn't save Alex.*

She was trapped beneath the disfigured steering wheel.

—And pregnant!

The shock rocked him.

"Kirkland, help me!" Cassidy grabbed her stomach. "I'm in labor."

Cassidy trapped—pregnant—in labor—it was too much for any person to process. His mind kicked into automatic, pushing him to do what needed to be done. He did a quick assessment of the situation. Cassidy—the woman he couldn't get off his mind because her body danced in his dreams every night—was pregnant, trapped behind the wheel of her mangled car. Cassidy—the woman his brother had started dating a year ago—in labor. It didn't take a rocket scientist to come to a conclusion. He pieced it all together, digested the harsh reality, and took charge. He delegated someone to check on the arrival of the police and emergency services. He assigned a woman to slide into the passenger's seat and hold Cassidy's hand through her contractions. He called over the biggest men in the bunch and they tried to remove the steering wheel. When that didn't work, they pooled their strength and tried to move the seat enough to pull Cassidy out. The best they could do was to recline the seat and place an extra inch or so between Cassidy's belly and the wheel.

"It's coming!" Cassidy announced as the men gathered around the car. Someone cursed the police and ambulance for taking so long. "My baby's coming now! Kirkland!"

He was there in a breath. "I'm here." *To do what?* He had no idea what he was doing. He removed his shirt and wiped the perspiration away from her face, stalling for time.

"My baby's coming now."

A man parted the crowd, announcing the police were clearing away cars and making way for the ambulance. "Five minutes."

"I can't wait five minutes," Cassidy cried. She bore down, clenching her teeth together to fight the pain.

Everything happened so fast Kirkland would never be able to tell the story with any accuracy. Screaming and pushing. Angling his body into the car. Someone holding a flashlight over his shoulder so he could see the emergence of life. The head was there—Cassidy couldn't wait. As if he doubted her claim. And before he could be afraid—the head, the shoulders, a baby in his hands.

The crowd collectively blinked in silent amazement.

Seconds passed that felt like hours as Kirkland stared down at the tiny baby cradled in his palms.

"Why isn't my baby crying?" Cassidy shouted.

The woman in the passengers seat tried to console her.

*Crying?* A baby should cry. Crying meant the baby was breathing. He knew that much. The baby's color looked bad—a dusky blue. He held the baby, limp and lifeless, in his hands. *If I had been there I could have saved Alex.* Acting quickly, he covered the baby's nose and mouth and gave two rapid puffs. He gave two more breaths, then remembered he should have checked for a heartbeat somewhere in the sequence. He placed two fingers over the crease in the baby's elbow—the brachial pulse. His CPR training came rushing back.

"What's wrong with my baby?" Cassidy screamed.

No pulse. *"The paramedics said he had no pulse when they arrived,"* Mother Galloway had told him. *"There was nothing they could do to save my son."*

Cassidy was yelling, "Why isn't my baby crying?" She stretched her arms out to her baby, but the steering wheel stopped her progress. "I don't hear my baby crying!" she yelled over and over.

He cradled the baby in the crook of his arm and began depressing the tiny area of exposed chest. He tried to keep count, but Cassidy's wailing cries threw him off. He covered the baby's nose and mouth with his lips and exhaled two more puffs of air. Compressions. Cassidy screaming. Breaths. Cassidy crying. Compressions. Cassidy yelling at him to give her the baby! Breaths.

Crying.

The baby yelped, followed by a weak cry. As the baby's lungs filled with air, the cries became stronger. Color filled her cheeks. She kicked and cried.

"My baby," Cassidy said, near hysterics. "Give me my baby."

The police were running toward the scene with the paramedics behind them. Someone mumbled about their terrible timing.

He wrapped the baby in his shirt to keep her warm and handed her to Cassidy.

"It's a girl." She looked at him as if he had been sent from above to nobly answer her call for help. "Thank you, Kirkland. Thank you." The hysterics were replaced by tears of joy.

The gravity of it all worked through the adrenalin fogging his brain. A baby. He had brought life into the world. And reacted quickly—giving CPR when the baby was in distress. He had never, ever experienced anything like this before. He could have never imagined how spiritual it could be to hold a new, innocent life in his hands. Surreal.

He had saved a life—wait until he told Alex this one! Sadness crushed his chest. Alex was gone. There would be no retelling of this story over beers at their favorite spot.

"Congratulations," the paramedic said as they checked the baby. The crowd gathered around, slapping him on the back. Firemen worked to extricate Cassidy from the car. She reached for him, and he rushed to her side, taking her hand in his. Finally, he'd done something good and wholesome that no one would ever be able to take away from him.

Kirkland never left Cassidy's side. In the ambulance, the emergency room, and her hospital room, he stayed with her. He remained silent, observing every little thing. He stood in the shadows with his sandy-brown hair, suntanned skin, and watchful eyes the color of warm, hot rum. He didn't speak until the baby had been settled in the nursery for the evening, and all the medical staff had left her room. His first words to her: "Is she Chevy's baby?"

"Chevy?" She was genuinely stunned, but could see how he would have misunderstood. "Chevy's, no."

He stepped closer to the bed. He looked annoyed. "You were dating my brother just a year ago."

"Chevy and I went out three times." Her eyes dropped to the weave of the hospital blanket. "He and I didn't seem to click."

Kirkland's face softened, but quickly hardened again. "Should I call your husband?"

She shook her head. "I'm not married." Scandalous behavior in the small, prehistoric town of Hannaford Valley.

"What about your boyfriend? He'd want to be here."

She turned toward the window. "There's no husband. There's no boyfriend." She looked back to Kirkland. "I'll call my folks in the morning. They're not exactly happy to be having an illegitimate grandchild." Before he could ask any more questions, she shifted the direction of the conversation. "I can't thank you enough for everything you did. You delivered my baby and then you saved her life."

"No need." He walked around the bed until he was facing her. The color of his eyes swung from rum to honey under the influence of the bright overhead light. His gaze was intense, insightful, and distracting. His eyes were filled with the wounds of a much older man. There was so much pain behind the inquisitive orbs Cassidy had to look away.

"You'll always be a hero to me." She reached out and brushed his crumpled shirt. Her fingertips grazed his abdomen and she felt the iron ripples of his lean body.

"I should go."

She nodded, but she didn't want him to leave. She wanted him to sit with her. She wanted his sandy-brown presence to comfort her. She had wanted to explore the possibilities since they collided in Sutton's foyer a year ago, but Sutton had warned her. Her brother-in-law couldn't be trusted, she'd said. Chevy was a much better prospect, but there was no spark between them. Cassidy always had the feeling there was another woman monopolizing Chevy's attention.

Kirkland, she couldn't keep out of her mind. Not when she dated Chevy, hoping something permanent would come from their friendship—she wanted to marry and have a child so desperately. Not when Sutton told her Kirkland was trouble.

Not when she found out he was nine years younger than her. Not when she turned thirty-three and panicked about her biological clock. He had become her mind's focus when the doctor told her now or never, and she had cooked up the idea of having a child on her own—with the aid of a sperm bank.

"You're flushed." Kirkland stepped forward, rattling her from her musings. "Are you going to be all right?"

"I'm fine. Tired."

He smiled, spreading his luscious brown lips into a seductive grin. "You have a good reason to be. The baby's beautiful."

"She is. Thank you." She reached for his hand and squeezed it tight.

Their eyes met and he shifted uncomfortably. "I should go. I have to go back to the capital tonight." He pulled his hand away and walked to the door. He stopped and paused before turning to her. "Do you mind if I call and check on you in the morning?"

Her heart leapt. "No."

He watched her for a long moment, hesitating as if there was something he wanted to say. "Well, good night." He turned and left, leaving the power of his presence to linger long after he was gone.


After a night of sleep made restless by the continuous pumping of adrenalin in his system, Kirkland dressed and hurried to the hospital. He had to wait a half hour before visiting the nursery, but when he stared into the face of the baby girl he'd delivered, it was all worth it. His mind reeled, but retained no thoughts at all. A cluster of emotions swirled, immobilizing all rational thought. His heart burst with every gurgle. With those piercing eyes, the baby would grow up to be as pretty as her mother. She had Cassidy's glowing almond complexion. Her hair was dark and thick, jet black just like her mother's. He stood with his nose pressed to the glass until the nurse took her away.

Fatherhood had always been something he'd run away from. He took extra precautions in all his affairs with women. Alex had instilled the importance of practicing safe sex after his "scare" with his mistresses. The last thing Kirkland wanted to do was bring home an illegitimate child to his mother. With her obsession about being accepted by the town it would devastate her. As he watched the nurse wheel the baby away in her bassinet, parenting took on a new meaning. It had only taken a split second to steal his heart and win his undying devotion. It had happened the moment he breathed life into the helpless baby and she inhaled, crying to tell him she would be all right. His mind fast-forwarded to birthday parties, dating, and graduation. He would be there to protect her. She would always feel wanted, and know how precious she was to the world. She would want for nothing. First thing, he would set up a trust fund for her—put his money to good use. He made these vows as he watched the tiny, innocent baby kick in protest of a diaper change.

"Which one's yours?" A man joined him at the window, offering a cigar with a blue band. The question tossed him, and all his newly discovered emotions, into a brick wall. Cassidy's baby was not his baby. He could make all the promises he wanted to, but he wasn't the baby's father and he had no right to insert himself into her life. Many people had been called upon to deliver babies outside of the hospital. It didn't give them any paternal rights.

Kirkland listened to the man prattle on about his perfect son, wondering where Cassidy's baby's father could be. She had swiftly changed the subject when he'd asked. Thank goodness, she'd cleared up the thought that Chevy was the culprit. If the father could see this perfect, beautiful baby, he'd want to be in her life forever.

*In her life forever.*

*In Cassidy's life forever.*

Where he wanted to be. Where he needed to be from the day he'd bumped into her in Greyson's foyer. He'd tried to accept that she was Chevy's girlfriend, but it never seemed right. He couldn't imagine her experiencing the same magic with Chevy as they'd shared when he looked into her eyes for the first time. He watched the nurse swaddle the baby, wondering who could have ever walked away from this sweet family? He pondered the absurdity of it as he made his way to Cassidy's room.

"Kirkland!" Cassidy beamed when he walked in. She began to fuss with her hair, her cheeks coloring with embarrassment.

He laughed, sitting on the edge of her bed. "I've seen you at your worst. I've seen too much of you." His observation shined light on the intimate gesture of sitting on her bed. He moved to stand. She stilled him by placing her hand on his forearm.

"I just left the nursery. What are you going to name her?" he asked.

"I was thinking of Sara or Lori, but after what you did for me, I think Courtney is more appropriate." Her thick lashes dropped to her cheeks. "It's the closest I could get to Kirkland."

A lump formed in his throat.

"If you don't mind."

"Don't mind? I'm flattered. You don't have to—"

She squeezed his hand. "I want to."

He liked the way she found reasons to touch him. "I just left *Courtney*. The nurses were fussing over her."

Cassidy smiled.

"When do you get to take her home?"

"Tomorrow. Normally, I would have gone home today, but under the circumstances of my delivery, the doctor wanted to keep us an extra day."

He pulled a chair next to Cassidy's bed and spent the morning getting to know her. He never put much value on getting into the psyche of women. Too much of an emotional commitment. But it came easily with Cassidy. She proudly described the nursery she'd been preparing since becoming pregnant. They relived the birth, over and over, changing the details a little every time, making him a grander hero in each version. He listened as the doctor and nurse gave Cassidy the instructions she'd need once she was at home. Volunteering to stand in for the missing father, he helped when the nurse brought Courtney in and instructed them in baby care. By late afternoon, when he had to leave to take care of business, he noticed Cassidy's family still was not at her side. "Should I stay until they arrive?"

She pulled her eyes away from the baby long enough to answer. "No. They won't be here until later. My mother doesn't drive. She has to wait until my father gets off work. They're coming from the capital."

"Is that where you were going when you went into labor?"

She nodded. Her full attention was back on Courtney. "I was going to stay with my brother and his family until the baby was born."

"Will you go there when you're released tomorrow?"

"No." Cassidy cooed to Courtney. "We're going home."

He watched the loving scene for a few minutes longer before he tore himself away. But he knew he wouldn't stay away very long. Cassidy must have felt the pull between them too, because she was delighted, but not surprised, when he arrived at the hospital the next morning with flowers and a full layette, insisting on driving her home.

# Chapter 2

Kirkland listened to the developer's spiel, his mind some miles away. He was thinking about Cassidy and Courtney. Wondering how inappropriate it would be to show up on their doorstep, uninvited and without calling. He couldn't call, he reasoned; he didn't have her phone number. In all the excitement of taking them home, he'd forgotten to ask. Maybe if he brought a nice gift.

"Mr. Ballantyne?" Pete Frawley tried to regain his attention. "Should we reschedule?"

"No. I've heard enough. Leave your proposal. I'll take a good look at it and give you a call." He stood and offered his hand.

"I know Hannaford is up in arms about the possibility of developers coming in and modernizing the town, but it's time. Hannaford needs a little modernization. Who best to do it than two people with ties to the community?"

Kirkland wasn't sure Hannaford would accept modernization no matter who was the catalyst.

"I love this town," Pete said as they walked to the door. "I know how to put it on the map. And it'll be for the good of everyone. Whether they understand it now or not."

Kirkland stopped abruptly, a tight frown taking over his face. "Let's get something clear, Pete. Flattering me won't get you the contract to develop my land. I'd prefer brutal honesty. You don't care any more about this town than I do, or else you wouldn't even *consider* destroying it with stone and concrete. So don't stand in front of me and blatantly lie about your intentions."

Pete's mask slipped away and for a brief instance, Kirkland wanted to rethink his plans for Alex's land. Pete nodded. The tone of his voice changed, turning dark and somewhat sinister in their conspiracy. "The people in this town are suffocating and they're too backwoods to know it's their own hands around their necks. We understand how this place can choke the life out of you." For emphasis he clenched his hands together, pretending to choke someone's neck. "My parents could never seem to cut ties with this place. Now I'm left living the *legacy*. I won't die here. I'll use whatever I have, do whatever I need to do to make enough money to leave this place in style." As if remembering he was in a job interview of sorts, he straightened his back and added, "I'm the best man for the job. I can clear the land and build the industrial park you want for a fair price. All while being very discrete."

"Discretion is the key." Or he would have gone with one of the hundreds of developers he'd worked with in the past. This project needed to be done quickly and quietly. Ground should be broken weeks before the town discovered his plans, giving him leverage as they fought in the courts to stop him.

"I can be very discrete, Mr. Ballantyne."

Before Pete could continue, Kirkland opened the door. He attributed Pete's reckless attitude to his age. He had not long ago graduated from college and was searching for a big project to make his name in the construction world. As small as Hannaford was, Kirkland didn't remember Pete from around town. It seemed odd when Pete tried to advance their friendship by talking about people they both should know. Kirkland knew the folks he mentioned. He just couldn't place Pete in the picture. He was a stranger, but not a stranger. It raised his guard. They shook hands and Pete left without glancing back.

He watched Pete trundle down the stairs of his childhood home, fighting memories sure to make him regret the actions he was taking. He used the house abandoned by his family, when he was in Hannaford. His parents had long ago moved into the new home Greyson built them when he returned to town. Once Greyson married Sutton they moved into a grand home he had helped design, but was no longer welcome in.

His childhood home was still furnished with the sofa he'd spilt juice on as a child. He could still hear the rowdy conversations that took place over lunch with his two older brothers at the dining room table. The threadbare carpet, like the rest of the ailing house, was clean, but in need of repair. The rooms had shrunk over the years. They were now unable to accommodate his towering height and wide shoulders. There just didn't seem to be enough room in the tiny house for his body, his memories, and his sudden onset of guilt.

He stepped out onto the porch, taking a deep

breath and exhaling the guilt, only to be assaulted
again when the aroma of roses wafted up to him.
He took a seat on the porch swing. He looked out
at the bed of roses his mother had left behind. He
remembered the hours she spent with her flowers,
starting as a novice and quickly becoming an expert
who could crossbreed her own roses. He pushed
against the splintered wood flooring of the porch
and the swing jerked backward, squeaking. He fell
into the rhythm of the swing's movement and accompanying sounds.

Warm memories of childhood innocence touched
him. When had the naïveté left him cold and willing
to destroy the town that had nurtured him into a
man? Greyson had given up everything to return to
Hannaford Valley. He came armed with a plan to
save the ailing town, and he'd been more successful
than he could have imagined. Chevy devoted his life
to forestry, living deep in the woods and sacrificing
his personal life to preserving the town. Even the rumors about his bizarre sexual appetites didn't sour
him on the place. He had never left it and probably
never would.

Kirkland tried to understand why he was wired
differently than his brothers. He lived Alex's vision.
He wanted more than Hannaford could offer him.
He'd left the town to go to college and never came
back. He moved to the capital after graduation and
made a comfortable life in the city. Like Alex, he
felt no emotional ties to Hannaford. It was his
birthplace, nothing more.

His childhood had been good—the answer wasn't
rooted there. Sure, they had wanted for things other
kids took for granted, but he couldn't blame his fa-

ther for supporting them the best he could. When he became a teen, Greyson and Chevy didn't like having him around much, thinking they were too grown to hang out with a kid. But Alex had come along and filled the void left by his brothers. College had come too easy for him, leaving him with too much free time. Free time he quickly learned could be filled by women—as many women as he wanted, if he said the right words and did the right things. No, Kirkland couldn't complain much about his life growing up.

Things fell apart when Alex Galloway died. Kirkland's family—Greyson mostly—tried to make him feel it was wrong to grieve for his best friend. Greyson and Alex had never liked each other and Kirkland was expected to align himself with the Ballantyne boys. He couldn't, and he didn't. Alex was more like a brother than either Greyson or Chevy.

And then Sutton showed up on his doorstep, upset about her discovery of his part in Alex's countless deceptions in their marriage. Everything went downhill from there. Finding out Alex had left him the old Galloway place added a new dimension of betrayal.

He didn't know what he had expected Sutton to feel when he told her he had possession of the Galloway land. He wanted her to understand how he was trying to spare her more hurt. He couldn't sell the land or transfer it to anyone else for two years. Alex stipulated it in the will. Sutton had been left penniless. What good would telling her have done? She and Sierra were going through enough turmoil. He didn't want to add more pain.

The emotions washing over him made him want to fight to keep them at bay. He couldn't handle too much more regret. He'd done what he'd done, thinking it the best thing to do, but being totally wrong. Maybe Sutton was right: he and Alex were too much alike. She had no idea how deep the betrayals went.

Missing his friend and fighting a fit of guilt made him need comfort. Release. With everything he had going on, he hadn't had time for women lately, but a soft, hot, willing body beneath his was what he needed to assuage his guilt right now.

Hannaford Valley was too small to select from its pickings of available females, spend a night, and walk away. There would be huge repercussions. His parents would pay the price. His mother in particular would be ridiculed when she had spent her entire life trying to fit in. No matter how low he had sunk, he couldn't do that to her. She was the light of his life.

As his body tightened with need, he could picture no face from his past that made him want to undertake the long drive into the capital. He spread his arms across the back of the porch swing and closed his eyes, letting the rhythm of the swing take him to a quieter place. He drowned himself in darkness, the sound of chirping birds helping him meditate as gentle heat waves washed him with the sweet aroma of roses. An unfamiliar emotion snaked through his body, massaging him with the knowledge that everything in his life would be all right. He fell deeper into the warm darkness of his meditation, and his heartbeat pounded slowly, confidently. This new emotion lured him into recesses of his heart he had never explored. He felt himself going under, deeper, until he came to the place where he either needed to wake himself or allow his body restive sleep. He gave himself over to sleep, feeling the decision meant more than a quick nap on the front porch.

*Kirkland,* he heard, as a vision of Cassidy's face appeared before him. Startled, he sat upright, his heart beating rapidly.

He'd tried to suppress his thoughts of Cassidy Payne, but now she appeared in his dreams. She marched in carrying his guilt as he planned to turn Hannaford Valley into an industrial city of wealth. Now even his time of quiet reflection was overrun with images of Cassidy.

He hadn't seen her since driving her home from the hospital. A wide smile covered his face as he thought of how beautiful Courtney looked in the layette his mother helped him choose.

He wondered how Cassidy was handling motherhood. Maybe she needed something. No, he needed to stay away from that volatile situation. There was an absent father lurking in the background and running into him could mean an explosion he didn't need or want.

He had to admit it was strange. The way he couldn't keep Cassidy out of his head. He'd fought her presence when she'd dated Chevy. Now he had to forget about her because she had a child by another man.

He took a trip down a forbidden road. What if he and Cassidy were Courtney's parents? He brushed the thought away. He wasn't ready for a family. Matter of fact, having a wife and kids was never to be a part of his agenda. Still, Cassidy had the power to make him suppose.

"You took Granddad's inheritance and bought yourself a baby." Darius held his niece with the casual ease of a parent who had three children of his own. "All I bought was a house."

"Uncle Darius thinks he's a comedian." Cassidy nudged him in the shoulder before handing him Courtney's bottle. He cradled Courtney in the crook of his arm and looked around for a place to sit. "It's been pretty hectic around here," she apologized as she set a stack of old newspapers onto the floor.

Darius sat down and fed Courtney the bottle, cooing and making a connection with his only niece. "Jamie and I can take Courtney for the weekend. Give you a chance to get adjusted."

She sank down next to him on the sofa. "She's only six weeks old. I'd go crazy if she wasn't here."

"You don't trust me with my niece? Jamie and I do have three kids, you know. I think we can handle a baby who doesn't do anything but eat, poop, sleep, and spit up."

"I know you guys can handle her, but I would be on the phone every minute checking on her. No, it's too soon for an overnight." She tugged at Courtney's tiny foot.

"Well, the offer stands."

Soon the bottle slipped from Courtney's lips and her eyelids closed under the weight of sleep. Darius placed her on his shoulder and rubbed small circles over her back.

"Hey," Cassidy said, "you're pretty good at this."

Darius shot her a look of exasperation.

"She's usually fussy after she feeds," she explained, soothing his feelings. "I'm glad you stopped by. I miss you and Jamie and the girls."

"We miss you, too. I'll be in town on business a couple of days a week from now on. I'll be sure to check up on you two. I might need to borrow your sofa every now and then, too. Driving back and forth to the capital gets old fast."

"What are you working on in Hannaford?"

"Hannaford's city council got wind of a developer trying to move in and destroy a good chunk of land. They've called my firm in to formulate an alternate proposal."

"You don't know anything about developing."

"No, but I know about increasing revenues through revitalization. CPAs do more than add and subtract, little sister."

"Little by one minute."

"One minute or ten years, it still counts. I'm going to scrutinize the efficiency of Hannaford's existing businesses, compare it with research from other towns this size, and put together a plan to pump revenue into the town without destroying its natural charm."

"Sounds like a noble undertaking."

"Um-hmm. Hey, I'm going to meet with your friend's brother, Greyson Ballantyne. The paper mill is a good model to pattern other businesses after. It doesn't invade the town and provides jobs, and he collaborates with environmentalists so as not to destroy the land." Darius laughed at Courtney's hearty belch. "Have your parents come by to see the baby yet?"

"*My* parents?"

"When they act like this, they're your parents. My parents are more sensible."

"With us being twins, it makes it pretty hard for us not to have the same parents."

"Yeah, well." Darius left the room to put Courtney down for a nap. Very few saw any resemblance between him and Cassidy. Darius was tall and skinny, still possessing a teenage lankiness. He was dark, like their father, with a perfectly edged mustache. His voice was a low bass, but backed with the ability to articulate intelligently on many subjects. From sports to rap music to world politics, Darius had a head for it all.

Cassidy had always been a little tall for a woman, and much too skinny—until Courtney came along. She, too, had held on to her youthful high school looks, but now she'd filled out. She didn't fuss about losing her "baby weight." She finally had hips and dips. And curves: thighs and booty to cushion her seat.

"So nothing from Mom and Dad, huh?" Darius asked when he returned.

"They called the first week I was home. Left a message on the answering machine."

"But they're still not on board with modern medicine impregnating their only daughter instead of some nice, rich bloke." Darius used his best impersonation of an English accent.

"Now, you know Mom will kick your butt if she hears you trying to make fun of her accent."

He laughed, returning to the sofa. "You'd think

her accent would have faded after thirty-five years of living in the States."

"Nothing ever fades with Mom. Once she gets something in her head, good luck trying to change her mind."

He gave his sister a tight squeeze. "Don't worry, they'll come around."

"You've always been in my corner. Is it too much to ask my parents to accept my decision?"

"I guess so. I don't understand what the big deal is. There are a lot of single women raising children, and they turn out just fine. Mom and Dad want the best for you, and to them that's getting married—"

"To some rich bloke—"

"And then having a houseful of kids to seal the deal. I promise you they won't be able to stay away from that precious little girl you have. Once they start coming around you won't be able to keep them away."

"I think Dad is okay with it. He's just sticking by Mom."

"And he always will. Keeping up the united front, and all. No matter what went on when we were growing up, they fought it out in private and then punished us collectively."

Cassidy laughed, remembering some of their exploits.

"You have to understand where they're coming from, Cassidy. Look at everything Dad went through to marry Mom and bring her home. A black man in the army trying to marry and bring another black—a foreigner at that—into the country when he wasn't welcome here himself." Darius shook his head sadly.

"They don't want your life to be any more complicated than it has to be."

"I know. I have to give them time."

"Right. Time." He paused, then changed the subject. "We're taking the kids to dinner with the grandparents this weekend. I'll work on them. Don't worry." He gave her one last squeeze before playfully pushing her away. "Now tell me the story about how you delivered my niece on the freeway again."

# Chapter 3

Frazzled, Cassidy rushed to answer the door before her visitor went away. "Kirkland." She snatched away the scarf covering her crumpled curls. Crossing her arms over the beat up old sweatshirt hid the stain of Courtney's drool, but she couldn't hide the matching cutoff shorts riding her thighs.

He was laughing. "I didn't have your number so I couldn't call. I hope you don't mind."

Courtney wailed.

"Go ahead." He motioned in the direction of the crying. "I'll wait here."

"Come in." She unlocked the screen door before disappearing around a corner. "Make yourself at home." She realized how difficult that would be with her house looking like someone had detonated a Fisher-Price-laced bomb beneath the slab of its foundation. She gracefully hopped over piles of clothes, toys, and other baby paraphernalia with ease. She'd learned to navigate the mess in the dark, in the middle of the night, on two hours of sleep.

No time to wallow in embarrassment, she lifted Courtney from her crib. She'd had very little time for anything lately. She paced the nursery, bouncing

Courtney on her shoulder and singing a lullaby she hoped would quiet the baby's shrill cries. Kirkland joined her after several minutes of pacing and bouncing. "Having trouble getting her to sleep?" he asked.

"She's been fussy," she answered over Courtney's cries. "She always fusses a little after she eats, but it's been much worse lately."

"Can I try?" Kirkland asked, but he was already taking Courtney from her shoulder. He cupped Courtney's head and bottom between his strong hands and peered into her eyes. He concentrated all his attention on her twisted face as if he were communicating without words. Amazingly, she began to settle down. When her cries became intermittent whines, Kirkland placed her against his chest and soothed her until she fell asleep.

"How did you do that? Do you have kids of your own?"

"No. Sutton's first husband, Alex, was my best friend so I spent a lot of time around Sierra when she was a baby. As a matter of fact, Alex left her with me quite a bit." He looked up with a hidden message. "Sutton doesn't know about that."

The meaning was clear. "She won't hear about it from me." Cassidy didn't pry in other people's business. She had enough going on in her own life. "Let me put her in the crib."

"No. I can do it." He walked the length of the room, watching Courtney sleep in his arms. He seemed reluctant to put her down. When he did lay her in the crib, he carefully covered her with a pink blanket, smiling when he recognized the layette he'd purchased as a homecoming gift.

"It looks like a tornado struck your place," he said when they returned to the living room.

"I know. I look a mess too."

"No. You don't." The flash of his eyes showed he meant it.

An awkward moment passed while Cassidy couldn't think of anything clever to say.

"She cries after every feeding?" he asked, sounding like a trained medical professional.

She nodded. "It's getting worse."

"Maybe she's lactose intolerant. Sierra went through the same thing—crying and fussing every time she drank her bottle. Alex told me it was because she couldn't digest something in the milk."

"Sounds serious. Lac—"

"Lactose intolerance. The doctor changed her formula and she's been fine ever since. She takes a supplement when she eats dairy products, but I'm sure you've seen it's no biggie. You should take Courtney to the pediatrician."

And with that advice, she burst into tears.

"What?"

The harder she tried to stop crying the more tears fell. Her hormones had been on overdrive lately, but there was no excuse for breaking down in front of Kirkland.

"What did I say?" He drew her into his arms, but she still couldn't stop the tears. He pulled her close. "I hate seeing you upset this way. I'm not saying Courtney is lactose intolerant. It just sounds like Sierra when she was a baby. It's not life threatening. You'll take her to the doctor and she'll be fine. Where's the phone? We'll see if Dr. Carter can see her today—until you can get an appointment with the pediatrician."

"Oh, God. I'm so sorry." She pulled out of his embrace. The sudden void she felt after leaving his arms shocked her system, sobering her.

"You're worried. It's okay."

"It's not okay, Kirkland. I'm Courtney's *mother* and I didn't think of this lactose thing. I didn't make her an appointment to see the doctor. I thought she was just being fussy." She moved away from him. "I'm in way over my head. My mother was right. I can't do this alone."

"You can't know everything."

"But I should know what's wrong with my baby."

"You're overwhelmed." Kirkland remained calm, watching her behind sandy-brown lashes so thick and lush they shouldn't have belonged to a man.

She kicked a pile of old newspapers. "Look at this place. It's a mess."

"You'll clean it up when you have time."

"Stop being so understanding, Kirkland."

"You don't want me to be understanding? Too bad. I'm your friend. I'm supposed to support you." He shook his head. "This is what I don't understand about women. I'm genuinely concerned and trying to comfort you, but somehow it's the wrong thing to do."

They had bonded as friends, Cassidy realized. The circumstances were weird, but they were friends. "If you're a true friend, you'll tell me the truth. I'm not a good mother." Saying the words aloud made her throat constrict. She'd been feeling blue lately, overwhelmed by being responsible for another life, trying to return to work, mend her relationship with her parents, and keep a decent house. Today, it had all crashed down on her and she'd lost it in front of Kirkland, collapsing in tears. "I'm failing at being a mother. Other women have more than one child and they can keep the house clean and still know when their baby is sick. My brother has three kids, and they manage. His wife runs their house like a well-oiled machine."

"You want brutal honesty, Cassidy? That I can do." He crossed the room, determination on his face. "Maybe trying to do it alone is the problem. You're raising a baby by yourself, and you shouldn't have to. Where's Courtney's father?"

Cassidy had decided long ago she would be open and honest with her daughter about her conception, never allowing secrets to rule her life. "Courtney doesn't have a father."

Deep sadness crossed Kirkland's face. "What do you mean? Is he dead?"

"No. He never existed."

He shook his head and ran his fingers through the thicket of tight brown curls. His hair was a little long for a man's, but big Afros had made a comeback. She remembered it being longer a year ago. It looked soft and touchable—his crown of glory. "I don't understand. What do you mean he never existed?"

"I was implanted at a sperm bank."

He laughed. He tossed his head back and laughed so heartily his wide shoulders shook. He leaned forward, would have doubled over if there had been enough room separating them. She crossed her arms over her chest, tapping her foot in rhythm to his laughter. Suddenly, almost violently, he sobered. "You're serious?"

"Not the reaction I expected."

"How?"

She gave him a twisted look.

"Strike that. Why?"

"I haven't shared this with anyone outside of my family, so I'd appreciate it if—"

"I won't tell a soul. Why?"

"I was thirty-three years old. I'd never been in a serious relationship, and it didn't look like it was going to happen for me anytime soon. My biological clock started to tick. I developed some *female* problems and the doctor told me now or never." Her obstetrician had performed a minor medical procedure after Courtney's birth that would exclude her from having any more children.

"Wait. There's a lot to digest here. You had to have a baby now, or you wouldn't be able to have any because of a *female* problem."

She nodded.

"Is it catching?" he asked with a mischievous smile. "Just breaking the tension," he added when he saw her shocked response. "And you've never been in a serious, committed relationship?"

She shook her head, no.

"Are you a virgin?" He laughed at her facial expression. "Tension breaker."

"I'm glad you think this is funny. It's not. It's my life."

"Hey." He grabbed her arms, stopping her from walking away. "You have to admit this isn't a story you hear every day in Hannaford Valley, West Virginia. Give me a minute." He closed his eyes, a tran-

sient smile crossing his full lips. When he looked at
her again, the playful attitude had disappeared and
been replaced by something so hot Cassidy felt herself melting under his gaze. His voice had dropped
an octave. "So there's no man in your life?"

"No." She braced herself for his judgmental
speech about the choice she'd made to become a
single parent.

Kirkland didn't give her a speech. He stepped
forward as he pulled her into him. "Good," he said
before lowering his head and kissing her. He kissed
her gently—a direct contrast to the way he held her
body against his. He gave her one kiss that
amounted to no more than a faint brushing of
their lips, but had enough impact to make Cassidy's
legs buckle. He released her and she took a shaky
step backwards.

"Get out." Her voice croaked.

"What?"

"Leave."

"Why?" He stepped towards her.

She separated them with the sofa. "Leave, please,
Kirkland." She was so stunned by the effect of his
kiss she didn't know what to say, or do, so she threw
him out of her house.

"You're mad."

"No. It's just—You should go."

Here she was looking beaten and worn, a single
mother nine years his senior and he had the nerve
to kiss her like she was a *Playgirl* centerfold. It was
enough to rattle anyone. It didn't help that he was
the star of her *Playgirl* fantasies, and she hadn't
been able to keep him off her mind since she met
him in Sutton's foyer.

"I won't go if you're upset with me. I don't want to leave it this way."

"I'm a little tired." She gestured to the messy room. "And I have a lot to do."

He watched her for a long moment before he agreed to go. "Let me know how it goes with Courtney at the doctor's."

"I will."

He stepped quietly to the door.

She collapsed on the sofa when she heard his car speed off. "What just happened here?" she asked aloud. Her life was in disarray and she couldn't complicate things further by starting a relationship—if he even wanted a relationship. She had no idea what Kirkland thought he was doing by kissing her . . . and painting her with his passion.


Cassidy stepped out of the pediatrician's office, carrying Courtney on her hip. Kirkland had been right: lactose intolerance. Her mother would have a field day if she learned the news. "Another good reason not to have a baby from a bloody test tube," she'd say. The sperm donors were thoroughly screened, but predicting lactose intolerance hadn't been an area of focus in the testing. The pediatrician assured her all serious diseases and mental disorders had been ruled out. She had to trust her physician, otherwise she'd become sick with worry. Other than the lactose intolerance, which only required a change in the type of baby formula she drank, Courtney had received a clean bill of health. Cassidy counted her blessings and prepared to write a check for her insurance deductible.

"Your friend took care of the entire bill, Ms. Payne," the receptionist informed her. "Here's your next appointment date."

Somewhat bewildered, she took the card but didn't question the payment of the bill. Romance cover illustration was good work, but she wasn't rich. She figured the "friend" who paid the bill was actually her brother. She thought Darius was the only one who knew about her appointment today. She realized how wrong she was when she stepped out into the lobby.

"Everything go okay?" Kirkland greeted her. The only man in a lobby full of women and children, his muscular body made him appear out of place. He smiled with ease, oblivious to the stares.

"You were right," she answered, keeping her voice down.

He approached, carrying a portable baby seat.

"Someone has been shopping."

He placed the seat at her feet and watched Cassidy for a long moment. Courtney babbled, becoming restless in her arms. He smiled and gently lifted Courtney off Cassidy's shoulder. After exchanging a few unintelligible words, he buckled her into the seat, lifted it, and headed for the door. "Are you ready to go home?"

She stayed frozen in the middle of the waiting area. She summed up the situation, without concept of time, as Kirkland stood at the door waiting. A too sexy man, nine years her junior, had kissed her and now he had come to check on Courtney at her doctor's appointment. When Cassidy looked at Kirkland she saw a young man who was bold and reckless, hot and spicy. He had a body designed to be a woman's playground. His smile made the most sanctified woman a sinner. Men like Kirkland didn't pay pediatrician doctor bills and buy baby seats.

What were his motives? His sister-in-law had warned her he couldn't be trusted. She'd also heard rumors about his conquests. He had a reputation for being an educated, well-off, ladies' man. Handsome and suave, he had a gift for getting what he wanted, and smiling like an adoring little boy the entire time he took what he needed. Hard to believe this Kirkland was the same man who delivered her baby, looked at her like she was a precious jewel, bonded with Courtney, and kissed her like she was the object of his greatest desire. Too many men wrapped into one. Her life was too complicated for casual sexual encounters, and she couldn't begin to figure out how he would fit into her and Courtney's life in any other way.

She didn't know her own motives when it came to Kirkland Ballantyne. The thoughts she had about him late at night made the steamy romances she drew covers for seem like kiddie picture books. He scrambled her mind and warmed her body. As she watched him standing at the door of the clinic, she realized she needed a man in her life. She wanted a man in her life. A strong man who could rule her body and run her household. A man to raise and protect her baby. Her mother might have been right about a couple of things after all.

This thought was enough to horrify her. "What are you doing?"

"I'm taking you and Courtney home."

"Why?"

Kirkland shifted the baby seat from one hand to the other. "Do you want to discuss this right here?"

She watched him, feeling a little defiant.

"I assure you that what I have to say will embarrass you much more than it will embarrass me."

Her gaze swept the room. Yeah, everyone was watching, already speculating about Kirkland finally becoming a father because of his careless exploits. With all the dignity she could muster, she hiked the diaper bag up onto her shoulder and strutted out of the doctor's office.

"I hired a cleaning company to send a maid three days a week," Kirkland announced, closing the front door behind him. "It should take some of the pressure off of you. Help you get adjusted to being a single mother."

She threw him a look, but remained quiet as she opened the straps on Courtney's baby seat. "I'll be right back." She put Courtney to bed for her midday nap and returned, hands on hips, ready to do battle with Kirkland "Butt-his-nose-in" Ballantyne. "I can't afford maid service."

"I can afford it." He casually took a seat on the sofa, unfazed by her anger. "Consider it a gift to Courtney." He gave her the coy grin that was beginning to bug her. "You wouldn't deny me the right to give Courtney a gift, would you?"

He had her. "I'll pay you back, then."

"I won't accept it." He stood, and approached with swaggering confidence. "Let's talk about more important things." His body keyed in on hers, targeting her emotions and ensnaring her with his hypnotic posture. The cool wall pressed against her back.

"Why did you kick me out when I kissed you?"

"The question is: why did you kiss me? I don't want you to get the wrong idea about our friendship."

"Friendship, huh? You're calling our relationship friendship?"

"What do you call it?" *Wait!* "There's nothing going on between us other than friendship."

"Maybe I haven't gone about this the right way." He placed his hand on the wall next to her head and leaned his weight into her. "Would you like to see what all the talk is about?"

"Arrogant—"

He laughed. "Just kidding."

"Releasing the tension."

"Right. Releasing the tension." He hooked his finger into the collar of her T-shirt. "Speaking of tension release . . ." He boldly leaned in to kiss her. She placed her hand flat against his mouth. He gripped her wrist, kissed her palm, and then drew a circle in the middle of her hand with his tongue.

"What is with you?" She was flustered by his brazen attempt to seduce her.

"I'm very attracted to you."

"You're much too young for me."

"I can make you forget my age."

She pulled her hand away. Right then she couldn't remember her *name.*

"I can make you melt . . . with one kiss." He leaned into her again, his mouth inches from hers before she could stop him—before she could find a good reason to stop him.

She fought through the heat storm developing between them. The inferno fueled by their combustible chemistry made it too hot to breathe. She inhaled deeply and forced a snappy comeback. "Must be a potent kiss." She knew from her quick sample the other day that it would be.

"Wait until you see what I do to make you call my name."

Cassidy swallowed—hard. "Is this all about sex for you?"

He blinked, revealing too much. Beneath the quick wit and bold attempts to fluster and seduce her, he was hurting. And the pain was raw and new. "No," he answered in a husky whisper, "but it's the way I show you how I feel."

"And it might work if sex meant the same thing as having a loving relationship based on trust and respect."

He released her shirt. "Trust and respect."

"You've heard of those."

He nodded. "They don't always exist in my world."

"Your sex appeal has gotten you everything you've ever wanted with a woman."

He worked his jaw back and forth, absorbing the truth of her blow. "Up until this point."

"And you're happy with what you've gotten?"

His gaze slid away.

"Your parents have a good relationship," she observed, keeping the advantage she'd gained.

"They do." He peered at her. "I went about this all wrong."

She nodded, wondering if he would have thought

so if they were rolling around in her bed right now. "Depends on what you were going after."

His eyes narrowed. "I hope I didn't ruin our friendship."

She shook her head.

Kirkland straightened. "I'm going to leave now before I make this any worse."

She watched him walk to the door. The removal of his body heat left her cold and feeling alone. He was preoccupied. She'd given him something to think about. She wanted him to answer her question. What was he going after with his kind gestures and flirty appeals? As much as she needed him to stay, she needed him to leave. There were so many reasons that starting something with Kirkland was wrong. So many, but she couldn't remember a single one as he moved closer to the door.

He stopped with his hand gripping the doorknob. "I'd like to call you. If it's okay."

"Making a phone call is what a friend would do."

# Chapter 4

First Sunday dinner in the Ballantyne household had grown to be a meal of epic proportions. Mama Ballantyne was in all her glory, cooking for two days straight—cakes and pies, biscuits and breads, roast, ham, chicken, and too many sides to name. Anticipating the circus, Kirkland arrived early to have some time alone with his mother. He considered her a saint, having survived life in a houseful of stubborn, headstrong men. Growing up the baby, his mother kept a close eye on him. He was never a part of the shenanigans Greyson and Chevy got into. He was the one who told everything to his parents, hoping to steal some of the attention from his older brothers.

The attention always came from his mother, and he'd grown to adore her. As an adult, he made it his business to be her outer ring of protection, his father being the innermost layer. It pained him to see her striving for the town's approval. For whatever reason, Hannaford's elite circle of women didn't include her in their set. Over the years she played down the importance of their friendship, but Kirkland knew his mother well enough to see she was hurting every time they shunned her at social events.

While his older brothers had left home, he remained emotionally attached. He knew the details of his parents' finances, helping them manage every aspect of their household. Pop called him when he needed one of his son's help with a project. He often ran errands for his parents, and was always ready and available to help whenever they needed it. He reminded his father of Mama's birthday and the date of their anniversary. He was the one who took Pop shopping, helping him select something nice his mother would love. Let his brothers call him a mama's boy. There was no harm in wanting his mother to be happy.

As Kirkland greeted his mother in the kitchen with a kiss and long hug, he cringed at what she would say if she knew his plans for the town. He had never disappointed her. He needed her support of his business endeavors. Knowing her desire to be accepted by the town snobs, he would have to break the news to her very gently. He'd have to show her proof of the good his industrializing the town would do. If anyone would understand his quest for independence and to prove himself, she would. He looked down into the loving eyes of his mother. If he believed what he was thinking, why hadn't he shared his plans with her yet?

"Is everyone going to make it?" He hauled the center section of the dining room table from the utility closet.

"Everyone's coming. I'm so excited. It's been months since I had you all here at the same time."

He added the table extension, locking it into

place. She smoothed a white linen tablecloth over the surface. He was placing the chairs at the table when his father entered the dining room.

"Douglas, I need your help out back." Pop left without waiting for a response.

Whenever his father addressed him by his middle name, what followed was never good. Oblivious to it all, his mother hummed her way back into the kitchen.

He followed his father, catching up to him in the backyard. He joined his father at a pile of white-washed wood. "Yeah, Pop?"

"I'm building your mother a gazebo for our anniversary. I'd like you boys to he'p me so I can finish on time."

"No problem."

"I need you up front 'cause the design is complicated."

"No problem." His experience in reading blueprints would make the project go much smoother. Having him pitch in meant only a phone call and he would be there. It didn't explain his father calling him *Douglas* and needing to see him alone.

"Douglas, I had to put in a phone call to Sutton to get her to come to dinner today. You know anythin' about that?" He stuffed his hands in his trousers, waiting for an explanation.

"We've had words. We don't seem to be able to get along since Alex died." A sharp pain pierced his chest, as it always did when he thought of his best friend.

"Sutton didn't say much more than that either. You kids been having differences since you were six years old. I know something's going on 'cause she'd never skip Sunday dinner to avoid you over nothing."

"Sutton and I will work it out, Pop."

"You see that you do. And without upsetting your mother. You're her favorite, and she's crazy about Sutton and Sierra. You two settle whatever you're fighting about." Pop paused to give him a pointed look that said the matter wasn't negotiable. "I'm going to clean up for dinner."

Kirkland walked the backyard, seemingly measuring the space to be used for the construction of the gazebo, but he needed time to think. He didn't know what to do about Sutton. Things had been strained between them since she'd confronted him in his apartment after Alex's death. He couldn't control Alex any better than she could. Alex was reckless, fun loving, and a bit selfish. Other than their friendship, Kirkland didn't know many who actually liked him. But he and Alex had been best friends and would have done anything for each other. Alex had been the one who encouraged him to pursue a career in construction. Alex set up business meetings for him with people he'd never have had access to on his own. Alex supported him emotionally—they were brothers. So his friend asked him to babysit secretly. Or pull a few strings to get strange women jobs. Even doing the front work for renting apartments in other cities didn't seem like too much to ask from a friend.

He cared about Sutton too. They'd all grown up together. They were inseparable—they were friends. He had warned Alex about seeing other women. He'd told him over and over again Sutton would leave him one day. It was the only thing they ever fought about: how Alex treated Sutton.

"I know how to handle Sutton," Alex would say. As cocky as ever, he'd tip his glass back, then slam it on Kirkland's bar. "When you going to get yourself a woman so you can stop worrying about mine?"

"I know you love her."

"More than anything. I am who I am. Can't change it. I have my father's genes."

Alex lived in a world created for his own enjoyment. The only way to make him see the truth was to produce tangible evidence. Kirkland left the room, but soon returned with a photocopy of pregnancy test results.

"Kirk, man, why you bring that up?" Alex hopped down from the bar and slouched down on the sofa. "I won't make that mistake again. Wear a raincoat. Always wear a raincoat."

"If she had been pregnant—"

"She wasn't," Alex snapped, tired of having his indiscretions thrown in his face.

"And Sutton had found out—"

"She wasn't pregnant, and Sutton doesn't know anything about it. And she never will. Unless you plan on telling her."

"Every time she suspects you're messing around, I get a call."

"I've told you what to say. I can handle Sutton."

"I don't like to see her hurting, and I don't like being in the middle."

Alex had risen slowly from the sofa, panic, betrayal, and anger merging at the creases of his forehead. "I thought we were friends, Kirkland."

"We are." He crumpled the paper, tossing it into the ashtray. He knew, and Alex knew, that he would never betray his best friend.

"I'm trying," Alex said earnestly. "Do you think I like sneaking around on Sutton? It's just—just—going home to the same woman night after night. There's so much stress at work. And the women are always there, throwing themselves at me. Gorgeous women who are satisfied with one night."

Kirkland knew it wasn't as simple as Alex wanted to believe. He paid a price to be with these women. Fancy dinners, expensive gifts, elaborate trips, furnished apartments. Not to mention the emotional turmoil of lying and arranging multiple schedules while maintaining his productivity at work.

"I've gotten better," Alex said. "I'm only seeing one other woman. I'll break it off with her. I need a little time. I'm going to make Sutton and Sierra happy. I love them. I just need a little time to get myself together."

"You have to take care of this, Alex." Kirkland tried to sound stern, but knew his message hadn't gotten through when Alex showed up on his doorstep a few months later crying because Sutton was really going to leave him this time.

"Kirkland," Mama Ballantyne called from the back porch, rousing him from his memories. "Come on in and get ready for dinner." She looked worried as she absentmindedly dried her hands on a kitchen towel.

He'd seen this expression before. The day she entered his apartment the morning after Alex's death to find him destroying the place.

"Kirkland?"

"Coming."

By six o'clock everyone had arrived and they sat down for dinner. Polite chatter and compliments to Mama moved the conversation. Greyson sat between his wife and his stepdaughter, preparing their food and being the head of his family. His tender but authoritative gestures reminded Kirkland of why Cassidy had refused his advances. She'd discounted him because of his age, and dismissed him because of his slick rap. He'd seen Alex pick up women with less effort, but it'd never work with Cassidy. She needed a real man in her life, and if he wanted it to be him, he had to change his approach.

As he continued to watch Greyson interact with his family, getting Cassidy became his mission. He couldn't figure out how she'd stolen his heart so easily. From the first time he'd bumped into her, he couldn't stop thinking about her. It had killed him to know she was dating Chevy. Running into her in the middle of her crisis had to be some sort of omen. It was his second chance to win her. And he wanted her so much.

Sierra chattered to Greyson. She looked up at him with huge brown eyes as if he had the answers to all the questions in the universe. As far as she was concerned, Greyson could make everything all right. Most would have tuned out Sierra's endless rambling, but Greyson swung his body in her direction, asking questions that encouraged her to go on and on. When Sierra settled down, he angled toward Sutton. He poured gravy over her roast beef, added a biscuit to her plate, and started cutting her meat. Sutton seemed to pay the gesture no mind, and Kirkland wondered just how spoiled she actually was. Until she stopped in the middle of her conversation with his father to thank Greyson with an intimate smile. Her eyes sparkled when she looked at her husband. Kirkland could feel the warmth of love between them across the table. He wanted Cassidy to look at him the same way.

"Kirkland, tell us how you delivered Cassidy Payne's baby," Mama said.

Kirkland's gaze slipped to Chevy.

"I hadn't heard about that," his brother said.

"Stop being a hermit," Greyson chided Chevy. "You're really starting to live up to the rumors."

"I'm busy with work."

"Yeah, work," Greyson mumbled. "Get *unbusy* with work. Cassidy's a good woman. Obviously she was ready to settle down. Cassidy and her baby could be sitting beside you right now."

"Or beside Kirkland." Chevy stabbed at his plate.

"What do you mean, Chevy?" Sutton peered across the table at Chevy, a scowl already on her face.

"Greyson didn't mention Kirkland's been spending a lot of time with Cassidy and Courtney? Cassidy named her baby after him." Chevy lowered his head over his plate, satisfied to have turned the tables on Greyson.

Sutton turned in her seat. "Greyson?"

His lashes lowered as he cast sheepish eyes around the table. "Mama said something about it."

"And you didn't mention it? I *like* Cassidy. She's a friend of mine."

"What's that supposed to mean?" Kirkland asked.

He didn't like the implication that because Cassidy was a friend, she was too good for him.

"Anyone for dessert?" Mama asked, standing at the end of the table.

The doorbell rang, interrupting an awkward moment.

Pop spoke. "Kirkland, get the door. Dessert sounds good, Mar-beth. Sutton, why don't you help her?"

Sutton followed Mama into the kitchen, throwing Kirkland an angry look as she left the room. He ignored her and went to open the door to four neighborhood boys—two sets of brothers who all looked around the same age. One stepped forward, too confident for a kid around nine or ten years old. "Can Sierra come out and play?"

Kirkland smiled. This would be good. "One minute." He reentered the dining room and took his seat. "There are some kids at the door for Sierra."

"Can I be excused?" Sierra asked Greyson with a smile not to be denied.

"You don't want dessert?"

She shook her head, sending her long red braids flying.

"She can have dessert later," Pop tossed in. "Let her go play."

"Go ahead." Greyson watched her run down the corridor. "I didn't know she had friends in this neighborhood. I hardly ever see kids playing around here."

"Those four little boys did look a little older than Sierra," Kirkland said.

"Four *boys?*" Greyson was out of his chair in a shot. He hurried down the corridor.

Kirkland and Pop shared a laugh.

"Sutton!" Greyson's voice roared through the house a minute later. When she appeared from the kitchen, Pop pointed her in the direction of the front door. Minutes later, a chorus of raised voices brought chaos to the dinner table. Pop pushed his chair back and mumbled his way to the front door.

"What's going on?" Mama asked, coming out of the kitchen.

"Sierra has company," Kirkland answered, "and Greyson is learning what Mr. Hill must have felt like when we were kids."

Mama rushed to the scene. Kirkland's mischievous smile faded when he looked across the table at Chevy. His relationship with Chevy was much different from his with Greyson. They were closer in age, so when Greyson left home, they remained behind. Neither moved far away from their childhood homes, which meant they spent a lot of time together. Chevy was more diplomatic and attempted to understand his relationship with Alex. At the very least, he tolerated Alex, not criticizing Kirkland's choice of friends. He and Chevy could talk honestly about anything. Rarely did they understand the other's logic, but they respected each other's opinion. Based on this, Kirkland owed his brother honesty without the sugar coating.

"I like Cassidy. A lot. I'm going to go after her."

"How did that happen?" Chevy asked, his face

still too blank for Kirkland to know how he felt about it all.

"I'm not sure." He sat back in his seat and met his brother's glare. "I was attracted to her the first time I met her, but I never did anything about it. Now I want to."

Chevy shoveled a spoonful of mashed potatoes into his mouth.

"Is this going to cause a problem between us? Do you still have feelings for her?"

His brother chewed slowly, contemplating his answer. "No problem."

"But you're upset about it."

"No," Chevy answered sadly, shaking his head.

"I know you, Chevy."

"If I have a problem with it, are you going to just forget about her?"

He held his brother's intense stare. "No. I'm not going to forget about Cassidy."

"Then what does it matter if I have a problem with it, Kirkland?" He pushed back his chair and stormed from the room. He left through the kitchen, undoubtedly not wanting to explain to everyone why he was too upset to stay for dessert.

Kirkland watched him go, but didn't try to stop him. Chevy and Cassidy were no longer dating. From Cassidy's account, nothing had happened between them. He couldn't walk away from her to assuage Chevy's ego. He knew his brother's history of trouble with female relationships, but giving up Cassidy wouldn't help him on that front. Chevy needed to find the right woman. Once he did, he would understand why Kirkland couldn't walk away from Cassidy—even for him.

* * *

Kirkland pulled up in front of Cassidy's house later the same evening. The house she lived in had belonged to her grandfather. The country cottage sat between the homes of Old Lady Polk and Mr. Calor. They were both widowed and had lived in these houses as long as he could remember. Seniors who frequented church and didn't believe in sex before marriage owned most of the houses on the street. They insisted upon living in the bubble of the past that engulfed most of Hannaford Valley. Knowing Cassidy had used a sperm bank to become pregnant, he wondered why she didn't sell her grandfather's home and move to Charleston. Sentiment about family values and legacies lost probably held her in their grip. If his visions for renewing the town came true, she'd have to abandon those notions and learn to live the glamorous life he wanted for her.

He gathered the dinner sent by his mother along with the long-stemmed red roses from her garden—they had worked for Greyson when he pursued Sutton, so he'd give them a chance. Just as he was about to get out of his car, Cassidy's front door opened and a bulky man with long blond hair and tanned skin stepped out onto the porch. He watched as the man folded himself inside a Corvette and sped away.

*Is this more the type of man Cassidy wants?* He might be a lot of things, but a family man wasn't one of them. He knew women went for the muscle-bound, sports-car-driving type, but he hadn't seen it in Cassidy. She had pushed him away because she wanted something more serious than sex, she'd said. Her dismissal had caused him to re-think what he wanted from her. He allowed his feelings to become involved, and now he finds out she's dating a Fabio look-alike? Thoroughly peeved, he stormed the porch.

"Kirkland. You said you would call." She smiled tentatively. "Come in."

He thrust dinner at her. "My mother sent you dinner."

"She didn't have to do that."

"There's only enough for one. But then again, you probably already had dinner."

"No. I haven't. I—"

"I can guess what you were doing, Cassidy. Is Fabio the family man type?"

She suddenly laughed. "Fabio?"

She actually laughed at him when his insides were twisting. His emotions were so confused. He didn't understand why he wanted to kill the man who had just left her house. He couldn't rational-ize the anger directed at Cassidy. He had the urge to protect Courtney from the opportunistic man who had just driven off in the expensive sports car. Where would they put the car seat? "I don't see what's so funny, Cassidy."

She fought the giggles and raised an eyebrow at his tone. "Shh, Courtney's asleep."

"These are for you." He shoved the flowers at her.

"Thank you." She sniffed the flowers and started to sneeze. "I'm allergic—" sneeze— "to flowers."

Great. Nothing would come easy when it came to winning Cassidy Payne. He couldn't even impress her with flowers. He took the roses and dropped them outside the front door. "I bet Fabio knows you're allergic to flowers."

Cassidy crooked her head to the side, watching him. "Kirkland, are you *jealous?*"

"Jealous?" He laughed at the absurdity of it. He didn't get jealous. Women were jealous over him and his free-wheeling lifestyle. "Please." He wrapped his arms across his chest.

"Okay." She turned on her heels and danced off into the kitchen.

He followed. "You aren't going to explain?"

"It sure sounds like you're jealous to me." She was smiling again.

"I'm not jealous." He sat at the small kitchen table, his knees scraping the underside. "I'm just worried about the impression you're making on Courtney."

"If I didn't know you were speaking from jealousy, I'd be very offended by your remark. So offended I'd ask you to leave."

Kirkland dropped his eyes. He knew Cassidy would never do anything to harm Courtney. "I didn't mean it that way."

"How did you mean it?"

"Not that way."

She turned to hide her smile. "Do you want something to eat?" She pulled the Tupperware containers from the bag. "You were wrong. Your mom sent enough food for two."

She was grinning again, while his insides were burning. How could he eat with this sick, nauseating feeling?

"Did you come over just to bring me dinner?"

"Yes," he mumbled, still angry about the Fabio

look-alike. "I thought you might be too busy, or too tired, to cook."

"You're very thoughtful. I'll have to call and thank your mom, too." She prepared her plate and sat down to eat.

"You aren't going to tell me who the guy is?" he finally asked, unable to wait her out.

She chewed slowly, watching him. "He's a model."

He grunted in disbelief.

"I'm a cover illustrator for a publishing house in New York. They send me photos and blurbs about books and I paint the covers."

"He didn't seem like a photo to me."

"Occasionally, I use live models. If I meet someone who would make a good cover, I paint them and sell the artwork to the publishing house."

"Do all the models look like him?" Sarcasm fueled the question.

"The majority of my covers are for romance novels, so yeah, most of my models look like him."

He watched Cassidy take another bite of her dinner. The thought of men coming and going didn't sit well with him.

"Would you like to see some of my work?"

He followed her into the third bedroom, which had been turned into an art studio. There were hundreds of pictures strewn about the room. A small pedestal draped in purple fabric sat opposite the only window. A pasteboard with photos of men and women in seductive poses filled one wall. On her easel was a painting of the man who had just left her house.

"You live in this world." He checked out her paintings.

"What do you mean?"

He turned, giving her his full attention. "You live in a world of hunks and beautiful women who find love and live happily ever after."

"And where do you live?" she asked with unsolicited tenderness.

Her question surprised him. "Not here."

Cassidy sat down on a huge red, satin pillow. She held out her hand and he joined her on the pillow across from her. "Tell me about where you live, Kirkland."

"In my world, love that lasts a lifetime ended after my parents' generation. My world is about families with two working parents and latchkey kids. Divorce happens twice as much as marriage, and you'd be hard pressed to find a marriage not touched by infidelity."

"Greyson and Sutton are happy."

He thought of Sutton's first marriage to Alex, but didn't comment on it. "They're an exception. They grew up together."

"So, do you think I'm foolish to hold out for true love?"

He looked into the depths of her eyes. Any man would give her all she needed to be happy. "No, I think you'll find it."

"And what about Courtney? Have I condemned her to a life of infidelity and divorce?"

As precious as Courtney is, Cassidy would have to fight the men off with a stick. "I think she'll be okay."

"If it's possible for other people, why don't you think you can have it?"

He'd walked right into her trap. But he didn't

mind discussing his hopes and fears with her. She truly cared where his head was at. She wasn't judging him, only trying to understand him. "Do you remember Alex Galloway?" he asked.

She nodded. "Hard to forget Alex Galloway. He was 'the man' in high school."

"Alex was more of a brother to me than my own brothers." The pain pierced his chest as expected.

"And he taught you his cheating ways, and jaded your perspective of love."

"I don't want it to sound like he corrupted me, because he didn't. Alex got me into some trouble here and there, but I reciprocated. He looked after me when I needed it. If it wasn't for him, I would have dropped out of college."

"What did he do?" Cassidy asked in a quiet, soothing tone.

"I was having a hard time in an upper-level math course. The concepts were too far over my head and my instructor targeted me for failure. I started to give up, spending more time in the bars chasing women than at school. To me, I was going to flunk out, so I was biding my time until I did and had to tell my parents.

"When I called Alex, he came to town on the first flight he could get. He sobered me up and got me a private tutor. He encouraged me to take on my instructor. Once I told the teacher I would pass his class, or die trying, he backed off. After that, I became more determined in college. Instead of just passing to keep my parents happy, I took the hardest courses and fought for A's. Alex helped me realize college was about me, and my future. He told me to do it for me and not to let anyone keep me from what I wanted."

"Alex was a good friend to you."

Something in the tone of her words touched him. Maybe it was because he could actually talk about Alex to someone without them countering with all his faults. Whatever it was, the pain piercing his chest expanded until his emotions seeped from the wound.

"You miss him. It's okay," Cassidy said before pulling his head to her chest. She placed an arm around his shoulders and pressed her palm on his cheek. "His death must have been hard for you. He was more than a friend. He was your brother."

With that simple acknowledgment, Kirkland let himself grieve his friend's death. He hugged Cassidy tight, burying his head in the safety of her chest, and let his emotions flow. She held him for a long time, never uttering a word. She stroked his back and encouraged him to face his pain. She shared his emotions without judgment. She became his safe place.

# Chapter 5

Cassidy lifted Courtney high into the air. She cooed and made funny faces, causing her to chortle. Cassidy brought Courtney close, inhaling the intoxicating scent of her freshly bathed baby. Courtney was in her best mood after her morning bath. The baby grabbed a lock of Cassidy's hair, clutching it in her tiny fist. Cassidy kissed her soft cheeks, loving every minute of motherhood. For all her fears and doubts, this moment assured her she'd made the right decision about becoming a single mother. She rocked Courtney in her arms, thankful she'd been given the chance.

She couldn't forget Kirkland's part in it all. If he hadn't come to the rescue . . . she didn't want to think about it. He had, and everything had turned out wonderfully. She'd be forever grateful to him for it. Everything he'd done since had come from his heart, and not obligation. She'd come to rely on his friendship. Having his support in a small town like Hannaford meant a great deal. Many residents still held on to old traditions and values, which was the root of her problems with her parents.

Courtney cooed again.

"Yeah, you like Kirkland, too. Don't you?"

Courtney's arms flared.

"I do believe you've grown attached to Mr. Ballantyne." She carried the baby into the kitchen, propping her on her hip while she checked the warmth of her formula. They'd developed a workable routine. Darius had suggested that a schedule would help to bring order to her house again, and it had. After Courtney's bottle, she would grab a quick breakfast. Afterward, Courtney would take a short nap during which Cassidy would work on her illustrations. Right around the time Courtney woke again, the maid service would arrive. While the service straightened up, she would take Courtney into town to run errands. They would return around lunchtime. Courtney would take another bottle, then a long nap. This was when Cassidy got most of her work done.

Evenings were always quiet. Courtney still woke during the night, so Cassidy always turned in early. She liked the days Kirkland unexpectedly stopped by. It broke up the monotony. There were other reasons she liked his visits, Cassidy admitted to herself. She had begun to look forward to his random visits. He brought energy into the house. Even Courtney brightened up when he arrived. He would never stay long, but she enjoyed the time he was there. Sometimes he'd arrive in time for dinner, and join them in the kitchen, telling her about how the construction business operated. Some nights he would rock Courtney to sleep and put her down for the night to give Cassidy a couple of extra hours to work on her drawings. Other times, he'd join her in the middle of a movie, letting himself out when she dozed off on the sofa.

Things were easier when Kirkland came around. The routine was no longer monotonous. Motherhood didn't seem so draining. Courtney wasn't as fussy. "Kirkland is a special friend," she told herself, knowing she wasn't being honest with herself. "A friend."

The paper mill was Greyson's brainchild, but Kirkland and Chevy had enthusiastically invested in the idea. All three worked to make it a success and brought Hannaford Valley back to life through economic prosperity. Kirkland divided his time between the mill and his construction job in Charleston. He went over reports at his desk, thinking of the irony of his latest business venture. Would he ever get his brothers to come on board with the idea? He tapped his pen against the edge of the desk. No, it wouldn't happen. He'd have to develop the project himself and show positive revenue before they'd even consider the good an industrial project would do for the town.

Sutton stuck her head into his office. "Got a minute?"

Where was his secretary? And why wasn't she a tenacious gatekeeper like Greyson's or Chevy's?

"You want to see me?" he asked, shuffling papers to give the illusion he might be too busy to talk.

She came in uninvited, and took a seat in front of his desk. She pulled out a notepad and poised herself like a reporter. "I'm doing a research project for my Ethics of Environmental Law course. I thought you might be able to help."

"Me? Chevy's the bleeding heart, always trying to save a whale or keep a forest from being destroyed."

The right side of Sutton's mouth lifted in sarcastic amusement. "Funny. No, I think you'd know more about this. I'm interested in what you're going to do with the land my philandering husband left you."

"Greyson's your husband now."

The set of her jaw faltered for a quick second. "So, any plans?"

"Nothing definite." A half-truth.

"There seems to be a buzz amongst the developers. Something about an industrial complex."

He worked hard at maintaining a neutral expression. "Small towns are famous for rumors."

"So there's no truth to it then?"

"Sutton, why don't you tell me why you really came?"

She flipped her notebook closed with a snap. "You don't fool me, Kirkland Ballantyne. Your family might be wearing blinders. You might even have Cassidy convinced you're a nice guy, but I know what Alex was and I know you're his clone."

"You've talked to Cassidy about me?"

Again, her jaw slacked. "Cassidy? I warned her about you."

"Does your husband know you're trying to cause trouble for me? What did you tell her?"

She studied his face. "Why are you more concerned about what Cassidy thinks about you than what's happening to the old Galloway land? Could it be because you already know what's going to happen to the land?"

He didn't answer. His sister-in-law was beginning to scrape his nerves.

"Cassidy is a single mother, for God's sake. Don't play with her."

"I know what Cassidy is. I was there. Remember? Why don't you let Cassidy and me handle our own business?"

"Someone has to protect her."

"Like no one protected you from Alex? Like I didn't protect you?"

"You were my friend."

"And now I'm your brother-in-law. Sutton, I know what Alex did to you was wrong, but it's wrong to take what he did out on me. Alex was your husband—not me. The ultimate responsibility for the failure of your marriage had to be between you two. My friendship with Alex and your marriage are two separate things." He regretted the harshness with which his words were delivered, but they needed to be said. Since he had stepped over the line that would bring Greyson's wrath to his door, he might as well throw everything behind it.

"You insinuated yourself in the middle of our marriage."

"How? By being a friend to Alex?"

"By doing his dirty work. By helping him lie to me. Can't you see your responsibility in all this?"

"No," Kirkland said flatly. "No, I can't."

"I guess that's why we have a problem."

"Why do we have a problem, Sutton? Alex is gone. Why can't we remember him for the good things?"

"Do you think it's easy, Kirkland? I thought I had

forgiven him. I was in a good place until you told me about the land he gave you. You knew what Sierra and I were going through and you didn't do anything."

Unshed tears glazed her eyes. He didn't mean to make her cry. Despite the turbulence of their relationship, they had all been best friends once—she'd married his best friend, and his brother—he cared deeply for her. Sierra was his niece twice over. He didn't want Sutton to fall apart whenever he came around. "We're both still hurting . . ."

Sutton clutched her notepad to her chest, stood, and left his office.

"Damn." He didn't know what to do for Sutton. She should turn to Greyson. He wasn't even sure it was his place to intervene. Just a few days ago he was huddled on Cassidy's floor grieving for Alex. He didn't know how to help Sutton get over Alex's wrongs. And they were too busy blaming each other to share their grief.

# Chapter 6

Cassidy smiled when Kirkland pulled up to the curb in front of her house. She was sitting in a rocker with one hand idly rocking Courtney's bassinet. She wore red shorts and a matching tank top that revealed the new fullness of her breasts. She looked up and, as if seeing him for the first time, a wide, bright smile filled her face. He could never fully describe the feeling that moved through him when he saw her. She was happy to see him. He couldn't remember anyone ever being this happy to have him near.

Kirkland grabbed the bag on the seat next to him and sprinted to the porch.

"Hi," Cassidy said.

He handed her the shopping bag and peeked in the bassinet at Courtney. He bent down, letting her wrap her hand around his pinky. He answered each of her chortles with unintelligible words he had dubbed "their secret language."

"Kirkland, you don't have to bring a gift every time you stop by." She stuck her nose into the shopping bag and gasped. She held the white satin and lace christening gown up in front of her. "This is gorgeous." She searched for the price tag. "This had to set you back—"

"Don't worry about it." He hid his embarrassment by directing his conversation to Courtney.

"I—we—can't accept this. I don't know how I'm going to pay you back for the maid service—"

"I never asked you to pay me back for the maid service. I don't want you to pay me back for the christening gown. We're friends. Friends do these kind of things for each other." He glanced at her and she was watching him as if she didn't believe his motives were purely friendship related.

"We are friends," she said cautiously.

"Exactly. So let me take you and Courtney to dinner. Have you eaten?" He'd purposefully left the office early to catch her before she'd prepared dinner.

"No, but—"

"No, buts." He continued to play with Courtney.

"Hey."

He stood and turned to face the screen door in one motion. A man stepped out onto the porch. His eyes dashed between Cassidy and the man, asking a million questions. His gut tightened and he stepped in front of the bassinet as if he needed to protect Courtney from her mother's indiscretions.

"Kirkland, this is my brother, Darius."

He felt relieved as he offered his hand.

"Darius has work in town so he's going to stay the night. Maybe we can have dinner another night."

Darius took in Kirkland's protective stance, his obvious jealousy, and the christening gown and made an astute assessment of his intentions toward

Cassidy. "I don't want to disrupt your routine. Go to dinner. Courtney and I will be fine."

"Leave Courtney?" She looked worried.

"You could bring her along," Kirkland offered.

"You'd better take me up on my offer," Darius said. "You never know when I will again. Courtney and I will be fine."

"Yeah?" Cassidy asked, her apprehension clear.

"You deserve a break from motherhood for one evening," Darius prodded.

"We'll only be away for a couple of hours," Kirkland said.

"I do deserve it, don't I?" Cassidy asked rhetorically. "Okay. Give me a minute to change?"

"Take your time."

Cassidy stepped up to take Courtney from the bassinet, but Kirkland shooed her away, lifting the baby and cradling her to his chest.

Darius grabbed the bassinet and they all moved inside.

"So, you delivered Courtney?"

"It was amazing," Kirkland said.

Darius nodded. "I have three of my own and I was in the delivery room each time." He paused, reflecting. "It changes a man forever. To see his child, someone he created, brought into the world."

Kirkland didn't know what to say to that.

"So, you been hanging around since Courtney was born?"

"You make it sound like I'm an opportunist."

Darius stared at him, blankly.

"Darius," Cassidy called from the bedroom, "leave Kirkland alone. He's a good friend."

"Friend?" Darius bit at his cheek, an obvious reflection of his doubt. "Are you so loaded you can give all your friends expensive gifts?"

Kirkland placed Courtney in her bassinet and prepared for a battle with Cassidy's brother. "Did I do something to offend you?"

"Some men would see Cassidy and Courtney here alone, no family close by, and think this is a good setup to step into and take advantage of."

"I agree, that's why I'm looking out for them."

Darius nodded, not giving away his thoughts.

"You don't give Cassidy enough credit. She's tough. She can take care of herself."

"But I'm her big brother, so it's my job to do that."

Cassidy stepped into the living room. "You're my big brother by two minutes." She looked to Kirkland. "We're twins."

He saw no resemblance. Matter of fact, they were complete opposites.

"Two minutes counts."

"Leave Kirkland alone," Cassidy said, ignoring the way Darius's eyes bugged out of his head. Kirkland hid his response. No ogling in front of the overprotective big brother. "Did Darius tell you he's working with Greyson?"

Darius jumped in. "I didn't have a chance."

Something passed between them Kirkland didn't want to know about. "I need to make a quick call," he said, leaving them to fight it out.


"What are you doing?" Darius asked as soon as Kirkland disappeared.

"What?" Cassidy placed a hand on her hip. This

wouldn't be the first time he didn't approve of someone she was seeing.

"You're not interested in this kid, are you?"

"Kirkland's not a kid. Besides, we're just friends."

"Friends," he mumbled, tight-lipped. "He's definitely got more on his mind than being friends. Don't feel obligated to him because he delivered Courtney. It's what we do as high-level beings—we help each other in time of need. It doesn't mean you have to sleep with him as repayment."

"Darius! This overprotective brother routine is high schoolish."

He crossed the room and lowered his voice. "There's something about him that rubs me wrong."

"Just relax. Kirkland has been very nice to me, and to Courtney." She thought of the candid conversation she and Kirkland had had about the death of his friend. "He's gone through a rough time recently. He needs a friend, and I think he likes being here because it's a place where he can be himself. He overcompensates for my friendship by buying Courtney expensive gifts, but he's not hurting anyone."

Darius looked at her, dumbfounded.

"What are you worried about?"

"You've had a rough time recently, too. Having a baby isn't easy—especially alone and without Mom and Dad's support. I'm worried about you getting involved with someone who might not be the best person to get involved with."

Kirkland stepped out of the kitchen. "Cassidy, are you ready to go?"

She tossed Darius a silent warning, hoping Kirk-

land hadn't overheard their conversation. She
grabbed her jacket and left quickly, eager to assure
Kirkland she valued his friendship, and that Darius's comments wouldn't change anything. Once
outside, she started to apologize, but he stopped
her with a wave of his hand. He shielded his expression from her. Darius's comments had hurt
him, but he would never admit it. She helped him
protect his pride by dropping the subject.

She melted into the soft leather seat of his Lexus.
Her selection of a suitable casual dinner outfit was
severely limited by the extra ten pounds she was still
carrying after Courtney's birth, but she had decided on a sassy black dress that displayed the new
fullness of her chest with a deep neckline. She relaxed to the velvety crooning of the latest R&B sensation from the premium sound system. She
crossed her legs, enjoying how sexy the short hem
of the dress made her feel. She'd only had enough
time to fluff out the few curls in her hair, and now
it fell about her face in soft, dark waves. She'd never
been adept with makeup—having grown up with a
twin brother made her a tomboy—so she didn't
bother to do more than dab cocoa-colored gloss on
her lips.

The ride of the luxury car was smooth and relaxing. Kirkland expertly navigated the car on the interstate, heading for the capital. They laughed
when they reached the spot where he'd delivered
Courtney. "You saved the situation from becoming
tragic," she complimented.

"Now that's scary."

She remembered the relief she had felt when he
appeared in the crowd. She had called for him, des-

perate for his help. "You don't have to be modest
with me. I was there. I know what you did. You
saved Courtney's life."

"You're being dramatic."

"I was scared to death. The accident happened so
fast."

"Cassidy." He laid his hand on her knee. "Don't
talk about it anymore. You're going to get upset,
thinking about what could have happened."

She looked at the passing scenery, then back to
Kirkland. "Thank you. If I didn't say it, thank you."

"You've said it once and you don't have to say it
anymore."

Cassidy watched his intense concentration on the
task of driving. He exuded a seriousness too sophisticated for what she believed a twenty-six-year-old
should have. Somewhere, he'd lost that carefree, live-
in-the-moment invincibility men have when they're
still too immature to realize life is about consequences and actions. She watched his subtle, refined
mannerisms and thought he wore them well, as well
as the expensive suit clinging to his body.

She had always been a sucker for a man in a suit.
It had more to do with the intelligence of the
wearer than the way the tailored fit made her eyes
roam slowly over every sinewy muscle. At least that
was what she told herself. She was beginning to
admit it was probably a purely physical thing when
Kirkland turned to give her an incredible smile.
She tingled in places a friend should not have
made her tingle.

"You're quiet," he said, glancing her way. "You're
not still reliving the accident are you?"

"Just lost in thought."

His eyes swept her body. "Me, too."

She ran her fingers through her hair, suddenly wondering why she had limited their relationship to only friendship.

"Your brother doesn't like me. People usually have to know me a while before they come to that conclusion."

She felt sad for him, embarrassed about her brother's rude comments. "You overheard?"

"Enough to know he doesn't think I should be coming around you and Courtney."

"Don't let Darius bother you. I make my own decisions about my life."

"Really?" He exited the freeway and came to a stop at the red light at the top of the ramp. "So, if you wanted to hold my hand, you would?" He held out his hand, the stark white cuff of his shirt disappearing beneath the dark, crisp fabric of the suit. He exuded sex appeal, as his unique vibe bounced within the confined space.

The car behind them honked.

"The light's green," she announced, effectively avoiding his question.

He laughed, low and seductively, dispensing any doubt about his intentions.

"Why do you say things like that?" she asked.

"Like what?"

"You make negative statements about yourself."

"Do I?"

"Yes. Why?"

A shadow passed over his face, telling her it was somehow connected with his history with Alex Galloway. For Alex to have been his friend, he'd done a real job on Kirkland.

"You shouldn't do it anymore around me."

He whipped the car around a corner, sparing her a glance.

"Seriously. I won't tolerate it."

He grinned. "You've got the mother thing going on tonight."

She ignored his joke. "Don't do it." She paused. "Where are we going for dinner?"

"It's a surprise. Want to call and check on Courtney?"

"You know I do." Even though they'd been gone less than an hour.

He dug inside his suit and produced his cell phone. She wondered what else lay beneath the expensive fabric. As she pressed the buttons to dial her number, she imagined her fingers sweeping over the soft silk lining of his suit as she searched for his cell. She discretely perused his hard build. All legs and muscles, Kirkland had the perfect body. Mama Ballantyne had produced three fine men, but Kirkland was the best of the lot. His sandy-brown hair accentuated the bronze tone of his skin, making him distinctively handsome.

By the time she finished her call, they were pulling up to the guarded gates of an upscale apartment complex. The guard exchanged pleasantries with Kirkland, welcoming him home after a long absence.

"You're taking me back to your place?" she asked. Fear of her inability to exercise self-control crept into her voice.

"Should I be worried?" He looked amused as he pulled the Lexus into a reserved parking space.

"Maybe I should be worried."

"Maybe you should." He liked toying with her. The more flustered she became, the bigger his grin grew.

"Did you have this planned?" she asked as they stepped into the lobby.

"What kind of man do you think I am, Cassidy Payne?"

They stepped into the elevator and Kirkland pushed the button to take them to the penthouse.

"I thought you were living in Hannaford Valley?"

"I spend a lot of nights in my parents' old house when I'm working, but I haven't been able to give up my place here." The elevator quickly arrived at the top floor. Kirkland had just slipped his key into the door when it swung open. Not expecting anyone to be there, thinking maybe they'd surprised a robber, Cassidy stepped back and behind his broad shoulders.

"Mr. Ballantyne." An older man with dark hair that shined from overuse of chemicals stood in the doorway. "Good to see you."

Kirkland drew Cassidy from behind his back. "She's a little jumpy."

The man stepped aside, allowing her to enter the apartment. Although she had never seen an "apartment" with high-beam loft ceilings made from rich dark wood, and a winding staircase up to the next level. Not to mention the two patio doors monopolizing the expanse of the living room. She tried not to gawk as she imagined how large the apartment could be.

"Cassidy," Kirkland said, "this is Guy. He looks after my place when I spend a lot of time in Hannaford."

Cassidy exchanged pleasantries with the man. He didn't have the refinement of a butler—did people even have butlers these days?—but he seemed to be an employee of some sort. She knew Kirkland was financially stable with partial ownership in the paper mill and his construction career, but she'd never imagined he was wealthy enough to live like a prince.

"The staff is waiting for you," Guy told him. "I'll be back tomorrow, early afternoon."

"Where's he going?" she asked after Guy hurried out. A mood was being set she wasn't sure she was prepared for. Having dinner with Kirkland in a crowded restaurant was safe and friendly. Eating alone in his apartment was sensual and definitely not conducive to remaining just friends.

"He doesn't live here." His hand was at the small of her back, guiding her through the apartment. "He takes care of the apartment for me, but when I'm here, he usually goes home. I like my privacy. He was on Alex's payroll, and now he's on mine." Something painful flickered across his face. "I've tried to take care of Alex's people."

Another example of his goodness. He hid it well, wearing a costume of flirtatious bravado, but underneath he was a caring man who had experienced too much pain in his life.

"What did he do for Alex?"

Kirkland looked uncomfortable, but her gaze didn't falter, pressing him for an answer. "Guy helped Alex take care of certain *situations* requiring discretion."

With her understanding came a dislike of Alex. Everyone had heard bits and pieces of the circumstances surrounding his death. If half of what Cassidy had heard in the beauty shop was true, and Kirkland had anything to do with it all, she understood why Sutton held such contempt for her brother-in-law.

"I've said too much. You're looking at me the same way Sutton does."

She lowered her head. She hadn't meant for her emotions to be so easily read. A long silence stretched between them. Kirkland was a dangerous temptation. He was young, and ambitious, with many life experiences in front of him. She had been where he was going, and didn't necessarily want to repeat it. But he was kind and decadently sexy, too. When he wasn't around and she found herself thinking about him, she could always list the reasons she should stay away from him. When he came near, looking like creamy milk chocolate waiting to melt in her mouth, she couldn't imagine anything but being the seducer in their relationship.

"Sutton is your friend. Does the truth about my friendship with Alex change your opinion of me?"

"You're a friend, too."

"I would understand if it did. Everyone judges me by my friendship with Alex."

"I don't know enough about your friendship with Alex to have any opinion on it. Truthfully, it really has nothing to do with me. I didn't even know you then. Besides, I wouldn't judge you by who your friends are." She felt some desperation with the thought of losing her friendship with him. He had grown to be important in her life. She didn't want to end their acquaintance yet. "Sutton and I are friends, yes, but I wasn't a part of her relationship with Alex. I know you in a different way. I don't want to get mixed up in the middle of your past with Sutton and Alex. I want to be your friend now."

"I don't think anyone has ever seen me as Kirkland Douglas Ballantyne before."

"Who do they see you as?"

"The youngest Ballantyne brother, or Alex's friend."

"Are you projecting these feelings onto other people?"

"You're analyzing me."

"You should focus on being yourself. You're intelligent and caring. Don't live up to the rumors and stereotyping. Be yourself. You're a good person with a good heart."

Kirkland watched her, astutely sensing her feelings for him. She reexamined her words. They'd been innocent enough, but her hands pressing against his chest swayed their meaning. She emotionally pulled away, embarrassed her feelings had gotten so out of control without her noticing.

"You see me this way?"

She tried to take her hands away.

Kirkland stopped her. He took her hands in his, caressing her palms with his thumbs. His touch caused a shiver of emotion to wave through her body. She hadn't felt this nervous since her first kiss with Billy Nelson in ninth grade. She'd grown up and discarded thoughts of perfect relationships and giddy stolen moments. Kirkland's lazy caress touched her in unfamiliar ways. One simple gesture opened doors she had welded closed a long time ago.

She cleared her throat and moved the conversation onto safer ground. "So, you sent Guy away. You've stolen me away from my precious baby and driven me to the capital. Are you setting me up for something, Kirkland Ballantyne?" She smiled, trying to bring humor into the heated moment.

He gripped her shoulders and gently spun her around, continuing their journey through his home. "Yes, I am."

They'd passed through several rooms of the apartment, and still his hand pressed her forward. The rooms were expansive and well decorated. Each room was a burst of color, conservative while festive. Everything was in its place, neat and orderly. Cassidy found herself thinking again that he lived the life of a much older man. He had an old soul, drowning in grief over his best friend's death. She felt a certain kinship with him on that level. She missed her parents more than she had let on to Darius, but they had made the decision not to be a part of her and Courtney's life. They would have to accept her life choices and love her in spite of them.

"You have servants?" Cassidy asked, still trying to find a safe topic of conversation.

"Not exactly."

"What exactly?"

"I have a few employees who take care of the things I know nothing about."

"You're in construction. What can't you take care of?"

He grinned, but didn't reply. He was being mod-

est. Trying to hide another one of his good qualities. He gazed at her with serious brown eyes. They
sparkled hopefully, a hazel dream for her. He
leaned forward, slowing the passage of time. Her
lips parted in anticipation.

The cook burst through the kitchen door. "Mr.
Ballantyne, I'll be serving dinner now." The door
swung closed.

"No problem," Kirkland answered.

She didn't recover as quickly. The moment was
lost, but she waved in the aftermath, still feeling his
warmth.

The man in the white cook's uniform came
through the swinging door again, balancing a tray
with two silver-covered platters. He placed dinner
on a small round table decorated with colorful
flowers and scattered candles. The table was set
with silver and gray place settings, which caught the
light from the flames in the fireplace.

He held out her chair. "The flowers are artificial."

In her awe, she hadn't remembered her allergy
to flowers. The table was so beautiful she would
have suffered through an attack to soak up the am-
bience. She hadn't remembered, but Kirkland had.
For a moment, she saw him as a prince in a dark
suit.

The cook poured them each a glass of wine and
said good night. He disappeared momentarily into
the kitchen before leaving through the front door.

"Why are you grinning?" Kirkland asked.

"Your employees are funny."

He laughed with her. "They're not exactly what
you would call refined—or subtle."

"It's so dark in here I can't see my food."

He went to the dimmer and added a little light. "Not subtle at all."

They sat at an elegantly decorated table, eating a fabulously prepared meal, but the atmosphere was lost on them. They laughed and ate with their elbows on the table, discarding the formality demanded by the elaborate table decorations. Discovering which of the gourmet foods they liked the best, Kirkland brought the remainders from the kitchen. He served her from a folding TV tray he found in the kitchen.

"This is really good," Cassidy said. "What is it?"

"I have no idea."

As they grew comfortable, Kirkland replaced the easy-listening music with R&B, then rap. She dropped her guard, becoming less inhibited. Rap music was not the usual way to seduce a woman. His intentions were to have fun. She had worried about her feelings for him needlessly. The warm emotions she felt toward him were based on friendship and their growing bond.

"Who is this?" Cassidy asked as the beat of the music made her head bob.

"Would you know if I told you?"

"No."

He left the table, giving her a private karaoke show. His performance was made original by the shaking of his narrow hips. He gyrated and crooned his way through the hook, never taking his eyes off hers. "C'mon, you can be my groupie." He grabbed her hand and pulled her up onto his imaginary stage. "You're too stiff."

"The beat is too fast."

"No, it's not. Just go with it." He moved around

behind her and grasped her hips, teaching her the way he liked to see them sway. "You know how to do this." He moved around in front of her, grasped her hips again, and helped her follow his rhythm. "Better."

"I've never danced like this in my life." She couldn't contain her giggles. "You *are* crazy."

"Sometimes you need crazy. Life's too serious." He spun her around, locking his arms around her waist from behind.

"I guess I did need a little crazy to take the pressure off."

"Me, too." His hands found her hips. "Now you've got it." He placed his mouth near her ear and added his own lyrics to the popular rap song.

She jumped into his fantasy, shimmering her body and rocking her hips like she'd seen on the explicit music videos. She slinked around behind him, giving the performance her all. She helped him off with his jacket, winding it above her head before sending it across the room. She tossed her head back and laughed at his shocked enthusiasm. He twisted around, grasping her hips and pulling her solidly against him. When she stopped laughing, she found him staring at her hungrily, his hazel eyes watching her. While she played, the music had stopped and the game had ended. He kept their rhythm alive by rocking their bodies together. He placed a hand on her cheek and lowered his head, his lips already parting.

"Don't," she whispered.

He ignored her, coming closer, his gaze locked with hers.

"Don't."

"Pull away," he demanded. "If you don't want me to kiss you, pull away."

She couldn't find the strength to meet his challenge, because only a tiny part of her wanted to.

"Pull away."

"Don't."

"Last chance, Cassidy." He pressed his face to hers, cheek to cheek. His fingers moved down her arm. "Pull away now." He breathed deeply, warming the side of her neck.

"Don't . . . stop," she whispered.

His fingers caressed the back of her hand. "Cassidy." He gently pressed his lips to the side of her neck.

"Kirkland." She tried to find the willpower to turn away, but his tongue tasted her cheek, effectively controlling her spirit.

"I'm so glad you're here," he whispered near her ear.

The warmth of his words caressed her. She had to retreat before she gave everything to this man. She didn't know his intentions. Hormones controlled her actions. There were so many reasons why she should pull away. As she began to list them in her head, he crushed her in his arms, locking her solidly against his body. "You're too young." It sounded lame even to her, but she needed to come to her senses.

"I'm a man." He punctuated his point by pressing his pelvis against hers. "Look at what you're doing to me."

He had done things to her body, too.

"Cassidy, you are funny and beautiful and understand me better than anyone. You don't judge me."

He sighed, raising goose bumps on her neck. "You're sexy as hell." His hand moved to the small of her back. "I've never met a woman who can stimulate my mind *and* make me hot as hell." He lifted his head and looked at her with seductive rum-colored eyes. "Don't ignore what's happening between us just because I'm a few years younger than you."

She opened her mouth to argue, but quickly discovered she didn't have a rebuttal. She stared into the depths of his sexy eyes and let him wrap her in the seductive comfort of his body. His muscles were hard, flexing as he squeezed her to him. He maintained the pressure of his pelvis, an open invitation for whatever she wanted.

"I don't know what to do here," he admitted.

She was clueless too.

He lowered his head to kiss her, but stopped just before meeting her lips. "Can I make love to you, Cassidy?"

*Make love?* She didn't know fantasy from reality. Every fear and delight she'd ever imagined crashed in on her. She needed an anchor to reality. She was a single mother, she reminded herself. She was thirty-four, and Kirkland twenty-six. She'd come to know him fairly well, but not well enough to know if he was a dishonest playboy, or simply misunderstood.

"Cassidy?" His unanswered question hung in the air.

If she were to make a decision based on attraction alone, they would have skipped dinner and made love as soon as they walked through the door of his penthouse. Over six feet of prime muscle with golden skin, sandy-brown hair, and light eyes could be hers for the exploration, with one word. *Yes.* Her insides quivered at the possibility of what she might discover. Every stereotype she'd ever heard raced through her mind. He possessed the aggressiveness of a young man, but he was also gentle—both qualities sure to make a good lover.

"Cassidy?" He cupped her cheeks in his palm, demanding an answer.

"One of us has to be rational."

He understood her meaning. Instead of being disappointed, he looked relieved. "You didn't say no." He smiled. "I'll ask you again. Another time." He stepped back, denying her the taste of his lips. "When we're both being rational."

# Chapter 7

"I don't know how to make this right between you two." Greyson lifted one end of a sheet of plywood. With Kirkland, he carried the wood over to the frame of the gazebo.

"I'm not sure you can."

Chevy joined them, and began hammering the wood into place. "You know," he said, "Sutton is stubborn. She'll come around."

Greyson ignored Chevy's assessment of his wife's behavior. "Pop came to see me. He wants everything to be nice and peaceful when we sit down together for the anniversary dinner."

Chevy stopped hammering and held a level gaze with his little brother. "It might help things along if you gave her the land, Kirkland."

"No," Greyson said firmly. Kirkland exchanged glances with Chevy, surprised. "I don't want any part of Alex in our lives. It took a long, long time for us to become a family. We don't need anything causing friction between us. We're doing fine financially. We don't need Alex's money."

"Don't you think it'll cause friction if you tell Sutton you don't want her to take over Alex's land?" Chevy, always levelheaded, asked.

"What would we do with it?"

Chevy shrugged. "Have you asked Sutton? She might have an idea. Maybe she'd leave it for Sierra."

"No," Greyson said sternly. "I'll provide for Sierra's future. Let's drop the idea of Kirkland giving Sutton the land."

"You don't want to talk to Sutton about it first?" Chevy prodded.

"I've made the decision." Greyson went to retrieve more plywood.

Kirkland exchanged another glance with Chevy. When Sutton found out Greyson had made a unilateral decision about the land, there would be trouble. The conversation had been effectively ended, so they joined Greyson in hauling wood.

By remaining quiet, Kirkland had avoided lying to his brothers about his plans for Alex's land. Plans Alex, and maybe even Mother Galloway, would approve of but certainly not many more residents of Hannaford Valley. As they worked on the gazebo, he justified the reasons an industrial park would be good for Hannaford. More businesses would move into town, bringing more jobs. With economic growth came the need for housing and entertainment. The sleepy town, forgotten by time and tucked away in the mountains, would grow rapidly, making life better for everyone.

He had begun to rationalize his actions a lot lately. What seemed like a good way to prove his manhood now seemed deceitful. He was hiding the truth from his family. He was keeping Alex's land from it's rightful owners. Guilt beat down on him underneath the hot sun. He worked hard, carrying lumber, hammering and planning—anything to keep from examining his true motives in industrializing Hannaford Valley.

Mama Ballantyne stepped out onto the back porch. "You boys wash up for lunch," she called.

He had planned to leave around the lunch hour to meet with Pete about the development. Meeting the budget for the industrial park required thorough planning and tight budgeting. Time was a factor with the mayor leading the efforts against changing the landscape of Hannaford. He was coming up for reelection this year and he'd made saving the environment the lead issue on his platform. Kirkland also needed to convince Greyson that upgrading the town was for the best of everyone. Once Greyson was on board, Chevy would follow, making it easier to get the town to accept change.

Chevy dropped his hammer and went inside for lunch.

"You coming?" Greyson asked, bumping his shoulder.

"I have a meeting."

"What kind of meeting?"

"Something to do with my construction work."

"Mama will miss you. She says you don't come around as much as you used to."

His mother stood in the doorway, watching them. Mama gained her happiness through the work she did at the church and taking care of her family. And she took care of her family best by providing them with big, elaborate meals. "Maybe I can move it back an hour," Kirkland wavered. He couldn't disappoint his mother.

"Good." They began to walk together to the house. "How's it going with Cassidy?"

He shrugged, fighting to keep the smile off his face as he remembered the rap show they'd performed together.

"She's a little older than you."

*Typical big brother concern*, he thought.

"An older woman is just what you need," Greyson added. "Maybe she'll be able to straighten you out." He tugged at the cap covering his wily curls.

"Didn't take one to get you in line."

"Oh, is that a crack about me being under Sutton's thumb?"

"I would have put it another way."

"That's it." Greyson took a boxer's stance, blocking his path. He responded, putting up his fists and planting his feet to the ground. They laughed, moving in a tight circle, jabbing, bobbing, and weaving. Kirkland's fist shot out, connecting with Greyson's shoulder. Greyson charged, grabbing him around the waist and wrestling him to the ground. Before Chevy separated them, they were rolling around on the grass like rowdy ten-year-old boys.

"What are you boys doin' out there?" Pop yelled from the bottom of the stairs.

"Nothing, Pop," Kirkland and Greyson answered together.

"You two still act like kids." Chevy shook his head, leaving them standing in the middle of the yard laughing.

"You boys are doing a good job on the gazebo." Mama touched Greyson and Chevy as they walked by.

"Thanks, Mama." Kirkland leaned down to hug

her plump frame. She exuded the welcoming warmth he'd come to associate with home. He felt the same way when Cassidy had held him and let him grieve over Alex.

"Hey," Pop said, "save some for me."

"Aren't you supposed to be helping the boys with this project?" Mama asked as he wrapped her rounded body in his long arms.

"Actually, we're supposed to be helping *him* build the gazebo, but he took off about an hour into the work," Kirkland answered.

"Still the tattletale," Greyson said, beginning a raucous debate.

Kirkland caught a glimpse of Mama's smile as she disappeared into the kitchen, happy to have her family at home.

"Oh, the baby!" Sutton hurried over to Cassidy's table in the diner. She bent down to the baby stroller and stroked Courtney's cheek, careful not to wake her. "She's beautiful."

Sutton hammered Cassidy with the usual questions. Is she sleeping through the night? Is she doing better with the fussiness since the pediatrician changed her formula? And then there were questions about Cassidy. How is motherhood? Is she exhausted? How is she juggling a new baby and work?

"Can you join me?" Cassidy asked. "It'll be nice to spend time with someone who can sympathize with achy breasts and dirty diapers."

Sutton slipped into the booth across from her.

"Maddie is locking up the library for lunch. You don't mind if she joins us, do you?"

"Not at all."

The waitress brought water and another set of utensils. "We're going to wait for Maddie before we order," Sutton told her. She clasped her hands together, and rested her chin upon them. "Watching Courtney makes me eager to have another baby."

"Are you and Greyson thinking about it?"

"Greyson has been thinking about it for twenty years." They laughed, and Sutton continued. "We had agreed to wait until I finish my bachelor's degree. Now I'm thinking law school will be too challenging, and having a new baby would be tough."

"So what has Greyson said about it?"

Sutton peered into her water glass. "I don't dare tell him I want to wait. His mother is pushing. My parents are pushing. Even Sierra has gotten in on the game."

"Greyson seems to be an understanding man."

Sutton shook her head. "Oh, he is. About most things. I'm not so sure about this." She smiled warmly. "Greyson loves me, and he treats me like a queen. But he's no pushover. Believe me, Greyson only lets me get away with what Greyson thinks I should get away with. Putting off having a baby will be a fight."

"You have an unspoken understanding."

Sutton rolled her eyes playfully.

Cassidy laughed. "Is marriage as much fun as you're making it look?"

"Yes! I got it right the second time around." Sutton quickly pulled out of her reflective fog. "What about you? You aren't letting Kirkland get under your skin, are you? I've warned him to back off."

"You shouldn't have done that."

"Why not? Was I wrong?"

She considered Sutton's position as Kirkland's sister-in-law. "I don't want to put you in the middle."

"I've already thrown myself in the middle. Looking at your expression, I'm thinking I might have interfered where I shouldn't have." She rushed on. "I didn't want you to get hurt. I know Kirkland, and you're my friend—"

"It's okay. You were trying to help."

"But I should back off." She leaned forward, dropping her voice. "Is there something going on between you and Kirkland?"

She thought back to dinner and the rap show at his place, and smiled. She dropped her eyes when she remembered the almost kiss. He wanted to make love to her. A twenty-six year old man with a perfect face and wonderful body found her attractive enough to desire. All emotion aside, it was enough to warm her in special places.

"Between us," Sutton assured her.

She braced herself to admit the truth to Kirkland's hardest critic. If anyone could help her see the brutal, rational truth of getting involved with him, it would be Sutton. "I think about him all the time."

"Oh, no." Sutton fainted back against the booth.

She laughed at the dramatic response. "What?"

"Those are every woman in love's last words: I think about him all the time. From there, you start doing what your heart tells you, and ignore your mind—and lose your good sense."

"Stop being so cynical now that you're an old married lady."

Sutton smiled. "All right, go on."

"There's nothing else. He stops by to see Courtney and we talk."

Sutton folded her arms over her chest and watched Cassidy disbelievingly.

"We went to dinner once."

"He's fed you? You've entered into the Ballantyne web of seduction."

"What are you talking about?" She hadn't laughed this much in a long time.

"The Ballantyne men have this thing they do with food."

She raised an eyebrow questioningly. "They do? I never pictured Greyson being kinky."

"Stop it!" Sutton hid her blushing cheeks behind her hands. "We're talking about you and Kirkland. Just how kinky has he gotten?"

"Nothing has happened. Nothing more serious than dinner."

"Should I point out he's—" Sutton paused to count—"nine years younger than you?"

"I know."

"Should I say one more time he's a jerk?"

"Sutton!"

The mood at the table became serious. "Cassidy, I love Kirkland. I really do. He's my brother-in-law, and he's been my friend since we were kids."

"You don't sound like his friend."

"He's family, and I'm his friend—not his fan. Kirkland was Alex's best friend and there's a reason for it. He has so much going for him, but he doesn't know how to treat women. When it comes to women, he's a liar and a cheat."

"That's harsh, Sutton."

"I wish someone had warned me about Alex."

"You're blaming Kirkland for how Alex treated you." She hesitated before asking, "What happened between you and Alex?"

Sutton measured her words. "Alex was a great provider of financial things. He wasn't so good a provider of emotional needs."

Cassidy nodded, not wanting to pry any further into her friend's first marriage. "I have to ask, where does Kirkland fit into what happened with you and Alex?"

Sutton's expression hardened. "I'm finding out more about that every day."

Maddie slipped into the booth. She defined hometown beauty. She devoted her life to caring for her aging parents, and readily sacrificed her happiness for others. She was the kind of woman who was gorgeous without makeup, but was not aware of it. Smart and focused, she didn't notice the men staring as she walked by their table to join Sutton and Cassidy in the booth. "Sorry it took me so long. Chevy stopped by as I was locking up."

"He did?" Sutton instantly jumped into matchmaker mode. She arched her eyebrow. "Did he ask to see your *books*?"

"You're terrible," Cassidy told her. "I'm glad you're here, Maddie. You can take some of the heat off of me."

Courtney began to whine.

"Let me get her." Sutton reached into the stroller,

lifted Courtney into her arms, but did not miss a beat. "What's the deal with you and Chevy, Maddie?"

"Deal? There's no deal," she stammered. She smoothed her fingers over her jet-black hair, repairing her bun.

"He just stopped by to pick up some books, right?" Sutton teased.

"Yes."

"Then why are you so flushed?"

Cassidy came to Maddie's rescue. "Sutton, maybe it's private."

"It's not *private*. We're friends. We all could be family one day." Courtney reached out and pressed her tiny hand against Sutton's lips. "I'm trying to help her get her man."

"What?" Maddie asked, thoroughly embarrassed. "Chevy isn't my man."

"But you'd like him to be." Sutton bounced Courtney on her lap. "Deny it."

"Don't you have any shame, Sutton?" Cassidy asked.

"Don't let me get started on you."

Cassidy threw up her hands. "You're on your own, Maddie."

"Having shame definitely isn't the way to get your man. Chevy is too reserved, and Maddie's too shy. One of you has to make your move."

"You don't think it's going to be me!" Shock made Maddie's eyes widen. "Chevy needs to make *his* move—if there's a move to be made."

Cassidy piped in. "So you *are* attracted to Chevy?"

"Told you," Sutton interjected.

Maddie leaned over the table toward Cassidy and whispered, "Have you seen his body?"

The women burst into laughter. Caught up in the moment, Cassidy began to think maybe it wasn't such a bad thing to be attracted to Kirkland. He was handsome, intelligent, and caring. She'd even witnessed his sensitive side. She wasn't naive enough to ignore the warnings Sutton had given her, but it was possible he'd changed after his friend's death. Emotional tragedy could bring about drastic change in a person. Sutton might be judging him by his past, and not the man he'd become. The bottom line for Cassidy was whether she was willing to invest her heart in finding out who Kirkland Ballantyne truly was.

"What's got you looking so serious over there, Cassidy?" Sutton asked once the giggles subsided.

Her gaze swung between Maddie and Sutton. She folded her arms on the tabletop and leaned forward conspiratorially. She whispered one word, opening the door on her suppressed emotions. "Kirkland."

"Yes?"

The women turned simultaneously to see Greyson and Kirkland approaching. Cassidy tossed Sutton and Maddie warning glances. She would die from embarrassment if they let on what they'd been talking about. What was she thinking? Asking her to make love with him did not mean he had any true feelings for her. It could have been the wine, or the music, or simply the moment. A little girl-talk and she'd lost her mind.

"Hi, Cassidy," Kirkland said.

She couldn't even look up and say hello.

"You were talking about me?" He looked at her as

if they were in a smoky nightclub alone, dancing to a slow, seductive tune.

Courtney's arms shot out in his direction. She started to bounce and gurgle with recognition. Sutton looked at Cassidy incredulously as she handed the baby over to him.

"Well, hello Courtney." He lifted her with easy familiarity. "Your mother is tongue-tied today." They shared a moment, speaking in their secret language before he slid into the booth next to Cassidy.

"What are you guys doing here?" Sutton asked Greyson.

"We're hungry." He kissed his wife. "Mind if we join you?"

Cassidy wanted Maddie to say she had to rush back to the library. She would make up an excuse and leave with her. She felt awkward, knowing she'd admitted her attraction to Kirkland to Maddie and Sutton. To their credit, they kept a straight face, refusing to tell Greyson what they'd been talking about before their arrival. She tried to follow the conversation, but how could she with Kirkland's iron-hard thigh pressing against her? Her daughter, the traitor, was cooing and rolling in delight with being held by him. How could Cassidy begrudge her? She'd been held in his arms, too, and it was a delightful place to be.

"I'll walk you ladies back to the library," Greyson said, picking up the check. "I have some things to do in town, and then I'll catch a ride home with you, Sutton." He placed a possessive arm around his wife's waist before kissing her cheek.

They said their good-byes, leaving Cassidy alone with Kirkland.

"You were talking about me when we came in," he said, boldly admitting he'd overheard. "What about?"

"Nothing."

"It looked like something."

She twisted her napkin.

"Why can't you look at me?"

"I can look at you."

"Look at me then."

She wrestled with her shame and her pride.

"Are you upset about the other night?"

"No." Her head shot up, and she instantly melted in his light brown eyes. "I was flattered by the other night. I don't want you to think you did anything wrong."

"Flattered, huh?" His grin revealed perfect white teeth. "Maybe flattery is why you're finding it so hard to look at me now." He bounced Courtney. "Is that it, Courtney?"

"Leave my baby out of this." She grinned. "You're a traitor." She stroked Courtney's shiny, dark hair.

Kirkland mimicked the gesture, stroking Cassidy's hair and letting his fingers linger over her earlobe. "I'd like to flatter you again tomorrow night. I'll bring dinner and some movies."

She still hadn't recovered from their almost-kiss. She couldn't be alone with him again so soon.

"Your mom seems to be speechless," he said to Courtney. "Would *you* like me to come over tomorrow night?"

Courtney wallowed in a world of happiness, playing with Kirkland.

"I guess it's a date then." He stood and placed Courtney on his hip. "C'mon. I'll drive you home."

# Chapter 8

Every sketch Cassidy drew resembled Kirkland. His sandy-brown hair, warm gaze, full lips, or stunning body appeared in every picture she painted. Her mind trailed off as her brush washed over the canvas, and when she came to her senses, Kirkland was staring back at her. Even Courtney seemed to be more energetic than usual, fighting her afternoon nap until the very end, seemingly in anticipation of Kirkland's arrival. Cassidy had to admit she couldn't wait to see him later that evening, either.

She chucked work and prepared for her date by giving Courtney an early bath and getting her ready for bed. Once she admitted her feelings for Kirkland, the knots in her stomach were replaced by butterflies. She bathed Courtney while the maid service cleaned her place. Once Courtney was dressed for bed, Cassidy gave her the last bottle of the night. Cassidy placed the baby in the playpen to exhaust herself while she spent too much time trying to decide what to wear. She ended up scolding herself for acting like a teenager. When Courtney fell asleep, Cassidy put her in the crib and took a hot shower. She dressed casually in blue jean shorts and a navy T-shirt.

"Casual is good," she told herself while brushing her hair. "Casual says friends." The doorbell rang, obliterating all masquerades of what the evening was about.

"You look nice." Kirkland stepped inside, handing her a bag of Chinese takeout.

"Thank you."

"Is Courtney asleep? Already?"

"It's late for her."

"I'm going to check on her."

She watched him disappear into the back of the house before going to the kitchen. Dark slacks covered his long legs. A kitten-gray dress shirt tugged at his muscular chest. He loosened his tie as he walked away. She knew he hated wearing ties, but his position at work required it. Tall and slim, his body was lean with muscles, as if he were naturally thin, but hard work had pumped up his mass.

"Do you think Courtney will wake up before I leave?" he asked, joining her in the kitchen.

"She usually doesn't wake up until five or six in the morning."

He looked disappointed.

"Can you grab something?"

He carried the soda and glasses into the living room. She followed with their dinner nicely dished out on her most expensive china plates. "What movies did you bring?"

"I pick out the best movies." He joined her on the sofa, kicking off his shoes and getting comfortable.

"Whenever someone says they pick good movies, they usually don't."

"I'll prove your theory wrong."

Knowing their different tastes in music, she

couldn't wait to see what he considered a good movie. He handed her the movies he'd selected. "I've actually heard of these titles."

He tasted his food, watching her with an amused grin.

"Okay. I should have had faith in you."

"You've underestimated me." His voice dropped. "Again."

Halfway through the psychological thriller, they ejected it from the DVD player. The masked killer made Cassidy's heart thump. She reminded Kirkland she lived alone and wouldn't get any sleep if they finished the movie. He ejected it without one teasing word and replaced it with a comedy.

"Wait for the popcorn," Cassidy called from the kitchen.

He appeared in the doorway. "We need extra butter."

She tilted her head toward the refrigerator. He retrieved a stick of butter and handed it to her. "How much?"

"The whole stick."

She smiled up at him. "I like a lot of butter, too." Her mouth watered—must be the unmistakable aroma of freshly popped popcorn. It couldn't have anything to do with the deep definition of his chest pressed against his tailored shirt.

"This is nice." He dumped the popcorn into a large bowl. "Being together like this."

Cassidy agreed; being together was relaxing. When her fantasies didn't cause a riot in her body.

They laughed and made fun of the corny actors in the B-comedy. After the movie, they tossed popcorn at each other as they debated over what to watch next. Kirkland seized the remote and flipped from channel to channel while fending off popcorn kernels. "One more hit and I'm going to have to fight back."

She watched the lift of his brow and decided to call a truce.

He settled on the comedy channel. "How about this?"

"This is doable."

They settled in, shoulder to shoulder, to laugh at the stand-up comedians. Hanging out with Kirkland reminded her of easier times. Days long ago filled with sleepovers with her best friends. She remembered the innocent fun of high school senior year—the picnics, the prom, and double dates with her brother. It was a time in her life when everything seemed possible, limited only by her dreams. She luxuriated in the feelings he awoke in her, settling into a easy rhythm with him.

The last thing she remembered was watching Kirkland grip the remote, depressing the channel change button in slow motion. In the soft light of her living room, her last coherent thought was to marvel over how his brown skin took on tones of red. She woke up gently, by degrees. Kirkland's smooth cologne entered her nose with even breaths. His face was inches from hers, close enough to brush her cheek with every breath he took. His strong arms encircled her thighs, securing her tightly in his embrace. One of her arms was looped over his shoulders, lightly caressing the muscles of his back.

"I was going to carry you to bed," he whispered.

"I fell asleep on you. I'm sorry."

"The baby. Work. It's a lot to manage." He paused, his arms still cradling her thighs. "It's pretty late." His sinewy muscles made contact with her arm, opening her to new sensitivities. His heat radiated over the surface of her skin. With him this close, his touch so intimate, she couldn't find the right words to say. "What were you talking about with Maddie and Sutton in the diner?" If possible, he moved a fraction closer. One millimeter more and their lips would touch.

Unable to meet his brazen gaze, she dropped her lashes.

"It was about me," he said, as if confirming facts.

"Girl talk. It was just girl talk."

"Girl talk—about me." He raised a disbelieving eyebrow. "Were you talking about your feelings for me?"

"It was just girl—"

"Tell me the truth," he gently prodded.

She came fully awake now. "It doesn't matter what we were talking about."

"It does to me."

"It wouldn't change anything."

"It would change *everything*."

"How? Why would it matter?"

He shook his head, discarding her attempts to avoid the issue. "Are you attracted to me? Is that what you were talking about in the diner?"

"Kirkland—"

"Cassidy." His voice cracked impatiently. "Are you attracted to me? Forget about our ages. Don't consider the negative things you've heard about me." His grip tightened around her thighs. "You know me in a way no other woman has ever gotten to know me. Is what you know enough to make you want me?"

"Want you?" She breathed, deep and long. Of course she wanted him. What she didn't want was him to look so sexy and masculine and vulnerable all at once. She didn't want him to be so close to her she was dying to kiss him, but afraid of what she would be starting. She summoned all the logical reasons why being attracted to him were wrong, but they couldn't compete with all the reasons she deserved to sample the happiness he offered.

"Cassidy, are you attracted to me? The real me. After spending all this time together, am I what you want?" His face came closer, their foreheads pressed together. His warm breath danced off her chin when he spoke. "If you don't want me I'll leave."

"Our friendship would end over this?"

"I'd have to go . . . and I couldn't come back."

"I don't understand."

"There's no way I could continue to come around here—wanting you this much—and you not feeling the same way." He moved closer still and his lips touched her cheek as he spoke. "I would rather give you and Courtney up completely than to spend time with you and not be able to have you."

Not see him again? Ever? Involuntarily, she took a deep breath.

"Tell me, Cassidy, can you see it in your heart to want someone like me?"

Her chest heaved and her breath came in short puffs. He met her lips, barely making contact with her mouth, as he took in every puff of air. All the emotions accompanying their previous almost-kiss rushed at her, making her head dizzy and her body flushed.

"I want you to stay," she admitted. The stark honesty of the confession surprised her. She thought to take the words back, but couldn't—they were the truth. She had wanted him for some time now. Every time she watched him play with Courtney, or he made her laugh, or helped her out in some obscure way, she wanted him more.

"Stay?" he asked.

"In my life. In Courtney's life."

"As what?" His hazel eyes sparkled with possibility.

"A friend."

"And more?"

"And more."

He crushed his mouth to hers, exhaling his relief. Very gently, restraining himself, he entered her mouth. His kiss ignited a long-lost fantasy in which she still believed in true love and happy endings. She gripped his shoulders, pulling him closer and marveling at the strength of his rigid muscles. His hold on her had not faltered. He held her firmly, but with the tenderness of precious cargo.

His gentle kiss grew more urgent. He'd been holding back too long. Self-control wasn't possible. He stepped backwards, bracing his back against the nearest wall.

His kisses were delicious. Soft and urgent. Rough and patient. He used his tongue as a weapon of possession, silently challenging her to name anyone else who had ever made her feel this way. He dared her to remove the lingering effects his kisses would have.

He shifted their combined weight.

She pulled out of his kiss long enough to whisper, "You can put me down now."

He bent to set her feet on the floor. Reluctantly, she untangled her arms from around his neck. He grasped her hips, surprising her with his possessive hold. He backed her against the wall, trapping her body with his.

"I didn't expect that," he said.

"Me either." She knew exactly what he meant.

"It was pretty fantastic."

She nodded. "It was."

"Let's do it again." He crushed her against the wall, greedily consuming her mouth. This was the hurried, probing kiss she'd first expected. He'd surprised her with his tender probing of her mouth. She had wanted him to hungrily ravish her. She wanted unbridled lust mixed with her passion, and she found it in his second kiss.

"That was pretty terrific," she mocked him.

"Yeah. Rap songs have been written about kisses like this."

She giggled at his ever-present sense of humor. His finger tapped across her shoulder, abruptly stopping her laughter.

"Should I tuck you in before I go?" A playful grin danced over his full lips, roughened by their kiss.

"I can handle it."

"Sure? I'd be more than happy to—"

She placed her hand against his chest. "Good night, Kirkland."

He let his fingers glide down her arm. He entwined their fingers, bringing her hand up to his mouth. He kissed the back of her hand, and then the palm, watching for the small intake of breath that indicated her shivering. He led her to the front door. "Good night, Cassidy." He gave her one quick kiss on her forehead before leaving.

# Chapter 9

Kirkland gripped the stem of the wine glass so tightly it snapped. Red wine splattered across the white linen tablecloth. The waitress appeared immediately, cleaning the spill and placing a dry cloth over the mess. She offered him another glass of wine and replenished the table with fresh bread.

"You're leaving her an extra large tip to make up for the mess you made," Chevy told him.

Greyson was more attuned to his abrupt change in mood. "What's wrong with you? You aren't paying attention to anything we're saying."

Right now Kirkland's attention was directed over Chevy's right shoulder. Across the room Cassidy was all dressed up, sharing a table with a man who looked like he stepped right out of an issue of *Muscle* magazine.

"Let's get back to work," Chevy said. "I don't want to be here all night."

As co-owners of the town's paper mill, going over the books and planning the future of the company was a task they took seriously. Monthly, they met over dinner to propose changes to help the mill remain a viable source of employment for the town. Chevy was rambling about preserving forestation, but Kirkland couldn't take his eyes off Cassidy. Her hair was pulled back in a tight bun and she kept reaching up to tuck an invisible strand of hair behind her ear. Flirtation or nervousness? She wore a springy dress, lavender—perfect for bringing out the golden flecks of color in her brown eyes.

"Kirkland, where are you?" Greyson asked.

He pulled his eyes away from Cassidy long enough to answer. "Cassidy's here."

Greyson and Chevy turned simultaneously in their seats and scanned the restaurant.

"Who's she with?"

"Grey! Don't ask him that," Chevy admonished his older brother.

"Why not?"

Chevy threw him a look. "He's seeing Cassidy, and she's here with another man. This town is too small."

"Oh," Greyson said, turning to Kirkland. "I'd go over there and find out what's going on."

"No!" Chevy tried to stop the madness before it began. "No, he shouldn't go over there. It'll cause a big scene. He should finish this meeting. He can talk to her privately—later."

Greyson lifted an eyebrow. "The hell with that."

"Yeah," Kirkland said, tossing his napkin on the table, "the hell with that."

Chevy called after him, but he kept walking. Each stride made him more determined. They'd just shared their first kiss and now she was on a date with another man. The kiss had been special to him—he thought it had meant something to her too. He would demand an explanation. He wanted answers. Each step brought a wash of emotions he wasn't prepared to deal with. Any hope of handling the situation in a dignified manner disappeared when Cassidy tossed her head back in laughter. This man might try to touch her, or kiss her, or . . . His head throbbed.

"What are you doing here?" he asked, his anger forcing him to push the words out.

"Kirkland." Cassidy smiled, but the grin quickly faded when she saw his clenched jaw.

He caught sight of the man's hand lying on the tabletop, stretched in Cassidy's direction, palm up. Did he show up just in time to keep the man from making a move on her? His eyes locked on the man's chiseled jawbone. "And you are?"

"I think the question is, who are you? And why are you interrupting my dinner with this pretty lady?" He grinned at Cassidy, sitting forward slightly, obviously trying to impress her.

"What is it, Kirkland?" She tried to soothe his anger, but his anger had gone beyond the soothing point.

"Let's go."

"What?" Cassidy sputtered. Her hand went up to remove the invisible strand of hair.

"I said, let's go." He pulled his eyes away from the man to look at her. "Now."

"I can't leave. I'm having dinner with a client. Kirkland, this is—"

"I don't care who he is, or why you're here. Let's go." His rage drew the attention of the patrons sitting nearby.

"I think you should leave," the man said. His goofy smile was replaced by a stern look of dismissal. Evidently, he planned to take impressing Cassidy to the limit.

His eyes swiveled to the man challenging him for his woman. He had thought it was clear she'd become his woman when they kissed. He'd take that up with Cassidy later. Right now he had to make his position known to the guy hitting on her. The last fight he had been in was ten years ago when he and Alex had busted up a bar in the capital, brawling with three men over Alex's flirting with two women. Now he was the one being disrespected and he was ready to brawl again. He angled toward Cassidy and spoke calmly, but with conviction. "I want you to leave. You might be here on business, but he's hitting on you."

She tried to laugh off the seriousness of the moment. "Kirkland, you're embarrassing me in front of my client. I'm going to finish this business dinner, and I'll discuss this with you later."

"Not acceptable. We're leaving now." He reached out to take her arm.

The man rose from his seat. "The lady said she's not going with you."

Chevy and Greyson appeared at his side.

"Hi, Cassidy," Greyson said, sounding as if they had bumped into each other at the mall.

Chevy placed a firm hand on Kirkland's shoulder. "We need to get back to our table and finish up."

Kirkland shrugged him off and turned to the mountain of a man. "This is between Cassidy and me. We're leaving."

"I don't think so." The man unbuttoned the cuffs

of his silk shirt. He peeled the sleeves up to reveal thick arms meant to intimidate.

Kirkland stared up at the tank and then pulled off his suit jacket, dropping it to the floor.

"Oh, please," Cassidy said. "Cut it out, right now. Both of you."

The manager joined the scene. "Is there a problem?"

Greyson pulled him away, trying to calm the situation without drawing more attention.

"All right," Chevy said, "the entire restaurant is watching us. Kirkland, let's call it a night. Cassidy, I apologize."

"Don't apologize for me," Kirkland said. He addressed Cassidy. "I'm not going to sit back and watch you on a date with another man."

"This is dinner," Cassidy said.

Greyson reappeared. "Cassidy, please let Kirkland take you home."

"You don't have to leave," the tank said. "If this is what you have to go home to, maybe we should make it more than dinner."

"What did you say?" Kirkland stepped forward and the tank took a swing at him. The beefy fist knocked him off balance. He shook his head, trying to process all the action going on around him. Patrons raced from the restaurant. Chevy grabbed Cassidy and pulled her away from the table. Greyson fended off the manager and his reinforcements from the kitchen. The tank grinned, taunting Kirkland with words directed at his manhood—or lack of it. Kirkland regained his balance and swung at the tank. He landed a set of combinations, sending the tank back into his chair. One last blow and his head slumped over onto the table.

Greyson, the cerebral Ballantyne brother, enjoyed every minute of the fight. He snatched Kirkland's jacket from the floor and pulled his little brother out of the restaurant by the scruff of his neck. Their waitress followed, carrying the abandoned briefcase and files left on their dinner table. She handed them off to Greyson. He pulled out his wallet and handed her a wad of bills. "This should cover the damages. If it doesn't, send a bill to me at the paper mill."

"Give her a tip," Kirkland said, hurrying away.

Greyson peeled off several bills. "Where are you going?"

Kirkland didn't answer. He was too busy scrounging for his keys in the valet booth. Workers yelled at him, telling him he wasn't allowed in the restricted area. He was doing a lot of things he shouldn't this night. He ignored them, grabbing his keys and running through the parking lot in search of his car.


"Kirkland's still at the door," Darius said. "Do you want to see him yet?"

"No! Tell him if he doesn't leave you'll call the police."

Darius whistled before closing her bedroom door. This time he spared her the "I told you not to get involved with him" lecture.

Kirkland had been completely out of control at the restaurant. She'd tried to tell him her dinner was work-related. They had only kissed once, and look at how possessive he'd become. Granted, the emotional pull between them was strong, but one kiss did not give him the right to embarrass her. People in Hannaford Valley would be talking about the scene for weeks. In his defense, her model did push his buttons by implying there was more to it than a shared meal.

Darius tapped on her door as he entered. "I have to get going. I delivered your message to Kirkland and he took off."

She wanted to run to the window. Was he angry when he left? Hurt? She was mad at him; why did she care how he felt?

"How long are you going to keep avoiding him? Even if you don't want to see him again, you have to talk to him and tell him."

"I'm going to keep avoiding him until I'm not so angry I could slug him. And then I'm going to tell him I can't see him anymore." She cuddled a pillow to her stomach.

Darius stood over her with his arms crossed over his chest.

"What?" she asked.

"I don't believe you."

"You'll have to just wait and see, then."

He shook his head. "Kirkland is crazy over you."

"Crazy is right. You should have seen how barbaric he acted in the restaurant."

"And you're just as crazy over him as he is over you."

She sat up with a start. "*You're* crazy."

"If you really didn't want to be with him anymore you would've told him so the first time he came knocking. You don't want him to stop trying to see you."

She wanted to tell Darius he was wrong, but she couldn't. She was furious about what Kirkland had done in the restaurant, but her mind couldn't grip the concept of never seeing him again.

Darius knew he was right; she didn't need to confirm with words. "He's crazy jealous, which means he's probably falling in love with you. Or he's already in love with you."

"Kirkland is not in love with me."

"You're right." Darius made his way to the front door. "No more than you're in love with him."


Cassidy saw Kirkland sitting on her porch the moment she pushed Courtney's carriage around the corner onto their block. She couldn't make him out clearly because of the distance separating them, but she knew. She could feel his presence settle over her like a fuzzy blanket. Dressed in a black on black suit, he threaded his silk tie through his fingers, nervously awaiting her arrival. He must have come directly from work. She tried to remember seeing him in a pair of sagging jeans and an oversized designer T-shirt. Everything about him was different than the other men his age. At least that's what she had believed until he started the fight at the restaurant. With every step she contemplated how she should receive him. A week had gone by and she still refused to talk to him about the scene at the restaurant. She wasn't certain she was ready to speak to him now. Discussing the incident meant she'd have to confront her feelings for him.

"He wanted you," Kirkland said when she reached

the stairs. His brown eyes flickered with discontentment.

"I don't want to have this fight. No matter what he wanted, I was having a business dinner. More importantly, I wanted to be there, and you didn't respect that fact."

His back straightened, and arched with resentment. "And there's the problem."

"No, Kirkland, the problem is you embarrassed me."

"I asked you to leave with me."

"And I said no. You disrespected me and started a huge scene to get me to do what you wanted. You had a temper tantrum."

"Don't make this about my age, Cassidy. I'm a man. Was I supposed to sit there and watch this guy hit on you?" He stood slowly, every sinewy muscle tightening with anger. "If you ask me to stand by and watch you out with other guys, I can't do that. Could you do it? Could you stand to see me go out with other women?"

"We don't go *out*, Kirkland. You come *here*, and spend time with me and Courtney."

"What are you saying?" He raised his voice to a level she had never heard from him. He was always soft-spoken in their intimate discussions, choosing each word carefully.

"All these months and you have never even called me on the telephone."

"I do better than call you. I come here every chance I get. You won't give me any more. This is the relationship *you've* built for us," he was quick to point out. "Are you saying you want more?"

She hadn't meant for the discussion to be about

her behavior, or her desires. He had embarrassed her. He had accused her of cheating when they hadn't defined their relationship in those terms—in any terms. Courtney whined, saving her from answering.

"Let me help you with the stroller." He took the grocery bag and lifted the stroller onto the porch. Upon seeing him, Courtney's arms went up. This had become an automatic reaction whenever he came around. His smiling response had also become automatic.

"I came to apologize," he said. "I thought I could talk to you without fighting."

"You've come to apologize before, and I sent you away."

"I know, but I haven't given up." He held the stroller, waiting for her to unlock the door. "Do you want to do this on the front porch where all your neighbors can see and hear? I think I've given Hannaford enough to talk about when it comes to us."

He had her there. Her neighbors spent their days sitting on the porch enjoying the summer weather. Today was no different. She glanced around to see their heated words had already gained the attention of several people. Begrudgingly, she took her key from her purse and moved aside. She watched the easy shift of his muscles as he carried the stroller and grocery bag inside. He handed her the groceries and headed directly to Courtney's room. He lingered there for a while, joining her in the kitchen as she put the groceries away.

"Courtney was tired," he announced. "I laid her down in the crib and she went right to sleep."

"I should check her."

"You don't trust me with Courtney now?" He had moved without her knowing and now he was standing too close behind her. The soft fabric of his suit jacket swished across her bottom.

She didn't doubt him or his ability to care for Courtney. She needed a moment to gather her thoughts and subdue her emotions. "I like to check her." He followed her into Courtney's room, watching her discriminatingly as she kissed the baby good night.

"Where were you?" he asked when they returned to the living room.

"I needed a few things from the grocery store. We came home the long way. Courtney likes to watch the kids playing on the swings at the elementary school."

"If you need a ride, call me."

"I like walking. Hannaford's not big enough to own a car anyway."

He opened the top button of his jacket before sitting opposite her on the sofa. After a brief pause he jumped into the conversation they needed to have. "I shouldn't have reacted the way I did at the restaurant. I should have waited and talked with you in private."

She met him halfway. "I would've told you about my plans if I had spoken to you beforehand. It wasn't a date. Some of the male models do come on to me, but I never mix business with my personal life. I've learned to separate the two."

"Is safeguarding your career more important to you than safeguarding us?"

"What do you mean 'us'?"

"I'd like to think that, because of your feelings for me, you wouldn't go out with another man."

She drowned in the depth of his eyes. She couldn't answer him because she wasn't sure what he was asking. A long moment passed.

He took her hand, stroking her palm, giving her time to understand his meaning. "Every time you look at me, my chest explodes. You and Courtney need me. I feel it." He moved closer, wrapping his arms around her shoulders and pulling her close enough to press his forehead to hers. "We need to go to the next level, baby." He used the endearment as a weapon. She melted whenever he stepped out from behind the stiff shirt and crisp suit and spoke softly to her, dispensing of any formality. "I never meant any disrespect. There was a chance I'd lose you and Courtney, and I didn't handle it in the best way."

She slipped her hand away from him. "We're friends, Kirkland. I've never promised you anything more. I'm not sure I can give you any more right now. Things are complicated."

"How?"

She eased away from him, standing a safe distance away from the aroma of his richly blended cologne. "Your age."

"It means nothing."

"It means everything when we're in different places in our lives. I'm a single mother."

"Don't use Courtney as an excuse not to get involved with me. You know I care about her as much as I care about you."

She wasn't being fair, but fairness was hard to come by when he was so temptingly close. "I've already been where you are in your life. I'm not sure I want to relive it again."

Her words stunned him into silence. His long fingers went to the crisp crease of his collar. As he prepared his words, he traced the sharp cut of his lapel. "I tell you I care about you and Courtney and you respond by telling me you don't want to share my life with me?"

"Kirkland, I didn't mean—"

He didn't look at her when he left.

"I don't know what I did wrong in bringing you boys up, but when you fall for a woman, you completely lose your minds!" Pop stood front and center, peering down on his three sons, all lined up on the sofa. "Wipe the innocent look off your face, Chevy. You'll be the same way when you fall in love." He stepped backward, taking a seat in his recliner. "Explain to me what happened."

Greyson answered, his voice hinting at the pride he held in his little brother's actions. "You would've had to have seen it to believe it, Pop. Kirkland clocked this guy twice his size. I mean, he was a mountain, Pop."

Pop's intense gaze wandered to his youngest son. He might be upset with his sons for causing a raucous which might embarrass their mother, but he was proud his son had the grit to stand up for himself. "What made you do that, boy?" he asked, his voice stern.

"Greyson," Chevy interjected. "Greyson made him do it with his instigating."

Kirkland turned his thoughts introspectively

while his brothers argued and his father refereed. He couldn't explain exactly what had come over him in the restaurant. He'd never started a fight in his life. A woman had never affected him the way Cassidy did. Witnessing Alex's plight, he never let his emotions run away with him, something that carried Alex down the aisle when he still had an urge to sample the different flavors of women. Something primitive had come over Kirkland when he watched the tank drape himself over the table, smiling at Cassidy. He pictured this man taking his place in Cassidy's bed. He imagined this man taking his place in Courtney's life. He saw these things in his mind's eye and he erupted in angry jealousy again.

"All I know," Pop was saying, "is that you better make it right with your mother." He directed his words at all three of his sons. Pop ruled the household, but his greatest influence was over Greyson and Chevy. Kirkland lived for his mother's approval. She had always been the moral compass in his life, and so the best disciplinarian.

"Excuse me." He propelled himself from between his two brothers and sought out his mother. He knew exactly where she would be. Every evening after dinner she made her way to her rose garden. In the winter, she tended the herbs she grew in tiny pots in the sunroom. He kissed his mother's cheek and then settled on the tiny bench bedside where she was kneeling, tending her flowers.

"Did you do this to protect a woman?" Mama asked after hearing the complete story.

"Not exactly. She was having dinner with this

guy—I don't want him near her. I don't want any man near her," he growled.

One glance over her shoulder and he became more repentant. "I'm sorry. I know your reputation means a lot to you. I don't know what I was thinking."

"It's not like you to show your emotions so passionately." She stuck her trowel in the ground, displacing the black soil. "You've always been quiet, more reserved." She smiled. "More like me."

He squeezed his mother's shoulder, absorbing her warmth. "I'm doing a lot of things I wouldn't usually do lately."

"Like what?" She reached out a hand and he helped her up.

"Business." His meetings with Pete Frawley were eating at his conscience. He wasn't as happy as he should be about the progress they were making. He was beginning to question his decision to build an industrial park on the Galloway land.

"How so?"

He gathered his mother's gardening tools, placing them neatly inside the box she used to carry them. This would be the perfect time to confess his business plans to her. To tell her he might have acted irrationally, to spite those who didn't believe in his abilities. He wanted her to know he'd changed his mind, but the plans for the industrial park had somehow left his hands. It seemed someone else was controlling all the major decisions.

"Are there problems at the mill?" Mama asked as they left the rose garden.

"No, things are fine at the paper mill."

"What is it, then?"

"No matter."

"It does matter if you're upset about it."

His eyes were glued to the grass as they crossed the backyard. "Just business. It'll work itself out."

"Really?" Mama asked, doubtfully. "What about your feelings for Cassidy? Will that work itself out, too?"

"Cassidy isn't handled easily, but we'll work it out."

Mama stopped, removing her gardening gloves. "Maybe your mood has something to do with Alex's death."

His stomach sank, and he braced himself for the twisting sensation sure to follow.

"I talked with Sutton. She mentioned that she'll be visiting Alex's grave. Said he died three years ago this weekend."

He had put it out of his mind. His emotions weren't ready to be plowed up so soon. Three years sounded like an eternity. Sutton had gone on to marry Greyson. Sierra was growing up. Mother Galloway had settled into a routine in Chicago. Everyone had moved on. Except him. For him, it seemed like Alex had died three months ago instead of three years ago. The emotions were still too raw to handle. His best friend had left him.

"Are you going with Sutton?"

He swallowed. "I don't know."

"I know there's something going on with you. I'm your mother; we've always been close. This fight in the restaurant was the telling sign, but there's more—something bigger. You don't want to share it with your mother. It's all right. Some things can only be shared with another man. You might not be able to talk about it with me, but you seek out Greyson, Chevy, or your father. Don't let this eat you up."

He walked in silence, keeping pace with his mother. She knew him well; there was no sense in denying her claims.

"With that said, I want you to bring Cassidy to our anniversary dinner, and tell her to bring the baby I've been hearing so much about."

"Cassidy still isn't speaking to me. I'm not sure I can get her to come."

"Work it out with her before the dinner. I want to meet the woman who has my son jumping on men twice his size."

# Chapter 10

Kirkland watched Sutton and Sierra from a distance. His troubled relationship with Sutton was not enough to make him face visiting Alex's grave alone. Greyson soon appeared and led Sierra away by the hand, back to his Volvo wagon. They were the stereotypical Hannaford Valley family. He envisioned making a family with Cassidy and Courtney. It was refreshing to have them depend on him. Cassidy was an independent and strong-willed woman, but she had exposed her vulnerable side to him. No one had ever needed him before. Knowing Courtney could one day depend on him to secure her future made him warier about erecting the industrial park. He stepped out from his obscure viewing place.

"I didn't think you were coming," Sutton said without looking up.

"Does it seem like three years to you?" Even as he asked, he relived the day Mother Galloway told him Alex had been killed in a car crash—with a woman other than his wife.

"It seems much longer than three years. It seems an eternity since he was here."

"What do you think about when you come here?"

He needed to find peace with Alex's death. Maybe he could find it the same way Sutton had.

"I remember the good times between us." She smiled. "I mostly think about our time together in high school." She placed a colorful bouquet of flowers against the tombstone. Alex would have hated the flowers. He would have said it was too feminine. "What do you think about, Kirkland?"

He didn't want to think. Remembering Alex brought emotions too harrowing for him to handle.

"You two were so close," Sutton pressed. "Why?"

"He was like my brother." He had answered the question many times. His brothers wanted to know why he respected Alex more than he looked up to his own family. Mother Galloway wanted to know how she had inherited one of the Ballantyne boys as her surrogate son. Sutton wanted to know why he kept Alex's secrets. No one could accept the simple fact they were friends. "Does Sierra talk about him?" he asked.

"She does. She misses him."

"Me, too," he admitted. Sadness gripped his heart, tightening the muscles of his chest.

She turned to him, startled by his confession. "Who do you talk to? Now that Alex is gone."

"Alex was my best friend. That will never change."

"Alex is no longer here."

He kneeled on one knee, running his fingers through the plush green grass covering Alex's grave. The gesture was meant to look natural to Sutton, but actually her statement had caused such a sharp pain in his stomach it had knocked him to his knees.

"Kirkland, we have our differences."

He looked up at her, noticing for the first time how the clouds blotted out the sun. The gloom was not the making of his sadness. "We have our differences, but we're still family."

"I want us to get along."

She watched him for a long moment, searching for sincerity. His gaze did not waver. He didn't want to fight with his sister-in-law. Alex would want them to be friends.

"I don't want to fight any more either, Sutton."

Her voice dropped to a level of desperation. "Then tell me the truth."

"The truth?"

"Everything. Tell me everything. Alex leaving you the land—I know there's more."

He shook his head, denying without outwardly lying. This was not the time or place to discuss Alex's transgressions.

"You won't tell me."

He stood. "You're with Greyson now."

"Do you know how humiliating it was to find out about the land Alex left you? I don't want any more surprises. I don't want Sierra embarrassed."

"Sutton," he breathed her name, exhausted by the continuous merry-go-round ride with her and Alex and their marital troubles.

"You're not going to tell me."

"Sutton—"

"Sutton, honey," Greyson called, crossing the cemetery with quick strides. "It's time to go."

She waved at him, then turned to Kirkland. "I

know you're hiding something." She walked off, meeting Greyson.

Greyson kissed her cheek and whispered in her ear before joining him. "You okay?"

He nodded. "Today's a hard day."

Greyson locked his hands behind his back. "It's hard for Sierra too."

Kirkland wanted to comfort his niece. "I wish I could spend more time with her. She should know how much Alex loved her. I spent a lot of time with her as a baby. I miss her."

"You want to stop by later?" Greyson asked. "We could talk."

He caught Sutton watching him from the car. The expression on her face was full of animosity and unanswered questions. He didn't want to be alone with his thoughts today. Memories of Alex would haunt him if he didn't keep busy. But he couldn't answer Sutton's questions, which meant they'd be fighting, and he couldn't fight with her today. "No. I have things to do," he lied. Today, more than other days, he felt the void of being alone.

"The invitation stands," Greyson said.

Kirkland studied Alex's tombstone. *Beloved husband, father, son, and friend.*

"I should get going," Greyson said, slapping him on the back before walking away.

Kirkland was drowning in memories by the time he heard the Volvo pull away. The silence wrapped him in sadness, and pulled him against his will back in time. Having a friend who you could always count on was priceless. He didn't have that any more. His relationship with Greyson was growing stronger, but it could never replace Alex. He sat at the foot of Alex's grave, remembering.

*"This is a nice place," Alex said, rumbling down the stairs of Kirkland's new penthouse apartment. "You've made it, kid." He searched his breast pocket for his cigarettes.*

*"Don't light up in here."*

*"Punk."*

*They dropped down on the sofa pushed against the far wall to accommodate the packing boxes.*

*"I didn't know I had so much stuff in that little place."*

*"You need to get rid of some of this junk. I can't believe you made me move all this mess and you probably won't end up keeping half of it."*

*Chevy joined them from the bathroom. "I gotta get going."*

*"Big date?" Alex teased, knowing not having a personal life was Chevy's sore spot.*

*"Leave him alone." Kirkland punched his friend in the arm. "I ordered pizza. Sure you can't stay?"*

*"Long drive back to Hannaford."*

*"Thanks for the help."*

*"Anytime." Chevy left, quietly closing the door behind him.*

*Alex shook his head. "Is he still a virgin?"*

*"Leave Chevy alone. He's cool."*

*Alex hopped up. "Where can I smoke this?" he asked, waving a cigarette in the air.*

*Kirkland took him out onto the balcony. His apartment had a view of the cloud-covered mountains. He worried it might be too quiet living there after his cramped apartment off campus. Even though he'd been out of college for years, he remained a part of the college life by living so close to the school.*

"What are you going to do here all alone?" Alex asked, taking a long drag on his cigarette.

"Work, mostly."

"Well, kid, you've arrived."

They looked out over the mountains while Alex puffed on his cigarette.

"We should celebrate," Alex said, his tone giving away unscrupulous thoughts. "I know a couple of girls I could call."

Kirkland shook his head. He placed his foot on the railing, leaning over and letting his hands dangle over the side. "I don't want any part of that."

Alex took two more drags before he spoke again. "You're my moral compass."

He had looked over at Alex expecting to see a teasing grin, or some other expression of his joking nature. Instead, Alex watched him with solemn eyes. "I wish I could be more like you, Kirk."

"Like me?" He had laughed at the absurdity of it. He'd always wished he could be more carefree like Alex.

"I'm not kidding," Alex had confessed. "I wish I could be more grounded like you. You're focused. You're going to make something of yourself."

"You're successful."

"I make a lot of money. There's a difference." He mimicked Kirkland's pose on the railing. "They don't respect me at work. They keep me around because I make them money. Women are attracted to me because of the expensive toys I own. My marriage is a mess."

"You can change all those things."

"Really?" Alex snorted sarcastically. "How?"

"Find another job. Stop fooling around. Fix things with Sutton."

The country twang Alex practiced so hard to hide

*slipped back in place. "I'm not like you, Kirkland. I can't just put my mind to something and accomplish it. I try not to fool around on Sutton. Every time I do, I feel horrible afterward. I just can't stop."*

*Kirkland watched the clouds overhead, trying to place himself in his friend's shoes. He couldn't understand why a man couldn't control his actions. It was a foreign concept. Pop had always instilled in his sons a sense of pride and responsibility. Whatever mistakes a man made, he had to pay the consequences, even if he was remorseful.*

*"I love her, you know?"*

*"I know." He truly believed Alex loved Sutton.*

*"I just don't know how to love her. It scares me she might hate me if she knew who I really am. I've pretended to be a certain kind of man for her since the day I realized how special she is. If I ever showed her the true Alex Galloway, she'd run."*

*"Who does she think you are?"*

*Alex flicked his cigarette off the balcony. "Someone I'm not."*

*"You're real with me."*

*"Only around you. You're the only one in this world who doesn't want something from me."*

How many times had Kirkland needed to rely on Alex to pull him through, or help him out? Alex didn't know how to handle his marriage, but he gave Kirkland the best advice when it came to women. Alex would know how to handle the mess he'd made with Cassidy. He'd listen to the problem and tell him exactly how to make it right with her. It was uncanny, the way Alex was an expert on everyone's relationship but his own. He always said it was easier to see things from the outside.

Kirkland wanted to make a poignant speech over

Alex's grave, telling him how he was missed. The words wouldn't come. Three years after his friend's death and his emotions were still too raw to handle the gravity of being without him. He wandered back to his car, the overcast day making him sadder with every heavy step. Being alone in the world was cruel.

His cell phone rang. Greyson's number illuminated the tiny screen. He let it roll over to voice mail. He had his family, but he needed more than his relationship with them.

As he started the motor of his car, he tried to remember a time when he didn't feel lost and without purpose. A slow smile spread across his face, but faded before it could lighten his mood. He pressed the accelerator, determined to recapture the feeling. He couldn't be alone when he knew his heart yearned for companionship that was out there, available. He had a chance. It might be a slim chance, but there was still hope he could feel alive again.

# Chapter 11

"Is Kirkland with you?"

Cassidy secured the cordless phone to her ear with her shoulder as she shoved the last load of laundry into the dryer. "We had a disagreement."

Sutton exhaled loudly. "Kirkland and I have our differences, but I love him."

"I know."

"Today is the third anniversary of Alex's death."

"I'm sorry."

"I'm okay. I have Greyson. I ran into Kirkland at the cemetery. He was hurting."

Cassidy felt her throat thicken. "I don't know what I can do, Sutton."

The doorbell rang, giving her the answer. She disconnected when she saw Kirkland's car parked out front. After taking a peek at Courtney, she ran for the door. When she saw the sadness coloring his face, the fight in the restaurant seemed stupid. All the barriers keeping her from him shrunk to insignificance.

"Are you all right?" she asked, alarmed by his earnest appearance.

"I really need to be with you now."

She stepped aside, never questioning her role in comforting him.

He took her hands and led her to the sofa. "I apologize for the way I acted at the restaurant. I went nuts when I saw you laughing with that guy."

"He was one of my models."

"It doesn't matter. I realized today how much I need you in my life."

"We're friends. More than friends."

"More than friends," he repeated, savoring the word *friend*.

She pulled him to her, pressing his head against her bosom. It felt good to have him so close. It scared her to think she might have missed this opportunity because of a meaningless argument. She remembered the times he'd come through for her, offering her assurance about her parenting skills, saving her baby's life. She could never repay him, but she wanted to try to give him a measure of what he provided her. She cupped his face in her hands and was startled by his sadness. "Do you want to talk about it?"

"Alex died three years ago today."

She stroked his sandy-brown hair, noticing for the first time the flecks of gold embedded in the tight curls. "Tell me about it."

He hesitated, but then seemed relieved to be able to talk about such a painful time in his life. "The phone rang early that day, and I remember thinking if it was a telemarketer, they'd be sorry."

She gave him a reassuring smile, encouraging him to go on.

"It was Mother Galloway—Alex's mother—calling to tell me Alex had been in a car crash. He was thrown from the car on impact. His passenger was dead, too."

Her hand went to cover her mouth. "It must have been . . ." Her throat constricted, not allowing her to continue.

"What?"

"You must have relived Alex's death all over again when I was trapped in the car delivering Courtney."

"It hit me the hardest at the hospital, when I was watching Courtney in the nursery. I didn't know if you were married, or involved, or if the baby was Chevy's, but I knew I would protect her. It had to be some kind of sign, right? Discovering you in the same way I lost my best friend? It has to mean something."

"It means everything." She brought her mouth to his. She used the kiss to wash him in emotions. She wanted to erase his sadness and replace it with a fraction of the joy he gave her. He kissed her with equal enthusiasm. She closed her eyes and let herself become lost in this closeness with him. Her fingers danced down the cords of his neck and he hummed in appreciation. His arms encircled her middle, crushing her in his embrace. She pulled out of the kiss to capture a picture of the new expressions covering his face. He stroked her cheek with the tip of his nose, inhaling her scent.

He watched her attentively, absorbed in the play of emotions washing over her. "Can I make love to you?" He had promised her he would ask again. He smiled in recognition of her thoughts. "Are you ready for me?"

"Lift me," she panted. "Take me to bed."

He kissed her, sharing the flavor he'd immediately become addicted to.

"I want you." She tugged at the buttons on his shirt. "Pick me up," she demanded.

Kirkland wound his arms underneath her thighs and lifted her with ease. He placed quick kisses on her neck as she ripped at his shirt. She fought with the buttons in this awkward position, wishing he would run to her bedroom, drop her on the bed, and ravish her.

He kicked open her bedroom door . . . and Courtney wailed.

He froze.

She fought her hunger, switching into parenthood mode. "I'll check her."

Kirkland bent and set her down.

"Go get undressed. I'll be there in a minute."

He ignored her request and followed her into Courtney's room. "She usually doesn't wake up this soon." She checked Courtney's diaper, and finding it dry, she lifted her from the crib.

"Hungry, maybe?"

"Maybe, but she seems sleepy." She sat in the rocker, trying to coerce Courtney back to sleep. She had interrupted the ultimate in adult time. "I'm sorry," she apologized.

"Let me try." He took Courtney into the safety of his arms, speaking to her in their secret language. The baby fussed until he paced the room, bouncing her in his arms. "I don't think she's hungry." He grinned. "I think she misses me. She must have heard my voice."

Cassidy wasn't about to argue the logic behind his claim. Courtney never woke up this early in the evening. The way she quieted down as soon as he bounced her in his arms was shameless. Maybe Courtney had grown accustomed to having Kirkland around. Her mother certainly had.

Once Courtney fell asleep, Kirkland returned her to the crib. Cassidy joined him and they stared down into the bed, watching the baby fall into a peaceful slumber.

"I better get going."

"Stay," Cassidy said with pleading eyes.

"I should go."

"I want you to stay."

"I'm trying to do the honorable thing."

"What's honorable about leaving when a lady asks you to stay?"

He pulled his gaze away from her and watched Courtney.

"Kirkland?"

He looked over at her, clearly torn.

"Lift me."

He watched her carefully.

"Lift me. Carry me to bed. I want *you*. This is what you want. It's what I want, too. Let me give you the warmth and comfort you need."

"What can I give you?"

"You'll give me what I need." There was no doubt.

"How do you know this?"

"You give me what I need every time you come around." She held her arms open wide. "Lift me up into your arms, Kirkland. Take me into my bedroom, and make love to me."

He bent to kiss her, lifting her at the same time.

# Chapter 12

Cassidy stood nude between Kirkland's muscular thighs, her arms wrapped around his neck, taking in the exquisiteness of his body. Candles flickered, casting their shadows on the wall. His body was the playground of desire. From the brown curls on top of his head, to the sandy wisps of hair at the base of his penis, he was perfect. Tall and slender, his skin was rich and velvety. He had a birthmark on his inner thigh, a splash of dark color to assure her he was human.

He nuzzled her breasts. "Are you sore?"

"They're tender." She ran her fingers through his irresistible curls. "You're a breast man."

"How could you tell?" He smiled up at her. "Does it turn you off?"

"Not now that I have some."

"You're just right." He cupped her breasts measuring their fit. "You fit perfectly in the palms of my hands." He definitely had her in the palm of his hand. He placed a light kiss on the areola of her breast. "And you taste wonderful." He snaked his arms around her waist and rested his cheek against the swell of her belly. "You *were* a skinny little thing when I first met you." He pinched her thigh. "You were pretty then, but you're perfect now. Flawless. Beautiful."

She didn't always feel flawless or beautiful. Having a baby can do that to a woman. Skin stretches, permanent scars, a layer of body fat, and a pouch had been added that never seemed to go away. He touched her gently—none of these things mattered to him. He didn't see them. He looked at all the blemishes and still considered her beautiful.

His head snapped up. "I'm trying to fight the stereotypes and be very patient, but I have to tell you I'm about to burst here. Can we get into bed so I can make love to you?"

In answer, she kissed his adorable lips. He lifted her with the ease of a doll, and placed her on the bed. He stretched out next to her. The length of her bed barely accommodated his height.

"I'm buying you a bigger bed first thing in the morning," he said.

"First thing in the morning you'll still be here making love to me."

"Think you can hang, huh?" He trailed one finger down into the space between her breasts. "You know what they say about younger men . . ."

"I'm glad we can laugh about it."

"Don't laugh too hard. The rumors are true." He pressed their lips together while gathering her up in his arms. When Cassidy opened her eyes, dazed from the heated kiss, it took her a moment to realize he had palmed a condom. She peeled his fingers away and removed the plastic package. Glancing at him with hooded eyes, she ripped it open. He fell back, arms folded beneath his head, waiting. "You know what you want," he said, watching her lift his erection from his stomach.

"Yes, I do."

"And you don't play games about it. You'd never say no when you mean yes."

"Never." She laid the condom on his stomach. "Is this thing going to fit?" One side of her mouth quirked up into a grin.

"And you know how to flatter a man."

She savored ownership of his body. She didn't know what they had or how long it would last, but right now his body belonged to her. His skin was soft as silk, but underneath were layers of muscles hard as steel. There was a tuft of brown hair in the center of his chest usually hidden behind the button-up dress shirts. She ran a hand over the planes of his body, learning his sensitive spots. She liked the way his skin quivered in the wake of her touch, and the way his six-pack abs recessed when she hit an erogenous zone.

Boldly, she moved between his thighs, admiring what made him a man. She thought of wicked things she'd read in the romance novels she illustrated. Maybe the writers weren't working from a fictitious angle. Maybe they were privileged to a seductive secret. She would never read one of those books in the same way again. She lifted him, thinking it must be painful to be stretched so tight, to grow so rapidly. He was large, thick—any woman's dream.

She placed tiny kisses around his navel while she worked the condom down his erection. He sucked in a deep breath. He weaved his fingers into her hair, pulling her to him. She could feel the veins circling his penis become engorged by the stimulation of her touch. His breathing grew deep, slow, interrupted by sharp intakes of air between his lips. She'd never been so excited by a man's response to her.

"Come here, Cassidy," he said, sounding as if he were in pain.

She obliged, climbing atop his outstretched body.

"Kiss me, baby."

The endearment sent a chill down her spine. She braced herself near his shoulders, but when their lips met he pulled her down on top of him.

"I want to be careful. I know you're . . . tender."

"Let me do this." She answered his unspoken question. "Please."

His eyes blazed at her plea. He wove his fingers in her hair and pulled her down for another kiss. She placed him at her entrance. Her frenzy was growing uncontrollable by degrees. His kisses were intoxicating, erotic, and hot. Her body flushed with intense heat and she fit him inside. She closed her eyes, pulling away from the kiss so she could enjoy the initial shock of his size filling her. There would be only one first time.

She sat up, straddling his waist, sinking onto his erection. She worked slowly, giving her body time to become accustomed to his size. Once she had engulfed the last inch of him, she dropped her head back, resting her hands on his thighs for support. He stirred beneath her, fighting to restrain himself. He mumbled unintelligible words as he lifted his hips to meet her rhythm. He cupped her breasts, his arms trembling at his attempt to remain gentle.

Waves of pleasure began to build inside of her as his stroke went deeper. She bolted forward, dropping her palms onto his chest when he succeeded in caressing her G-spot. His handsome face twisted in agony. Sweat ran down his temples. He took deep breaths through clenched teeth.

"Kirkland, look at me."

Slowly, he opened his eyes. She fell into the depths of his gaze while working her hips. She pulled him into the crest of her climax, staring into the sexiest pair of brown eyes she'd ever seen. He petted her gently as she rode out the ripples of the explosion. She dropped her face to his chest, her cheek sliding against the perspiration pooled there. He rubbed tiny circles in the small of her back as she tried to catch her breath. Fine tremors were still controlling her body when he whispered, "I want to be careful, Cass. I'm trying to be patient."

"Don't be."

He growled an expletive. Gathering her body in his arms, he reversed their positions, dropping her on the mattress beneath him. She kissed his collarbone and pulled the skin on his neck between her teeth. He smelled of expensive cologne, perspiration, and their mixed musk. A movie of their lovemaking played on the walls, cast by the flickering candles. He growled again, warning her of the consequences of her actions. She grabbed the tight muscles of his behind, wrapped her legs around his waist, and dared him to take all she was willing to give.

He bucked wildly, pushing her knees back onto her chest for deeper leverage. He went up onto his knees, pulling out to the tip, sucked in a deep breath between his teeth, and claimed what she offered.

She stroked his shoulders until his body quieted, planting tiny kisses on his chest.

He waited until his breathing was normal before speaking. "Are you okay? I didn't hurt you?" They were lying on their sides, his knees touching her thighs.

"I'm better than okay."

"You did the right thing, Cass. Making love with me."

"There's no right or wrong. It's what we wanted."

He took her hand and splayed it over the tuft of hair on his chest. "I really care about you. I do. I want to do the right thing. I want to make you happy. I want to know you have everything you need."

"Kirkland—"

"I know you have some doubts about being involved with a younger man, but I'm going to prove how much of a man I can be for you and Courtney." Before she could respond, he gathered her up into his arms again, pressing her face against his chest.

When Cassidy woke up early the next morning, the sun was peeking through her window curtains. She was still naked beneath the sheet. Kirkland was gone. She came awake quickly, wondering what time it was, and why Courtney hadn't woken her for her morning feeding. She jumped out of bed, wrapping herself in a robe as she hurried to Courtney's room.

"Good morning." Kirkland was dressed and sprawled on the floor with Courtney between his outstretched legs. Giant alphabet blocks were spread around them. "Look who's up, Courtney."

Courtney turned to see her mother, arms springing upward.

"How long have you been up?" Cassidy joined them on the floor.

"Quite a while."

She lifted Courtney in her lap for a kiss. "Do you have time for breakfast?"

He shook his head. "I'll grab an early lunch."

"You dressed Courtney?"

He nodded. "I fed her the baby food in the fridge and a bottle of milk."

"Why didn't you wake me?"

He shrugged one shoulder. "Why? We made out okay."

"But . . ."

"But, what?"

But he had gotten up, dressed Courtney, and fed her. Without waking her to ask where or what or how. He was lying on the floor playing with her baby, while she recovered from his vigorous love-making. Her throat filled with an extra-large lump. These were the things a man does. These were the things the man she would love would do. "Thank you," she said, not knowing what else to say.

He looked at her, clearly concerned. "Is something wrong?"

She shook her head.

"Are you sure?"

"I'm fine."

He got to his feet. "I have to go." He bent low and

gave Courtney a kiss on the cheek. "Bye, sweet-heart." He kissed Cassidy's lips, lingering for a long moment. "I'll call you."

She let the sentimentality wash over her in warm, comforting waves. He made her feel so good. Recovering, she called after him, "No, you won't. You've never called me."

The front door closed softly.

Kirkland didn't call, but a brand-new bed arrived just after six in the evening. He came at eight, with designer bedding tucked under one arm and a huge teddy bear underneath the other.

"Stop buying me things," Cassidy scolded. "It's not necessary."

"Are you going to let me inside, woman?"

"You didn't call me."

"You're going to fuss at me about not calling when I sent you a bed? You must've really missed me."

"You said you would call."

"The bed?" He craned his neck to see inside her house.

"It came. Stop buying me things."

"The bed is for me. My feet were hanging off the end of your tiny mattress. Although, the new mattress has very little give, so it might be more for you." He thrust out his pelvis, making her laugh. "Are you going to let me inside?" He turned down the corners of his mouth with a mime's precise expression of exaggeration. "Please."

She stepped aside. "Come in. I made you dinner."

Courtney cooed when Kirkland took her in his arms, lifting her high above his head. Cassidy hid her smile, secretly tickled Courtney's response mimicked her own. She wanted to coo and jump in his arms, too.

"At least someone missed me," he said, amazed by the truth.

"Where were you today?" They moved to the kitchen.

Kirkland sat at the table, bouncing Courtney on his knee as he answered. "I worked at the paper mill today." He glanced her way. "You've never asked about my day before. This is very domestic."

"What do you do at the mill?"

"Nothing and everything. My work was really over when we finished building the plant, but because I'm part owner, I manage a department that really doesn't need to be managed."

"What about your other work? At the capital. What do you do there?"

"I manage projects for a company specializing in industrial construction. Boring, huh?"

"No." She placed a heaping plate of steaming hot food in front on him, and took Courtney to her high chair. "What do you do in your free time? For fun?"

"I spend my free time with you and Courtney."

"All we do is work. We should do something fun."

"Like what?"

"I don't know. We'll have to think of something."

They sat together talking about their work, getting to know each other with a comfort that only comes with the intimacy of making love. After Kirkland's second helping, Courtney's eyes began to flutter.

"I should put her to bed."

"She's not asleep yet." He lifted her from the

high chair, and cradled her in his arms while stroking her cheek. "I like holding her."

"You're going to spoil her, and then she won't sleep without being held."

"I guess I'll have to come over every night and hold her while she sleeps."

Once Courtney fell asleep, he put her in her cradle while Cassidy searched for something to watch on television. He joined her, slipping his arms beneath her thighs, as if to lift her, but instead, he drowned her in succulent kisses.

His fingers inched upward to her breasts, and she tensed at the contact. The wicked grin on his handsome face made him look as if he might laugh at her dilemma, but her expression warned him not to. He watched her as he pulled the hem of her T-shirt upward. She should stop him, aware her breasts were still tender five months after Courtney was born, but she lost all rational thought when his palm cupped her lacy white bra.

"Lift your arms above your head," he said, his face displaying his fight for control. She did as he asked, and he pulled her T-shirt off and threw it over the back of the sofa. "Lean forward," he said, searching for the clasp that would free her breasts.

She did so, and braced herself for the prickly sensation that usually shot through her breasts when they were manipulated. He tossed her bra over the back of the sofa. He placed his hands on her shoulders, and pushed her down.

"You're beautiful."

"I can't wait until my body gets back to the way it was." It should have seemed strange to be talking with a man about such an intimate female problem, but Kirkland had become a close friend she could share personal thoughts with.

"Why?" He shook his head, his eyes locked on her breasts. "They're great."

"You're good for my self-esteem."

"Really. They're wonderful." His gaze never wavered. "Plump and round and full. Engorged." He glanced up at her. "I can't wait to taste them."

Before Cassidy could explain she was too tender for that type of sensual play, she was looking down on the tight curls of Kirkland's sandy-brown hair. He cupped the underside of her right breast very carefully before making a wide circle around the globe with his tongue. He pulled away slightly and blew his warm breath over the trail. His heat mixed with his saliva, causing a chilling effect to radiate through her body. He dropped his head again, this time linking a straight line from the top of her breast to the dark circle surrounding her nipple. The bud jumped to attention, puckering and becoming erect. His hand moved to cup her left breast at the same time his mouth covered her right nipple. She arched her back. The initial contact was as shocking as she anticipated.

He continued his tender assault. His tongue eased over the taut nipple, once and then again, lavishing it in his secretions. She arched again as a dart of pleasure raced between the sensitive breast and somewhere much lower. He repeated the gesture until her body settled into the pleasurable sparks attacking her body. He pressed his lips together, clamping onto the tender bud and applying a soft suction. He built a new ache, licking and suckling her. She writhed at his touch, her back bowed and her nails digging into his shoulders. He ignored her tiny gasps and pushed onward to her pleasure limit. His lips tightened around her nipple and his tongue helped to apply a deeper suction. He successfully extricated the ache she'd been living with for weeks, uncovering a place that held deep delight. As she eased into his ministrations, he drank from her breast, claiming an honor no other had experienced.

A warm flush spread through her body. Her skin had never felt so sensitive. The fondling of her breasts had never felt so sensual, so provocative, so tantalizing. She moaned and weaved her fingers through his curls, encouraging him.

Sensing the height of her arousal, he moved his hand between her thighs. She parted for him, brazenly ready for his touch. He liked her response and quickly lowered her zipper. His palm pressed against her apex, massaging the heat radiating from her. A finger breeched the tiny elastic band and twisted in the density of her dark curls. He reached deeper, tracing her opening. He pressed, finding confirmation of her readiness. She stiffened as his finger moved upward, stopping its assent only when it found her throbbing center. She shivered as his finger swirled urgently around the tiny node. He drank deeper from her breast, applying pressure to the dripping bud until she exploded, melting in his hands.

# Chapter 13

Darius leaned against the doorframe of Cassidy's bedroom, arms folded across his chest, his face twisted with skepticism. "Is he living here now?"

"No. Why would you ask that?" She fussed with her hair in the dresser mirror.

"He's completely refurnished Courtney's room, he has a maid service coming here, the refrigerator is stocked with the foods he likes, and," he strolled over to the bed engulfing the room and flopped down onto it, "he bought this monstrosity."

The four-poster oak bed consumed the room. The oak had been stained to a dark, lush brown. There didn't seem to be enough room for the king-sized bed in her small bedroom, but somehow it fit perfectly. The large bed was dressed with the brown and gold comforter ensemble Kirkland had purchased. At night she sank into the rich bedding and surrounded herself with memories of hot nights. A monstrosity to Darius, it was an icon representing Kirkland's generous nature to Cassidy.

The things they had done on the bed! Kirkland's young body was strong and full of energy. His desire was never ending. They could make love for hours, but let her walk by in something skimpy and he reacted like a virgin seeing a nude woman for the first time. She shielded her grinning face, but Darius saw it in the reflection of the mirror. "What? He likes to buy things to show how much he cares. I've asked him to stop, but Kirkland is stubborn. It's the way he expresses his emotions."

"I don't like it, Cassidy. There's something about him that bothers me. I feel like he's hiding something."

"He's been completely open with me. He's admitted his past mistakes. He may seem a little reluctant about your friendship, but he's still dealing with Alex's death."

Darius looked skeptical, but offered no argument. "Where are you off to?"

"I have a business dinner. I'm coming straight home afterward. I can take Courtney with me if she's going to disturb your work."

"No. She'll be fine." He crossed the room on wiry legs, resting his hands on her shoulders. "I'm worried about you."

"Me? Why?"

"I don't want you to get hurt. I see how you feel about Kirkland. It's written all over your face. Courtney is attached to him, too. He might not have the same intentions you do."

"You don't know my intentions." She pulled away and sat on the side of the bed to slip on her shoes. "We enjoy each other's company. We're friends and we're lovers. We haven't sat down and psychoanalyzed our relationship to death. We're just having a good time together."

"Maybe I've got this whole thing all wrong. Maybe Kirkland wants something *you're* not willing to give him. Either situation is dangerous. I know you. It would kill you to think you hurt him."

She went to her brother. "Darius, I appreciate your concern. I do. But please let me have this. I like the way Kirkland makes me feel. I hope I make him feel as good. Right now, I want to savor this. Sooner or later we'll have to have a serious discussion, but not now."

Darius understood her feelings better than anyone. They were twins; he could read her thoughts as if they were his own. He could detect her emotions with the same clarity. She relied on this to persuade him not to worry. For once in her life she felt she was in total control.

"Don't worry," she said, interpreting his sudden change of mood. "I've got to go. I love you." She kissed his cheek good-bye.

"Hold on." He followed her out into the hallway. "What is it?"

"Your parents asked about you."

"They're still 'my parents'—this can't be good."

He shrugged. "They asked about Courtney. Wanted to know if I had a picture." He paused, trying to decipher her reaction. "I think they'd be open to you calling."

"Did they ask me to call?"

"Mom said she missed talking to you. Dad looked relieved she finally admitted it."

Cassidy had been waiting for an opportunity to make amends with her parents, but they would have to respect her decision. "I'll think about it." She turned to leave, not wanting Darius to see the sadness on her face. "I have to get going."

* * *

Cassidy opened the door to a grinning Kirkland. Her first time seeing him in casual clothing was immediately burned into her memory. The dark jeans were molded to his thighs, while the white pullover clung to the definition of his chest. A black baseball cap covered his sandy-brown curls. "Do you have plans for the weekend?"

"No."

"You do now." He stepped aside, directing her attention to the RV parked in front of her house, consuming more than its share of the street.

"What is that thing?" she giggled.

"It's the 2005 Marquis luxury motor coach by Beaver—and I rented it for the entire weekend."

"It looks like a big, brown bus."

"Wait until you see the inside. Total luxury for my girls: mirrored walls, oak cabinets, leather seating, and marble floors."

She crossed her arms over her chest, doubtful a "bus" could have all those things. "Does it have a bathroom?"

"Didn't I mention the whirlpool tub where I plan to taste every inch of you?" He snaked his arms around her waist. "Or the king-sized bed where we're going to make love? Maybe you'd prefer the double, so we can be closer."

"No bus could have two beds."

"Actually, it has three, nonbeliever. I thought you and Courtney and I could go camping in the mountains for the weekend."

"The mountains?" The thought of spending a romantic weekend with him isolated in the mountains was enticing. "It sounds wonderful, but I have work to do. I'm on deadline for Tuesday."

"Bring it with you. Can you image a more inspiring place than the mountains to paint?"

"No, I can't."

He held her hands in his. "Wait until you see the inside. It's a resort on wheels. We'll have a good time. C'mon." His lips trailed over her cheek. "Don't say no." He pulled her into the hard muscles of his body, tilting her head up for a kiss that would leave no room for negotiation. "What do you say?"

"I'll go pack."

Two hours later, Kirkland parked the motor coach amongst huge trees deep in the West Virginia mountains where deer roamed, grazing on the lush greenery. They parked a half mile away from the nearest campers, ensuring they would have complete privacy.

Cassidy sank into the soft leather of the copilot seat. "I can't believe this!" She pressed a button to operate the power sun visor. "I feel like a kid. Did you know there's a satellite stereo, 30-inch television, and a home theater system with surround sound in the living room area?" She grasped his arm. "There's a 22-inch television with a VCR/DVD combo in the bedroom."

"Don't forget the whirlpool." He leaned over for a kiss. "I plan to put it to good use tonight."

"This is great. What should we do first?"

"After I hook us up to the water and pump system, whatever you want." He watched as she bounced to the back. He was thrilled with the happiness he could bring her.

"Are you hungry?" she called from the kitchen

area. "I could cook dinner. There's a refrigerator, stove and dishwasher back here!"

"You know," he joined her, "you're setting the women's movement back years with your enthusiasm over appliances."

"Who lives like this?" She took Courtney in her lap and sat down on the creamy leather Euro-recliner, kicking her feet up on the ottoman with a satisfied sigh. She planned on taking advantage of every luxury the motor coach offered.

Kirkland relaxed on the sofa-sleeper across from her. Courtney's arms went out to him and he gladly took her into his lap. He watched the childlike joy coloring Cassidy's face. Being away from everything and everyone could become addictive if he could be with Cassidy and Courtney. "Very lucky people live this way. We should live this way."

She folded her arms behind her head. "Yeah, this would be nice. Traveling the country in a suite-on-wheels."

"Not to mention the company," he cooed to Courtney. When he looked up, Cassidy was watching him. Her eyes were filled with tearful emotion.

"Don't even ask."

"What was I going to ask?"

"You were going to ask what I was thinking that made me so emotional."

"Sure was. What is it?"

"I said, don't ask."

He smiled, taking her away from overwhelming emotions. "I better take care of the hookups." He handed Courtney to her mother before leaving the motor coach.

A light rain spoiled their plans to take a walk through the woods, but Kirkland couldn't complain. They explored the features of the motor coach like children on a field trip. The golden amber décor subtly highlighted the lavish accommodations. As they watched television with Courtney, he imagined them becoming a family. When the baby went to sleep for the evening, he wondered what it would be like to marry Cassidy and take long trips in their own motor coach. As late evening approached, the family atmosphere turned romantic. They dimmed the overhead dome lights and ran a hot bubble bath in the whirlpool tub. While Cassidy checked on Courtney, he prepared two glasses of chilled wine. Cassidy discovered the chocolate-covered strawberries in the refrigerator and brought them along to the bath.

He fit her between his legs, comfortably entrapping her thighs with his own. He scooped up a handful of bubbles and let his fingertips glide against the slick wetness of her back. She turned, beaming with a smile, and fed him strawberries. The feel of her slippery skin beneath his fingers excited him. Having her to himself in the isolated woods heightened his protective reflex. He kissed her shoulder aggressively. "I want to take care of you."

"You do such a good job of it."

He alternated his kiss to her other shoulder, embracing her around the waist.

"Hey, let's go hiking in the morning."

"Hiking?" He chuckled. "Didn't see you as much of a hiker, but okay." His remark saddened her. "What did I say?"

"My parents used to take Darius and I on a hiking trip every summer."

"Then hiking should make you happy, not sad."

She pulled her legs up to her chest, wrapping her arms around her calves, and resting her face on her knees. "I haven't spoken to my parents in over a year."

"Really?" He tenderly massaged her shoulders. "How come?"

"My parents expected me to marry and then have children. They weren't too happy about my decision to have Courtney on my own. Artificially at that."

"Once they meet her, they'll change their opinion. She's wonderful."

"If they ever meet her."

He finger-combed her hair, lifting it from her neck to plant a soothing kiss there. "Family is important. Your child has to know her grandparents."

"I know." She continued after a long pause. "Darius said they asked about me. My parents even mentioning my name is a huge step."

"Meet them halfway."

"I don't know."

He massaged the nodules of her spine, releasing the tension with small circular motions of his fingers. "You know it's the right thing to do."

"I know, but it's so hard to take the first step. If they reject Courtney, my heart would break. I couldn't forgive them for pushing her away. I think that's the reason I haven't tried to contact them. If they can't accept her, I'll have to cut them out of my life completely."

"Wait to deal with that if, or when, it happens. I don't think it will."

She watched him over her shoulder.

"Call your parents and invite them over for dinner. I'll be there with you."

"Oh, no. Meeting you and Courtney at the same time would not be good."

His massaging motion faltered, but he quickly recovered, not wanting her to know the stinging effect of her words.

"It's not you, Kirkland. My parents are very conventional. It won't be pretty, even if they do accept Courtney." Her voice dropped. "I couldn't handle defending my relationship with you, too. One battle at a time."

"I understand." He did understand, but it didn't repair his pride. It was his job to take care of them. It was what he did to prove how he felt about them. He didn't like having the responsibility taken away, even by Cassidy's parents.

"We should get out," she said. "The water's getting cold."

"The whirlpool is heated."

She gave him a seductive grin. "The bed will be much warmer."

# Chapter 14

"This was the best vacation I've ever been on," Cassidy said, standing back to marvel at the work displayed on her easel.

"You were supposed to be working." Kirkland stood next to her in her studio, equally as impressed with the painting she had done.

"I was so inspired I finished my work quicker than I expected." She approached the painting. Without him knowing, she had painted him playing in the grass with Courtney near the RV. Their laughter had been pure and innocent and she needed to preserve it. After spending several minutes watching them interact with such unguarded love, she'd picked up a brush and caught the moment on canvas. "This is my favorite piece. I'm going to have it framed, and then we'll hang it on Courtney's wall."

He was humbled by the gesture. He looked away, fighting an emotional display. She'd seen him become this way when he spoke of the good times he'd had with Alex. The emotional heat turned her insides to jelly. She watched the same heat turn his eyes to liquid lava as she leaned in to kiss him. His fingers strummed against her ribs. She moved into him, trying to get closer, to press their bodies together until they became one. His shirt blocked her progress, offending her. She fought to remain composed as she slipped the buttons from their holes and began working the shirt off his shoulders. It dropped to the floor with a *whoosh*. Her fingers swept over his warm, soft skin. He still smelled of outdoors. Inhaling the scent flooded her with memories of all the erotic moments of their impromptu vacation. She let her head fall back as a deep sigh rose in her throat. How could she want him so badly when they'd just spent the entire weekend making love?

His hand found her breast and he dipped to find her nipple erect, waiting for the ministrations of his mouth. His lips latched onto the tiny bud and clamped down on its hardness. The more he suckled, the more aroused he became. In one fierce move he shoved her shirt and bra up over the mound of flesh and returned to suckling her. He understood what each of her moans meant, and had learned the ways to flick his tongue over the nipple to get the most erotic response from her. He knew how hard to squeeze the flesh to make her hips rise up to him.

The floor fell away and Cassidy was surrounded in the warm safety of Kirkland's arms. He kicked off his shoes on the way to her bedroom.

"I love this bed," she said as he pressed down on top of her.

He grumbled unintelligible words as he worked at removing her shorts.

"I want to move it over to the window."

He rumbled again, sliding her shorts over her feet.

"Kirkland, let's move the bed."

"Now?" He didn't hide his surprise. "I'm a little busy right now." He opened the snap of his jeans, tore at the zipper, and let his pants fall to the floor.

Her eyes flashed over the bulge at the front of his underwear. "I want to look up at the moon when you make love to me."

"Cassidy," he pleaded. He let his eyes linger over his erection and then fall on her thighs. "Now? Can't it wait just a little while? I promise I'll move it before I go."

"Remember how romantic it was in the mountains?" They'd snuck out late one evening and made love on a blanket near the edge of the woods in the moonlight. Insect and animal sounds became their music, acting as a natural aphrodisiac.

"The mountains," he mumbled, reliving the moment.

She examined the anguish marring his handsome face. "Okay," she gave in.

He blew out a long breath. "Get up."

She jumped from the bed and pulled off her skewed shirt and bra while he moved the armoire to make room for the bed. She dashed into the bathroom and slipped into her most seductive gown. It accentuated her breasts with a dark purple lace. The thin silky material boldly displayed her nipples, while molding the thickness of her thighs.

She checked on Courtney. Sound asleep. When she returned to the bedroom, Kirkland was finishing his task.

"Better?" he asked. Seeing her in the gown for

the first time, his mouth clamped shut. "You're beautiful. Are you wearing that to please me?"

"Yes."

"Then I won't take it off. Come here."

She boldly strutted over to him, torturing him with the slow shift of her hips. She liked the brazen response she elicited in him. He wanted her and he wasn't afraid to show it. He stood on the opposite side of the bed, waiting for her to come to him. His fists were clenched and his body was tight. When she came to the edge of the bed, instead of going around it, she stepped up on top, standing in the middle of it, looking down on a perplexed Kirkland.

"What are you doing?" He seemed pleased with her flirtatious game.

"Lay down. Beneath me."

He complied without hesitation, anxiously anticipating what she would do next.

She gained her balance, planting her feet on each side of his torso. He rubbed her calves, her thighs, lifting her gown to take a peek at what lay beneath. He shivered, letting the sensation shake his body. She dropped to her knees and straddled his waist, startling him with the sudden, unexpected movement. She watched his pained expression as she ran her fingers over his chest. She followed with lingering kisses to his collarbone, nipples, and navel. He thrashed on the bed when her tongue lapped at the area beneath his navel, tickling his groin. He clamped onto her shoulders, pulling her to him.

She pushed at his hands. "Look at the moon."

He fought to pry his fingers away. She helped

him position his hands at his sides. His head fell back onto the pillow and he watched the moon through the window above. His thighs tensed when she moved her kisses lower to more sensitive areas. With every stroke of her tongue, he lifted his hips from the bed, not wanting the contact to be interrupted. He continued to watch the full moon as she brought him to the brink of explosion, then he pleaded with her to let him experience ultimate freedom.

She hurriedly applied the condom, more anxious than Kirkland to find release. She straddled his thighs again, carefully lowering herself down on his erection. He gripped her hips, his fingers biting into her skin as he fought to control her movements. She had taken him to the edge of ecstasy and she enjoyed the power it gave her over him. She tortured him with the slow lifting and lowering of her hips, leaning forward to plant quick kisses on his chest with each rotation.

With a surprising growl, he flipped her to the bed and took control of their combined movements. He kissed her neck, pulling the tender flesh between his teeth. "Look at the moon, Cassidy."

She watched the round fullness of the moon, lavishing them with bright rays as he drove her over the edge of sanity. Moonbeams illuminated his sandy-brown features as he lowered his head for a final kiss. He kissed her with unexpected gentleness as he reached his climax, never allowing his body to control the mood. She wrapped her arms around him, falling deeper into the emotions of his kiss. His body shuddered against hers, finding its release as her heart floated away on an invisible tide, beginning a new journey.

"I don't know if I'm ready to meet your parents."

Kirkland's hand stroked her arm, gathering her closer. "You've talked with my parents at church."

"Yeah, but talking at church is much different than *meeting* them." She tugged at a springy brown curl in the middle of his chest. "We've talked in passing. Social conversation."

"Does this have anything to do with the fact you used to date my brother? Because if it does, Chevy is cool about us."

"You've talked to him?"

He nodded. "He's okay with it."

She raised her head to look him. "Are you sure about this?"

"Yes, I'm sure. This is what couples do. My mother wants to meet you. I want you there with me." He placed a kiss on her forehead. "I want to meet your parents, too."

She stiffened. Spending time with Kirkland had helped her forget the problems with her parents. "That won't happen."

"Won't happen? I thought you didn't want it to happen right now. Why won't it happen? Are you ashamed of me?"

"No. Nothing like that. My parents are ashamed of *me*." She reached for her robe.

"Come back, baby. I didn't mean to upset you."

"You didn't," she lied. "I'm hungry."

"I'll help you cook dinner." He sat up, kicking his legs over the side of the bed.

"No."

"I did upset you."

"You can't cook, Kirkland. Get some rest. I'll wake you when dinner's ready." She padded down the hall. She stepped into a hot shower and tried to wash away the disapproval of her parents. Courtney was such a precious baby. If only they could know her. They were doing Courtney a terrible injustice by excluding her from the family. She was an innocent baby who deserved the love and support of her grandparents.

Kirkland eased the shower curtain back. He glanced at her as he adjusted the steaming hot water. He stepped in behind her, immediately wrapping his arms around her waist. "I never felt like I quite fit into the picture of my mother and father and two brothers," he said. "My mother and I are close. Pop and I have a good relationship. Chevy and I get along well, and Greyson and I have built a strong bond since he returned."

"It sounds like you fit."

He began to soap her back. "Separately, we fit. Together, we don't. I never have. Maybe it's because Alex and I were so close, while there were problems with his friendships with my brothers. There's a level of distrust we can't get around even now."

She knew he meant since Alex had died.

He turned her by the shoulders to face him. While the warm water rinsed her back, he soaped her front. "But we're trying. Every day, we try." He turned her back around, reaching around to help wash away the soapsuds. "You have to try, Cass. You have to try because it's eating you up inside." He kissed her neck. "And as long as your heart is breaking about your relationship with your parents, you won't be able to let me in."

They changed positions. She took up the shower gel and began working it into the hard muscles of his back while he dipped his head underneath the spray.

He turned and watched while she lathered his front. "I keep opening wounds."

"No."

"Why do I have the feeling I'd see tears running down your face if the water wasn't washing them away?"

She lifted her head sharply only to be pinned by his intense gaze.

"Work on it. Every day." He reached out to take her in his arms, but she stepped out of the shower and wrapped herself in a towel. If he would have held her at that moment the tears would have started, and she wasn't certain if she'd ever be able to stop them.

"Look who's up." Kirkland brought Courtney over to the stove so Cassidy could give her a kiss.

"Good morning." She kissed Courtney, and then Kirkland.

"Something smells good." He went into the refrigerator and removed several jars of baby food.

"What time do you have to go to work?"

He secured Courtney in her high chair. "Trying to get rid of me?"

"Never. We've had you all weekend. I thought it might be time to let you get back to work."

He found Courtney's dish and began measuring

out baby food into the separate compartments. "I'll go in to the paper mill later. I have to return the motor home first."

She watched him from the stove where she was frying hash browns and bacon. Her first impression of him had been so wrong. She'd seen him as a Casanova who wore designer suits, with an expensive education that left him speaking too properly. If she believed Sutton, he was conniving and used his good looks to help him obtain wicked pleasures.

Never did she imagine him adapting so easily to her domestic situation. From the day he breathed life into Courtney's listless body, he'd been her protector. They had a bond she could never envy, but found astonishing. They spoke a secret language—not meant to exclude her, but to bring them closer and solidify their relationship. Whoever came into Cassidy's life later wouldn't be able to sever the tie.

"What do you need to do today?" he asked. "Do you need a chauffeur?" Courtney reached out for his hand and helped him guide the spoon into her mouth. She gave him a toothless grin. He leaned forward and kissed her cheek.

"No. I have more work to do around here today."

So they were a couple. Dangerous ground to be walking on, Darius would say. Where were they going? Was it wise to let Kirkland get this close to Courtney when he might be replaced as the father figure in her life?

*He would make a good father*, Cassidy thought.

*He's a great lover.*

*Would he make a good husband?*

"You're staring at me," he said.

She turned back to the stove. A little rough

around the edges, but Kirkland was a good man. He was still struggling to come to terms with his best friend's death, but do you ever get over the death of a loved one? He had demons. Sometimes she watched him play with Courtney and something would come over him. Melancholy. When she would lie in his arms and talk about her hopes for Courtney's future, a dark mood would befall him. He had demons, but she believed they were of his own making. As soon as he realized that, he could find a solution and put an end to his silent suffering.

They ate breakfast together, reliving the weekend with smiles and laughter. She watched him devour breakfast while complimenting her on her cooking skills. She enjoyed seeing him carefree and guilt-free. He always seemed to be carrying an emotional burden, and whenever they shared a moment, he shied away from happiness as if he didn't deserve it. This weekend had been different. He'd let his guard down and enjoyed his time with her and Courtney.

"Do you have a pad of paper?" he asked as she began removing the breakfast dishes.

"Sure."

He took a pen from the inside pocket of his suit jacket and scribbled on the paper, pushing it over to her when he finished.

"What's this?"

"It's my phone number."

"I have your phone number. *You* never call *me.*"

"When I talk to you I want to see your face."

She smiled flirtatiously. "Don't they have video-phones or something?"

He grinned at her.

"So you're giving me your phone number, why?"

"I'm giving you all my phone numbers. My home, office, cell, and my parents."

She glanced down at the chicken scratches scribbled across the pad. All the numbers were there, labeled for clarity. "So you're giving me all your numbers, why?"

"Just because I don't call you doesn't mean you can't call me."

"You don't like the telephone."

"Not when it comes to conversing with you, no. But if you want to talk to me, you call. Any time. I'll be at one of those numbers." He left his chair and stood over her, his thighs pressing against her. He whispered in her ear, "You call and I'll come running." He kissed her cheek, then her temple.

She watched him lift Courtney for his kiss. "I'll see you ladies soon."

They watched him disappear into the living room. A few seconds later, she heard the front door close. A second after that, she began to miss him.

# Chapter 15

Greyson entered Kirkland's office at the paper mill, ushering Cassidy and Courtney in before him. "I ran into these two at the library."

"Sorry." Cassidy rolled her eyes at Greyson. "He insisted. I didn't mean to bother you at work."

"No, no, it's fine." Courtney's arms went up for him as soon as he approached. He took her from Cassidy's hip. "What were you doing at the library?"

"Courtney's been fussy all day. We took a walk into town and ended up at the library talking to Sutton and Maggie."

"Those three women are becoming an item," Greyson teased.

"We should go," Cassidy said. "I haven't gotten anything done today, and I have another deadline."

"Why don't you leave her so you can get some work done?"

"I don't know."

"Yeah, leave her," Greyson piped in. "I'm on the way to pick Sierra up from her grandparents' house. I promised to drive her to McDonald's. Kirkland can tag along. Sierra will get a kick out of the baby."

"I don't know," Cassidy hedged. "I don't leave her much."

The men flanked her like twin pillars. She looked from one to the other. Greyson smiled with a hint of mischief. Kirkland watched her as if he were eager to pass some test.

"Okay, but just for a few hours."

"Do you need a ride home?" Kirkland asked.

"No, I don't need a ride. I'll walk. It inspires me." She kissed Courtney's cheek. "You two be careful."

"We will. She'll be fine," Greyson said, taking Courtney's diaper bag. "I'm a veteran at this."

She turned to Kirkland. "I worry about her."

"I know."

She stood on tiptoe and pressed her mouth to his, ignoring Greyson's reaction.

He whispered against her lips, "I'll take care of her like she's mine . . . like she belongs to me."


Kirkland and Greyson looked down at Courtney. She had no modesty, kicking her legs heartily with her bare bottom exposed.

Sierra patted Greyson's leg. "Is Uncle Kirkland going to put a diaper on Courtney?"

Kirkland's eyes grew large. "I'm just learning to change her diaper," he said to Greyson. "You have a daughter. Don't you know how to do it?"

"Remember, Sierra wasn't in diapers when I became her daddy."

"Sierra, honey." Kirkland bent down to her level. "Do you know how to put a diaper on a baby?"

"Kirkland!" Greyson laughed.

"I'm desperate." He stood and looked down into

Courtney's smiling face. Her arms went up for him.
"What?" he asked Greyson. "I can't pick her up like
this."

Sierra giggled.

"Maybe we can wait until Sutton gets home,"
Greyson suggested.

"How long will that be?"

Greyson shrugged and looked down at Courtney.
"She's going to start crying if you don't pick her up
and then we're really going to be in trouble." The
doorbell rang, saving him. "It's the pizza. Be right
back."

Abandoned, Kirkland turned to Sierra. "I'm a
master's degree–prepared black man who is part
owner of his own business. I can do this. Right?"

Sierra shrugged her shoulders.

"Okay." He took off the jacket of his suit and
handed it to Sierra. She hurried to hang it on the
back of the nearest chair. She didn't want to miss a
minute of the comedy show her uncle and stepfa-
ther were putting on.

He rolled up his sleeves. "What's next?"

"You need baby powder," Sierra said.

He raised an eyebrow. "Are you sure you can't do
this?"

She giggled, hiding her mouth behind her hand.

"Baby powder." He grabbed up the diaper bag
and searched for baby powder. Finding it, his confidence rose. "Easy enough."

"And you need the white cream."

"White cream?" He gave her a playful roll of the
eyes and went back into the bag. He found two
tubes, read the labels and selected the correct one.
"Anything else?"

Sierra laughed. "You need a diaper, Uncle Kirkland. You're funny!"

"You get the diaper, smarty."

Sierra settled on her knees at his feet and pulled out a diaper from the diaper bag.

"You get it ready while I do this part." He reached for the baby powder.

"No! You have to clean her with the baby wipes first, then put the white cream."

He did as instructed. "How do you know about this stuff?"

"My dolls."

*Dolls, of course.* "What's next?"

"The baby powder."

He sprinkled the powder over Courtney's bottom.

"Now the diaper." Sierra handed him the diaper, open and ready to be applied. With her help, he fastened it.

"Not bad for my first try," he said, smiling down at Courtney.

Greyson returned. "How's it going?"

"I helped, Daddy."

"You're so smart." He scooped Sierra up into his arms.

"Just barely," Kirkland teased her. "You made me do all the hard work." He lifted Courtney and the diaper slid down her legs and fell onto the bed.

Sierra giggled, and Greyson roared with laugher.

Two tries later, the diaper was properly secured to Courtney's waist. Kirkland joined Greyson in his lower-level family room. Sierra entertained Courtney with her zillions of toys. They ate pizza and talked about things that would bring them closer together as brothers. Business and the paper mill never came up, and Kirkland liked that just fine. There was a time when he and Greyson had nothing to discuss but business.

"You and Cassidy seem to be getting along," Greyson said.

"You've been dying to get into my business all day."

"Can't deny it. How's it going?"

"Good." He looked over at Courtney. Cassidy had entrusted him with her most valued possession: her daughter. Things were better than good.

"Any plans for the future?"

"No. We're taking it slow."

Greyson nodded.

"What's the look about?"

"Your relationship with Cassidy is kinda weird. Don't you think?"

"Weird how?"

He took a long drink from his soda. "Incongruent would be a better word. You don't speak on the telephone, but you spend the night at her house. You're not really in a committed relationship, but you're close enough for her to let you sit with Courtney. Is she happy with the way things are going between you?"

"Did she say something to you?"

"No. No, she didn't say anything to me. Did she say anything to you?"

"We talked about having more fun together."

"See, there's the first sign. You're going along thinking everything's fine, but she's just watching to see if you're going to be a screwup. One day you'll leave the toilet seat up, and the next thing you know she's screaming at you to get out and never come back."

He chuckled. "I have no idea what you're talking about—and neither do you."

Greyson cringed. "Let me school you. I know you don't have much experience in the serious relationship department."

"I've dated plenty of women."

"Yeah, but having a lot of women isn't the same thing as being in a serious relationship. I'm talking the difference between what Alex had with Sutton and what I have with her."

He swallowed the pain of that truth. "So you think I have some work do with Cassidy?"

"If you plan on keeping her in your life." He sat forward, getting deep into the conversation. "You're younger than Cassidy, and you haven't been in any serious relationships. You're going to have to be open to learning, and ready to do what it takes to keep her happy."

"Cassidy won't respect a wimp."

"I'm not talking about being a wimp. I'm talking about showing her how much you care for her. Your mission in life has to be to give her whatever she needs to be happy."

"I'm there already." He scratched at the curls on his head. He hadn't really wanted to admit that to his older brother.

"I can see it. But giving her whatever she needs doesn't necessarily mean furniture and maid service. A woman wants to know you think about her. She needs to feel like you respect her and want her to be happy with *you*."

"Is this how you trapped Sutton into marrying you?"

"Sutton is damn lucky to have me."

He raised an eyebrow. "Does she know about this?"

"I'm still working on the fine details." Greyson laughed. "Seriously, if you treat her like you can't live without her, she won't be able to live without you. It's not a game if you really feel that way. I love Sutton and Sierra. I *couldn't* live without them. Not one day." His gaze veered to Sierra playing with Courtney.

"I hear ya," Kirkland admitted quietly.

Greyson got back to business. "This is what I'm saying. You're younger than Cassidy, and your generation dates a lot differently than my generation. You call a woman and have her meet you at the movies or restaurant. I would pick her up, help her on with her coat, and open doors for her. You think living together is a commitment. I think living together is a cop-out and is the best way to show a woman there is no commitment. See what I'm saying?"

"I need to treat Cassidy more like a lady. Take her out and be a gentleman. Make sure she understands how I feel about her."

"You've got it."

"I think I've been doing a pretty good job."

"'Pretty good' isn't good enough for a woman who's special to you. If you were Courtney's father, would 'pretty good' from some guy be good enough for her?"

"I get the point."

"I like Cassidy a lot. She's good for you." Greyson

fell back against the sofa. "You've changed a lot since you started seeing her. You're more settled. You still need to let go of Mama's apron strings, but we want you to take baby steps."

"See, you were actually giving me good advice. Don't start working my nerves."

"Ready to call it a night?" Cassidy let her camera dangle from the strap around her neck. "I think I have enough shots here to illustrate several covers."

Donté broke pose and stretched his tired muscles. "I didn't think posing for a book cover would be this much work."

"You and every man I've ever photographed. Just be glad you don't have to pose while I paint you."

Donté ambled across the room and checked out some of the paintings. "This is great." He looked at her and flashed a spectacular smile. "You're good." He pointed to the man on the canvas. "You gonna make me look this good?"

"You're quite handsome on your own."

"Do you do any other stuff? Could you paint a portrait of me for my girl?"

She was commissioned for private portraits all the time. With a new baby, she could use all the work she could get. She discussed the terms of consignment while they looked at other samples of her work.

"I didn't mean to keep you this long," Donté said when the doorbell rang.

"No problem. I enjoyed talking to you." She raced off to answer the door. "I'll be right back. It's my little girl." She threw the door open and took

Courtney from Kirkland's arms. She cuddled her closer having missed her the hours she was away. "She's sleeping so hard."

"Sierra wore her out." He stepped inside hauling the car seat and diaper bag.

"Excuse me, Cassidy." Donté entered the living room. "I gotta get going."

She saw him out, with him promising to follow up with her about his personal portrait. She watched Kirkland's expression as she introduced the men. She held her breath when Donté extended his hand, waiting for fireworks to go off. Kirkland remained polite, saying, "I'll get the door while you put Courtney to bed." She watched him skeptically, but went to put Courtney down. He joined her in Courtney's room shortly afterwards.

"I'm so proud of you." She wrapped her arms around his waist.

"For what?"

"Don't act like you don't know what I mean. A few weeks ago you would have been wrestling Donté on my lawn."

"I listen to what you say."

"I see, and I'm very, very proud of you." She stood on tiptoe to give him a kiss that conveyed her appreciation.

"I trust you enough to be okay with the beef hunks parading through here, but it still gets to me. Can't you illustrate women for the covers of those books?"

"Kirkland," she groaned.

"I still need a little work."

She released him and they went into the living room. "Did Courtney give you any trouble?"

"None. She was great." He sat on the sofa and pulled her against his chest. "It gave me and Greyson some time to talk. I wouldn't mind doing it again."

"I'll keep that in mind."

He kissed the top of her head.

"Can you stay with me tonight?"

"I want to, but I have to go." He pushed her up to see her face clearly. "Would you like to go out with me this weekend?"

"What?" A broad smile spread across her face.

"A date. With me. Just the two of us. Greyson and Sutton can sit with Courtney. I asked."

"You did?" No man had ever made her feel more important.

"Is Saturday okay?"

"Saturday is good."

He stood to go.

She wasn't ready for him to leave.

"Are you going to tell me where we're going?" she asked.

"Is there somewhere special you want to go?"

She thought about it for a moment. "No."

"Then it'll be a surprise." He strolled to the door. "Can I get a good-bye kiss?"

She joined him at the door. "Will I see you before Saturday?"

He shook his head. "I don't think so. I have a lot of work to do at the paper mill."

"I'll miss you."

"Me too." He took her in his arms. He placed his lips next to hers when he said, "If you need me, call me. I'll drop everything to come."

# Chapter 16

Saturday morning Cassidy realized Kirkland hadn't told her what time he would be picking her up. Before she found the time to call him, Sutton called. "Greyson tells me we're supposed to have Courtney for the day."

"I hope it's no trouble. I should have called, but Kirkland said he took care of everything."

"He did. He and Greyson were cooking up mischief the other day. We're taking the girls to a carnival."

Greyson spoke in the background.

"My husband says to tell you to pack Courtney an overnight bag."

"Overnight bag? She's never been away from me all night. Did Greyson tell you where Kirkland and I will be all night?"

"Nope. Couldn't pry it out of him. Kirkland didn't say?"

"No. He didn't." She watched Courtney crawling across the living room floor, chasing a ball. She was wearing the matching pink shorts and shirt Darius had delivered as a gift from his wife. The shirt was made of soft Egyptian cotton that made you want to cuddle her in your arms for hours. Despite the lactose intolerance, she was a healthy weight; her arms and legs were plump and squeezable. "I don't know about an overnight."

"Courtney will be fine with us. You can call and check on her as often as you want. We're what, fifteen minutes away? You have to let her make friends with other kids."

"Girls," Greyson shouted in the background.

Sutton laughed. "He's having problems with Sierra's choice of playmates. All boys. Just like me," she added for Greyson's benefit.

"And look where it got you," he shouted back, laughter in his voice.

Sutton ignored the comment and came back on the line. "Look, you don't want Courtney so attached to you that she has separation anxiety and you can't leave her at school. This will be good for both of you."

*School?* Courtney wasn't a year yet. First-time-mother jitters plagued her. She couldn't even begin to think about sending Courtney off to school. "I don't know. I should talk to Kirkland."

"If you don't want to go out with Kirkland, I understand. Don't feel obligated."

"It's not like that."

"Are you sure?" Sutton sounded concerned, and not about Cassidy's apprehension about leaving Courtney.

"I'm sure."

"We're on the way then. See you in fifteen."

Sutton hung up before Cassidy could wheedle her way out of sending Courtney for her first overnight. She was still thinking about begging out of the date when Sutton arrived at the door. Sierra ran to Courtney and they greeted each other like old friends. Greyson slung the diaper bag over his shoulder and grabbed the car seat and stroller. After some discussion, they decided to take the playpen for Courtney to sleep in. Cassidy clung to Courtney until the last minute when Sutton took her away to secure her in the car seat.

Greyson ushered Sutton out the door. "Kirkland said to tell you he'll be here one hour after we leave."

"Why all the mystery?" Cassidy tried to smile, but her eyes burned with tears as she watched Sutton buckle Courtney in.

"He wants this date to be very special." He stepped out onto the porch.

"What time should I pick up Courtney?"

Greyson shrugged. "We'll meet you at my parents' house."

"Your parents?"

"Oops. Ruined part of the mystery. Kirkland's going to bring you for lunch tomorrow at my parents' house. Mama's planning a big cookout."

"Oh." She was distracted, watching Courtney, Sutton, and Sierra at the car.

"See you tomorrow."

"Okay," Cassidy whispered, watching him walk away. She went out onto the porch and watched until the brake lights on Greyson's Volvo wagon disappeared. She knew Courtney would be safe with Sutton and Greyson; it was just hard sending her away for her first overnight. She stood on the porch for a long time, expecting Greyson to come back around the corner because Courtney was crying for her mother and they couldn't comfort her. It never happened. She remembered what Greyson said about Kirkland arriving in an hour, and went inside to get ready.

Once she started preparing for her date, she felt better. She had the freedom to enjoy one night as a single, vibrant woman, and not a mother. She loved being a mother. She'd gone to great lengths to become pregnant, but when she thought of spending time alone with Kirkland, she wanted to be a woman, free of restraint.

She selected her outfit quickly. A golden yellow sheath dress that was elegant, but fun. She pulled a pair of strappy shoes from the closet, and didn't have to worry about the heels making her taller than her date. She added body to her hair with a curling iron, and applied summer colors to her cheeks and lips. She was contemplating calling Sutton to check on Courtney when the doorbell sounded.

"Do you like?" Kirkland held his arms out from his body and turned in a complete circle. She laughed as he stepped inside. He had traded his suit for washed denims and a powder blue shirt. He finished the outfit with black loafers, no socks.

She ran her hands over the tailored fit of the shirt. "I like a lot."

"Better than the suits?"

She let her eyes roam over the bulges and planes of his body. "I like this, but you wear a mean suit too."

"Just for tonight then." He kissed her lips quickly, before standing back to get a good look at her. He whistled. "You're extra pretty tonight."

"I feel overdressed, but you didn't tell me where we were going. I'm going to change."

"No. You look great."

She ignored him, rushing to her closet and changing into a blue summery slip dress, keeping the strappy sandals. She grabbed a matching sweater, touched up her makeup, and returned to the living room.

"This is even better," Kirkland said, his eyes observing the exposed cleavage. "Yeah, I like this a lot better." He gave her a kiss of approval. "Let's go."

Outside, he held the car door open while she angled inside.

"You asked Sutton and Greyson to keep Courtney overnight."

"Um-huh." He leaned down, to put them at eye level. "Something wrong?"

She looked at the eagerness in his eyes. "No."

He kissed her cheek before closing the door. She liked all the affection he was showing her today. "Can I know where we're going?" she asked once they entered the expressway.

"Don't worry. It isn't far." The corner of his mouth lifted in a smile. "Greyson will call my cell if there's a problem." Keeping his eyes on the road, he reached for her hand. "I want you to relax and have fun. Are you going to be able to do that without worrying about Courtney?"

"It's just . . . I've never left her overnight."

He glanced at her. "Should I change our plans?"

She mulled over the offer. "I need this, don't I?"

He nodded. "I think so."

She relaxed in the soft leather seat. "Okay."

"Okay, what?"

"Courtney will have fun with Sierra. Her first sleepover."

He squeezed her hand to show his approval and support. Minutes later, he parked in the back lot of a two-story red brick building with large windows. He banged hard on the huge metal door with Creative Arts Center etched across it. The door opened slowly, as if it weighed a ton to move. The face of the man struggling with the door broke into a wide grin when he saw Kirkland. "Mr. Ballantyne," he said, pulling the door open wide.

"How are you?" They exchanged handshakes before Kirkland introduced Cassidy. The man gave her a quick once over and smiled at Kirkland; a man's way of silently showing approval.

"Do you have everything ready for the opening?" Kirkland asked, pulling her inside.

"We just hung the last piece of artwork." He pushed the heavy door closed. "Are you going to make the reception tomorrow?"

"No, I won't be able to make it."

"A real shame. Especially since you had so much to do with getting the building ready. You're taking a look around, right? You have time for a quick look, don't you?"

"We will. I wanted Cassidy to see the exhibit."

"He told me you're a great artist."

She looked up at Kirkland, but he wore a blank face to mask his embarrassment.

"I have to get back to work. A lot goes into an opening. Call me when you're done so I can lock up." The curator scurried off, looking frazzled around the edges.

"What are we doing here?" Her voice carried in the deserted museum.

"You're an artist. I thought you might enjoy visiting an art gallery. Was I wrong?"

"No." She adjusted her tone to the acoustics. "The curator knew you well."

He took her hand and led her into the museum. "They were evicted from their old space to make room for a strip mall. I found them this building and helped renovate it."

"With your own hands?" She admired his giving spirit.

"I helped when I could, but mostly I talked the old owners into donating the building to the arts. I got a couple of contractors to donate materials and labor, and here we are."

They stepped into the museum and Cassidy looked upward at the tall ceilings. Sunlight was pouring in from the large windows on the second floor, casting a rainbow down onto the first floor. Artwork hung along the perimeter. The hardwood floors and brick walls gave the museum a funky contemporary feel. "This is a great space."

"Let's take a look around." He guided her back to the beginning of the exhibit. "All the artwork is from Iran. Most of it is done by women." He amazed her by pointing out the difference between watercolor, drawing, painting, and calligraphy. He explained the use of mixed media to create dynamic 3D pictures. He knew the history of most of the Iranian artists and the Tehran Museum of Contemporary Art where the artwork was usually displayed.

"How do you know so much about art?" Cassidy asked, watching him in awe.

He smiled down at her. "I came for a crash course yesterday. I wanted to impress you."

"It's working." He'd taken time to learn about the art so he could be a better guide for her. Taking an interest in what she enjoyed meant a lot. "You know more than I do about some of the media."

He took her hand again and led her to a stunning picture of Iranian horsemen. The horsemen sat astride their horses wearing gold and red military uniforms. It was like looking into a mirror, with the images portrayed in a repeating sequence, perfectly duplicated by the artist. The color scheme made it striking. The attention to detail made it a masterpiece. "I'm thinking about this for my mother."

She looked at him incredulously. "Can you afford a piece of art this valuable?"

"It's not polite to ask me how much money I have." He placed his hand on her shoulder, pulling her near. His fingers slipped beneath the strap of her bra.

"It's not polite to undress me in public either."

His fingers wiggled. His eyes were on the painting. "I think my mother would really like this for the living room."

"Are you really close to your mom?"

"Very." He searched her face for a reaction. "Does it bother you?"

"That you're close to your mother? No. Should it?"

He shrugged. "It might bother some. I think I'll

talk to the curator about this painting." He led her to the next piece of art.

"Did you tell your mother about me?"

"Yes." His fingers stroked her bare shoulder.

"Everything?"

He stopped and looked at her. "Everything like what?"

"I have a child and haven't been married. The folks in Hannaford Valley still frown on that type of thing. I've seen your parents at church. They look conservative."

"I told her," he answered, not giving any clue to his mother's reaction.

"Does she know how old I am?"

He scratched his sandy-brown curls. "I didn't mention it."

"Kirkland."

"What? I didn't tell her about our sex life either."

"Not the same thing and you know it."

His hand moved further underneath her bra strap. "My parents aren't as conservative as they seem. You'll fit right in. Don't worry about it. Sutton had Sierra when she married Greyson."

"Sutton was a widow when she married Greyson. It's not the same thing."

He moved them as a unit to the next painting.

"What if your mother has a problem with me?"

He stared at her for a long moment. "It would be a problem."

She returned his stare. "You're that close?"

"Close enough that I don't want to be forced to choose between the two of you."

"Because I'd lose." Her behavior had already driven a wedge between her and her parents. She couldn't stand inflicting the same pain on Kirkland and the Ballantyne family. She tried to walk away but his fingers curled around her bra strap, pulling her back to him.

"I wouldn't choose, Cassidy. I couldn't choose. It would be an ugly situation."

"You're not making me feel any better."

"It's a good thing. It means you care."

"Can you release my bra strap now?" She looked around for the little man with too much to do.

He smiled mischievously. "I have a trick for you."

"You're feeling spunky today. Trick or treat?"

"Both. Believe me." He pulled her into his arms and kissed her deeply. More passionately than she could ever remember him kissing her. Her mind went blank and she kept silently repeating, *He's a great kisser.* When he finally pulled away, he tipped her chin up to meet his devilish grin. Slowly, she recovered, raising her lashes to look up at him. Her eyes went to the object swinging from his finger.

"Oh my—" She wrapped her arms over her chest. "How did you . . . ?" She snatched at her bra, but he jerked it out of her reach. "Why did you . . . ?"

"I'm a breast man," he answered as if it were logical. He tucked her bra in his back pocket.

"Give it back, Kirkland. Before someone sees me."

He wrapped his arms around her waist and pulled her up on the tips of her toes as he kissed her. When he let her feet float back to the floor she couldn't remember what she had wanted from him.

"Let's go to dinner," he said. The male pride in his laughter bounced off the museum walls.

# Chapter 17

Dinner was not what Cassidy expected. After the private museum tour, she was learning not to underestimate Kirkland's resources, but she never would have guessed . . .

"I'm waiting for the Sheik to arrive," Cassidy said as Kirkland helped her to sit on a huge pile of oversized pillows.

"You'll have to accept me as his substitute."

The living room of his penthouse had been transformed into an Arabian palace, complete with servants and belly dancers. The music was as authentic as the food, delighting Cassidy with the attention to detail. They sat in the middle of a sea of purple and silver pillows enthralled by the dancers' performance.

"I can't believe you went to all this trouble." She rewarded him with a kiss.

"Nothing is too much trouble when it comes to you."

"How sweet." Her face ached from all the smiling she'd done tonight. "How did you pull this off?" she asked.

"I can't give you all my secrets." The belly dancers finished their last routine and Kirkland thanked them, sending them on their way. He pulled her into his arms. "Alone, finally."

She plucked a grape from a silver tray and popped it into his mouth. "I ate so much baklava I'll never get to sleep."

"Sugar high?"

"Some kind of high." She looked into his eyes, suggesting it might not have anything to do with food.

"Well, we should take advantage of your sleepless night." He arranged her so she was draped over his lap, fully exposed for his exploration.

"First the trip to the mountains, now this. You're going to spoil me, Kirkland."

"Good. It's my intention to spoil you and Courtney. I want you to need me as badly as I need you."

"We already do." She wrapped her arms around his neck, bringing him down to her for a kiss. Passion exploded at the meeting of their lips. He stroked her while letting his kiss trail down her neck. He cupped her breasts, chuckling at his handiwork.

"Can I have my bra back now?"

"You won't need it for the rest of the night." He laid her down on the mountain of pillows, covering her body with his. She ran her fingers through the silky softness of his brown curls as he pushed her dress upward over her hips. She responded by unbuttoning his shirt and working to remove his jeans. He undressed her slowly, kissing every inch of exposed skin as he went. Once he had her naked and writhing for his intimate kiss, he finished undressing himself, tantalizing her by standing over her and forcing her to watch as he shed his clothing.

She found her revenge when she applied the condom, taking her time to stroke his shaft as she unrolled the latex. Her fingertips teased as they slid upward and then downward, again and again. Losing all control, he pinned her hands beneath his and entered her in one long thrust.

The music continued to play in the background, transporting her to a land far, far away where the rules were much different. Kirkland felt it too, disregarding Western etiquette for making love. He was ruthless in giving pleasure, taking her to the brink of erotic unconsciousness. After satisfying her, he pursued his own fulfillment just as mercilessly. It was much more than making love: more sensual, more sexual, more connected.

He held her around the waist with a death grip, panting, trying to catch his breath. "I love you, Cassidy."

Her heart burst with joy. Relief washed over her in giant waves. She hadn't realized how badly she wanted him to love her until she heard the words aloud. Now she was free to love him too. "I love you, Kirkland."

Cassidy insisted they sleep on the purple and silver pillows beneath the purple scarves forming a tent above their heads. She awoke with Kirkland still holding her around the waist, his head pressed into the crook of her neck. He warmed her. It felt so right being with him in this intimate pose.

She thought of Courtney. Morning had come and she'd made it through the night without calling and checking on Courtney. Most of her time spent with Kirkland included Courtney, but yesterday had been different. Yesterday, he had proved his feelings for her weren't an extension of his affection for Courtney.

"I love Courtney, too," he cut into her thoughts.

She watched him, inches from her face, unblinkingly.

"Did you doubt it?"

"No. It's just—to hear it out loud . . ."

"It's overwhelming. I didn't plan to tell you how I felt, but I'm glad it happened." He kissed the tip of her nose, springing up from the pillows. "We should get dressed if we're going to make it to my parents' house in time."

He helped her up. "I thought I'd meet them for the first time at the anniversary party."

"You've talked to my parents in church."

She followed him to the bathroom. "We've made small talk in passing. This is different."

"Don't worry. Greyson, Chevy, and I are going to help Pop finish the gazebo. My mother's going to feed us while we do. It's very informal. Now the anniversary dinner will be another matter all together." He turned on the shower, testing the water temperature.

"Chevy will be there?"

"Chevy will be there." He spared her a harsh glance as he searched the medicine cabinet. "I've talked to him about us." He handed her a toothbrush. "He's fine with it."

"Are you sure?"

He turned to her, full body, and for the first time since meeting him, his size was daunting. "Chevy has moved on. Have you?"

"Don't ask me that."

"Why not?"

"I don't like you questioning my feelings for Chevy after I told you I love you. And I don't like the way you're looking at me."

"How am I looking at you?"

"Suspiciously. Like you're not sure if what I feel for you is genuine."

He found his own toothbrush and added toothpaste. "How do *you* feel about Chevy being at my parents'?"

He would be relentless about this. She watched him brush as she answered. "I thought it might be awkward for him—and for me. We parted friends, but I don't think he expected me to be in love with his little brother a year later."

He rinsed his toothbrush, concentrating too hard on the simple task. "It doesn't have to be awkward for any of us. I've talked to Chevy about it. He knows you'll be there today. You parted friends, just be friendly." He slid the glass shower door open and stepped inside, closing it firmly behind him and dismissing further discussion.

She brushed her teeth, joining him in the shower as he rinsed the sudsy water from the chiseled muscles of his chest. "I need to go home and change clothes before we go."

"I took care of it. There's a cute little outfit hanging in my closet with your name on it."

Cute was one word for it. Flimsy would have been more appropriate. The sheer material of the dress glided over Cassidy's skin, sparking sensitivity along her nerve endings. The aqua material was splattered with dainty flowers. The rich coloring made her skin glisten. Her multicolored strappy sandals went well with the summery dress.

"Why are you dressed like that, and I'm dressed like this?" She pointed a finger at the tan work clothes Kirkland wore.

"You're sexy. What's the problem? This is a working lunch for me." He smiled mischievously.

"I'm not overdressed?"

"Not from where I'm standing. Don't worry, I'll take a change of clothes with me."

She mumbled something about him being sexist, but he ignored her, taking her hand and leading her out of his apartment with a delighted chuckle.

Cassidy remained polite when she greeted Kirkland's parents, but she couldn't wait to get to Courtney. She left Kirkland and Greyson in the study planning the completion of the gazebo to find Sutton in the backyard with Courtney and Sierra.

"You missed her," Sierra said.

"Did you have fun?"

Sierra gave her a play-by-play of their sleepover as she joined Sutton.

"Sierra, honey, why don't you go ask Grandma if she needs us to help?" Sutton breathed heavily, watching Sierra run off to the house.

"She's a sweetie."

"Yes, she is, but she can talk you to death. She had a blast with Courtney." Sutton reached out and tickled Courtney's chin. "How'd the big date go? What did you do?"

Cassidy bounced Courtney, showering her with kisses as she told Sutton about her big night.

"Love?" Sutton didn't sound happy for her.

"Yes, we are officially in love with each other."

Sutton's eyes slipped away.

"How did Courtney do on her first official sleepover?"

"It was great. We really enjoyed her. We'd love to have her again. I think Greyson enjoyed her most of all." She lowered her voice although they were alone outside. "He really wants to have a baby."

"Don't you?"

"Yes. After I finish law school. He's afraid I'll try to hold off until I get my career started. He's a little older than me . . . he hears *his* biological clock ticking."

They shared a laugh and then Sutton became serious again. "He's accused me of stalling," Sutton said.

"Are you? Stalling?"

Sutton's gaze wandered off. She watched Mama Ballantyne and Sierra coming toward them carrying meat for the grill. She turned back to Cassidy. Painful indecision marred her face. "I don't know."

"That's serious, Sutton. You have to talk this out with Greyson and let him know how you feel."

"I'm not sure how I feel yet." Sutton smoothed Courtney's shirt down her back. "I look at Sierra and Courtney and I want a baby so badly I can hardly breathe." She shook her head. "I can't go through it alone again. I don't know how you do it."

"Who says you'll be going through it alone? There's no way Greyson would abandon you."

Sierra ran ahead of Mama Ballantyne. "Mom, Daddy wants you."

Sutton propelled herself up from the lounger. "I know he'd never abandon me. I know it here." She pressed her hand to her chest. "But it doesn't keep me from reliving my relationship with Alex."

"My daddy?" Sierra asked, too astute for a kindergartener.

"We'll make time to talk, later," Cassidy said. "Sierra, why don't you go get Courtney's car seat so I can help your grandmother with the grill."

Sutton mouthed "thank you" before going off to find Greyson. Sierra ran across the yard to get the car seat.

"That child is so busy," Mama Ballantyne observed. "I swear she has a touch of the hyperactivity disease." She watched Sierra struggle to drag the car seat across the grass. "She's a sweetie, though." Mama put the meat on the grill before sitting next to Cassidy and taking Courtney into her lap.

The men trouped out of the house, tools in hand. They went directly to the gazebo, although Kirkland gave her a big smile. The men were all tall and broad with similarly handsome facial features. She wondered how Mama Ballantyne had survived being the only woman in the house.

"Those are my boys," Mama Ballantyne said as if reading her mind.

"They're a handsome bunch."

"And a handful of trouble."

Sierra arrived with the car seat. With her encouragement, Mama placed Courtney in the seat so they could play. Mama joined her while she tended the grill. "Kirkland seems to have settled down since he started seeing you."

She didn't know how to respond. She understood they had a close bond, so the comment could be interpreted as positive or negative, depending on whether Mama approved of their relationship.

"He goes on about you and Courtney so."

"He's very special to me," she admitted. "Courtney's crazy about him, too."

"I love my son dearly."

She sensed a "but" coming.

"But, he's reckless."

Sutton's warnings about Kirkland swarmed around her head.

"Kirkland is reckless, but he has a good heart," Mama said.

"Why are you telling me this?" Cassidy's gaze went to Kirkland. He was laughing with Greyson, standing back while Chevy and Pop Ballantyne inspected the gazebo.

"Because it's the right thing to do," Mama answered. She sounded weary.

"Do you have a problem with me seeing Kirkland?"

"No." She replaced the lid on the grill. "No, I mean it when I say you're good for him." She paused, watching Kirkland for a long moment before she continued. "I hope he's as good for you and the baby."

His mother was warning her he might break her heart. Who knew him better? She felt her world come crashing in, as if her blinders had been ripped away and the monster in him revealed. Suddenly, the liberating love she'd confessed that morning began to smother her. Had she made a grave error in giving in to her feelings for Kirkland? Standing outside, surrounded by mountains and trees, she felt trapped inside a tiny box.

"Excuse me." She sprinted to the house.

"Are you okay?" Mama called after her.

"I'm fine. Watch Courtney for me, please."

"I didn't mean to upset you."

Her sprint caught the men's attention. Kirkland dropped his hammer in the grass and went after her. She navigated the hallways of the large house until she found the bathroom.

"Cassidy?" He knocked on the door before coming in. "What happened?"

She sat on the rim of the tub. She looked up at him with hopeful eyes, praying she hadn't made a huge mistake by ignoring Sutton's warnings.

"Tell me what happened, Cass."

She rested her elbows on her knees, dropping her head to escape his serious eyes.

"I don't like this. Tell me. Now."

She reluctantly met his eyes. "What are we doing?"

"What?" He stood above her truly perplexed.

"You and me. What are we doing?"

He crossed his arms over his chest. "What the hell did my mother say to you?"

"I can't do this. I'm too old for you. I'm a single mother. You're rich and I'm a struggling artist. You have this close family, and my parents have disowned me. We're so different." The more she listed the reasons to be apart, the more distraught she became. "It isn't logical—us being together. The right thing to do is to end it now." *Before she would hurt any more than necessary*, she didn't add aloud.

"You're not breaking up with me," Kirkland said definitively. He wet a cloth with cool water and sat next to her, handing it over to her. "Do you hear me? You are not breaking up with me. Not for no good reason."

"Kirkland, don't you see it?"

He lifted her hand, pressing the cloth to her forehead. "No, I don't see it."

"I didn't either until just now."

"I don't know what my mother said to upset you—I'll talk to her later—but we're not breaking up, Cassidy. We love each other. We're not breaking up."

"Stop saying that."

"Fine, but know it's true. I'm not ready to let you go." He paused reflectively. "I don't think I'll ever be ready to let you go." He shook his head. "If you think I can let you and Courtney walk out of my life, you're wrong."

"I don't have any say in it?"

"No."

"Kirkland—"

"No, listen to me. If I've done something wrong, I respect your right to tell me to get lost. It's not the case. Things are good between us. I don't care what my mother said to scare you, but we'll work through it. You don't just throw away a relationship like ours. I won't allow it." He turned her to face him. "I won't allow it."

She watched the love reflected in his eyes and wondered how he had become so worldly at such a young age. When she should have been strong, he had to be her rock. She should be the logical one, but he was forced to talk sense into her. Her heart couldn't see the logic in letting go of the man who owned her heart.

"You do know I love you, right?" he asked.

"Yes."

"Let's end this discussion." He pulled her into him, holding her for a long time and allowing her to compose herself. He kissed the top of her head. "No one knows what goes on between us, so no one should have an opinion about our relationship. I'll talk to my mother."

"No. She didn't mean anything."

"Something she said upset you."

"Yes. No. I'm just overly emotional today."

He watched her, trying to decipher the truth. She gave him a wry smile. He held her for a long time, patiently addressing her emotional needs. He offered comfort, making her feel as if they could stand against the world and defeat any obstacles thrown in their path.

"Did I embarrass you in front of your family?"

"Not at all. We've seen worse." He stood up. "Ready to go back outside?"

"Give me a minute."

"Five minutes, and then I'm coming back in." He opened the door, but ducked his head back inside. "Don't make me have to carry you out."

She took a minute to work through her unfounded fears and embarrassment. For a brief moment, she'd been so afraid of the power of her love for Kirkland she was willing to throw it away. She thought of the potential in him, the way he made her feel whole, and his strong relationship with Courtney. How could she have . . . ?

She vowed to never give up on him again. No matter what problems arose, she would not turn her back on him again. She touched up her makeup and prepared to return to the family and make her apologies.

"Hi." Chevy greeted her in the kitchen. He put down the beers gathered in his arms and pulled out a chair. "Can we talk?"

With the weird encounter with Mama Ballantyne, and now running into Chevy, she regretted coming for lunch. They sat across from each other at the kitchen table. His handsome presence still had the power to shift the mood of the room.

"Kirkland discussed your relationship with me."

She knew he would be direct. "I should've talked with you before I went out with him."

He shook his head. "We're friends. We couldn't push anything more." He captured her with the seriousness of his gaze. "No matter how hard we tried."

"I always felt you had someone else on your mind."

His eyes slipped away and she knew she was on to something. "I apologize."

"It's not necessary. I don't want it to be awkward between us."

"Sounds like Kirkland is going to be bringing you around a lot."

"Is this weird for you? Knowing I'm dating your brother?"

It took a moment for him to answer. "Kinda, but not because of jealousy. I see how happy Kirkland

is with you and I wonder why *we* couldn't find that."
He hesitated, his voice filling with sadness. "I wonder why *I* can't find happiness with a woman."

She reached out to him, covering his hand with hers. "It'll happen for you."

His mouth formed a slight smile. "You were always a good listener."

"We are friends. If you need someone to talk to—"

He stood abruptly, his male ego ruffled. "I'd better get back if we're ever going to finish this gazebo."

She watched him go, her heart mourning for him, but appreciating her relationship with Kirkland even more. She stood in the kitchen doorway watching the men complete the gazebo while Sutton and Mama Ballantyne worked the grill preparing lunch. Sierra was kneeling in front of Courtney, laughing and sharing her dolls. A twinge of regret moved through her. She needed her family. She had to make amends with her parents.

# Chapter 18

Kirkland stood at the back of city hall until he spotted Cassidy. She was casually dressed in blue jean shorts and a white blouse. He slipped into the seat next to her, whispering in her ear, "I want to kiss you, but I don't want to give the town gossips anything to talk about."

She smiled, her lashes dipping as a red flush colored her face.

Courtney's arms shot up in the air when she recognized his voice. He lifted her from the stroller onto his lap, greeting her in their secret language. "I didn't know you would be here."

"I thought you were working in the capital today."

"Didn't want to miss this."

"Darius is going to present his proposal to the city council. We're here to support him."

The mayor of Hannaford Valley addressed the town, impartially giving an overview of the situation regarding the commercial development of the town. The characters Kirkland had grown up with were on hand to offer their opinions. Rabbit stood and made a half-hearted speech about saving the town. An obvious ploy to impress any single women who didn't know his habit of wasting endless hours in the barber shop instead of getting a job. Carver and his wife—the town's biggest gossip—stood and speculated about what Japanese companies wanted to take over the town. Mrs. Carver's blood would curdle if she knew he held the biggest stake in developing the land. Little Man sat with the town's barber, taking in all the testimonies like tape recorders so they could play it back word for word the next day at the shop.

Kirkland sat forward, surprised to see Chevy take the stage. With the rumors and endless teasing from the children in town, he rarely ventured to community gatherings. The fact he had risked the taunting to voice his opinion spoke volumes about his passion for saving the land. "We've made a commitment at the paper mill to work with the environmentalists to preserve the land." He went on to explain the mill's plan to replenish the trees used in the production of paper products.

Kirkland watched with begrudging pride as Chevy spoke with an impassioned voice about the importance of maintaining the forests and lands for the animals and endangered species. With eloquence, he presented statistics about how destroying the environment would affect the health of Hannaford's citizens.

Kirkland felt the stirrings of guilt and regret, but managed to tamp them down, refusing to fall prey to sentimentality. He wondered if Alex would approve of his plans. Alex valued the land his father fought so hard to obtain, but he held no loyalties to Hannaford Valley. He worked hard to lose his country accent, something Kirkland had never been able to do. He often told colleagues he was born in

Chicago, denying his roots. And more than once, Alex and Sutton had fought about her telling his business associates about their life in the small town. Alex might have some regrets about selling his father's land, but Kirkland knew he would support any lucrative deal. Alex was about making money—lots of it.

There was that stipulation in Alex's will. The provision did not allow Kirkland to sell the land, or divulge his ownership of it for two years. He hadn't been able to figure it out. Knowing Alex Galloway, he was up to something Kirkland probably didn't want to know about. He'd spoken to Mother Galloway about receiving the land soon after he told Sutton, but she had gone on to live her life in Chicago, and was not concerned with "the workings of a backwoods town like Hannaford Valley." He took her attitude as approval for whatever he chose to do with the property.

The mayor approached the podium and introduced Greyson. Sutton and Sierra flanked him in the front row, a visible show of support. He spoke eloquently, challenging the town to block industrial development of Hannaford. "The town has survived worse economic times than these," Greyson continued. "We've never had to destroy the land. This is our home. We have to think of the future of our children."

As if cued, Courtney looked up at Kirkland and cooed. She was the future of Hannaford Valley. He had voluntarily taken on the responsibility for ensuring her future. *He* had stood in the hospital, watching her through the viewing glass, making promises he had somehow forgotten. He was beginning to have doubts. *What was I thinking?* Destroying Hannaford Valley in order to prove his manhood? His manhood was best substantiated by establishing a family—and leaving them a legacy to be proud of. Greyson's speech, fighting for the future of his children and the town, mocked him. He looked down into the big, brown, innocent eyes of Courtney and had an attack of conscience. "I have to leave," he whispered to Cassidy.

"Is something wrong?" Cassidy asked as she took Courtney.

"I remembered something important I have to take care of."

"Now?"

"It can't wait."

"Are you sure everything's okay?"

"Everything's fine." He kissed her cheek. "The dinner's set with your parents?"

She nodded. "Tomorrow."

"I'll talk to you after to see how it went."


Weeks had passed since Kirkland had visited Chevy at his cabin. Having never really taken to the sport of hunting, he still had a hard time being in the living room of the cabin with the animal trophies staring down at him. The detailed workmanship of Chevy's home could be seen in the stone fireplace and hardwood floors. Although the cabin was nestled deep in the woods, surrounded by flowers, greenery, and wildlife, it seemed isolated and cold. Chevy didn't seem proud to be living in the showplace he'd built with his own hands. He was lonely and his misery was beginning to manifest with a grizzly bear–like attitude.

"What are you doing?" Kirkland followed Chevy into the kitchen.

"I was out back cutting wood." Chevy draped himself over the refrigerator door. "Want a beer?"

"Yeah." He sat at the kitchen table. "Why are you chopping wood in the middle of the summer?"

Chevy tossed him a can of beer. "When do you think I should chop it? When it starts snowing?"

"No, I'm asking why you're working on the weekend. You're always working."

Chevy straddled the kitchen chair. "Why are you here?"

Kirkland ignored his brother's foul disposition. "Have you gotten any feedback from the city council?"

Chevy popped the top on his beer and took a long drink before answering. "The next thing that will probably happen is we'll get a court order to force the construction company to name the corporation they're working for." He left his chair and went to the kitchen window. "I think I'm going to have to get a dog to keep the rabbits away from my garden." He turned back to Kirkland. "Can't fight the enemy if you don't know who the enemy is."

Kirkland joined Chevy at the window. "When did you do all this?" A good portion of the land behind the cabin was now a garden of corn, tomatoes, and other vegetables.

Chevy shrugged. "Been busy."

"You want to go into the capital and get a drink tonight?"

"You're not going out with Cassidy on a Saturday night?"

"No. She's having a big dinner with her parents."

Chevy straddled the kitchen chair again. "You're not invited?"

"Family business."

"Everything going okay?"

"We're fine. She needed to take care of this alone. What about a drink?"

"Only if you spring for dinner at that expensive restaurant I like."

"You're on." Kirkland hesitated. "Can I talk to you about something?" He could be honest with Chevy, share the fears that made him want to destroy the town's landscape, and not worry about him being judgmental. Chevy would offer good advice and help him work out the problem. He was about to tell Chevy he was the hated developer the town wanted to hang when a car spitting gravel in the driveway distracted him. "Are you expecting someone?"

"Yeah," he answered, already heading to the front door. "Sutton's coming by to pick up some papers for Greyson."

Kirkland felt his stomach tighten into a huge knot. He and Sutton had been sociable at his parents' house, but only by avoiding each other as much as possible. He'd kept a close eye on her after his mother's little chat sent Cassidy running into the bathroom. He didn't want Sutton's badmouthing him to upset Cassidy further. He knew he had to deal with his sister-in-law and settle things between them, but he wasn't ready right then.

Sutton's smile dissipated when she entered the kitchen.

"Grab a beer," Chevy said. "The papers are in my office."

"Hello, Sutton." Kirkland took a long drag from his beer and felt the need for a cigarette although he had never smoked. It was Alex who chain-smoked when the going got rough. They were so close it was hard to distinguish between their personal preferences and subtle characteristics. He watched Sutton glaring at him, and he had the sudden realization he and Alex were the same person in her eyes.

"Kirkland." She pulled out a chair. "If I knew you were here, I would have come prepared to ask you some questions."

"Questions?"

"Yes. I've been working on that environmental project I mentioned to you weeks ago, and I'm finding out some interesting information."

"Really?" He was parched but didn't dare try to lift the beer with his trembling hands. "Like what?"

"Wouldn't you like to know?" She was too smug. She knew a little, but not enough to connect the deal to him. Or she knew a lot, but not enough to connect him to the deal.

"Yes. I'd like to know since you want to ask me questions about it. You must think I'm involved in some way."

"Now that's an interesting way to put it, 'involved'. With you being a lifelong citizen and business owner in Hannaford Valley, why wouldn't I want your opinion on what the developers are trying to do?" She watched him suspiciously.

As he matched her glare, he saw why his best friend and brother had both fallen in love with her. She was beautiful, smart, and tenacious. She was the one you wanted on your side when you fought city hall. But right now, her scrutiny was making him nervous and scared he could lose everything important in his life. He needed to get out of this land deal.

"Here you go," Chevy said, entering the kitchen.

Sutton rose slowly, not taking her eyes off Kirkland. "Thanks, Chevy. You're a good man."

Chevy's head swiveled between them, confused by the uncomfortable atmosphere.

As Kirkland watched Pete Frawley's slide presentation of the proposed industrial park, his conscience condemned his actions. Hadn't he realized how much of the countryside would be demolished? Had he known building an industrial park would spark more developers tearing down Hannaford Valley? Did he not think things through thoroughly enough? Were there other ways he could prove himself a man, and make a name for himself, without destroying his home?

*His home.* As much as he tried to detach himself from Hannaford Valley, the small mountainous town was his. The traditions made him who he was. The personalities of each resident were ingrained in him. All his childhood memories were spawned from his time in Hannaford. He was born here, raised here, nurtured here. The town was a part of him.

Like it would be a part of Courtney.

*I'm destroying Courtney's future.* He envisioned the baby's grin.

*What would Cassidy think about what I'm doing?* He felt her soft body in his arms.

His stomach bubbled. "I've seen enough."

Pete wore a crumpled suit and needed a shave. His emphasis remained on the labor he could do with his hands. His professional appearance was nonexistent. Most companies working with Pete tolerated his unconventional style because he was one of the best in the business. His building proposals were always well thought out and economical to construct. The quality of his work was superb. All these things considered, no one cared if he wore cheap suits and didn't shave often enough.

But today it mattered to Kirkland. Every tiny detail of his life was important today. He'd made a connection with Cassidy Payne he refused to jeopardize. He had to get out of the land deal. "I've seen enough," he repeated.

"I'm not done. There's more. You haven't seen the proposal for the factory—"

"We never discussed a factory."

"Yeah, but there are companies willing to pay a hefty sum to develop here. The labor is cheap and the square footage is less expensive than in the capital."

"I'm not trying to cheat people, or destroy Hannaford."

Pete watched him as if completely confused. "Destroying the town will be an unfortunate consequence of building the industrial park."

"What?"

"The town is a casualty of the times. It'll be destroyed in the name of expansion. It can't be helped."

"We need to find another way."

Pete cocked his head to the side, placing his hand at his ear as if to capture sound. "Find another way?"

"Yes." Kirkland grew more certain of his decision by the second. As Pete's disappointment over not being able to destroy the town registered, Kirkland realized what a huge mistake he had been about to make. "We need to find another way to develop Hannaford Valley."

"Do you know how many man-hours I've invested in this project?" Pete's face reddened with every word. "The plans have been made. Companies have been hired. We're ready to move to the next phase."

The next phase included securing the necessary permits to begin clearing the land. This wouldn't be easy with the growing protests from citizen groups like the one Greyson and Chevy belonged to. Somehow, Kirkland would have had to voice his opinion about developing the land, obtain the permits, and start the project without anyone finding out his role in it all. What had he been thinking? This was not right. He couldn't go through with it. As much as Alex wanted to get out of Hannaford, he never meant to destroy it. "We have to scrap these plans," he announced, grabbing the blueprints.

"Wait just a minute." Pete snatched the documents away. "We have a deal, Ballantyne."

Kirkland stood his ground, becoming agitated with Pete's insistence. He was glad the desk separated them, or he might have reacted physically without thinking. "I'm changing the plans. If you can't get behind it, you're fired."

"Bleeding heart," Pete mumbled. "You can't just up and change your mind without any warning!"

"Yes, I can. I'm hiring you, not the other way around. I've changed my mind about how I want to use the Galloway land. You have to get behind me here."

"I have invested—"

"And you're being well-compensated." He didn't understand Pete's level of anger over a change of plans. The construction business often changed its building plans in the middle of a project in order to meet regulations or solve structural problems. It was the nature of the industry. You learned not to stress over it early in the game. He watched Pete's face redden and his fists tremble, wondering what had caused such a violent reaction . . . until Pete's next words.

"I've made certain promises."

"What promises?"

"There are people who want this project completed. They want that factory built."

"What are you talking about?" Kirkland was coming closer to rounding the desk and pummeling the man. "Why are you making any promises about what I do with *my* land?"

"All you have to know is if this construction isn't completed, you'll never have to worry about working in construction again. I'll make sure you're ruined in this business."

# Chapter 19

"Your place is adorable."

"Thank you, Mom." Cassidy smiled, embracing her mother tightly. This was starting off on a good note.

"Cass, sweetie." Her father filled the doorway, hugging her and smothering her in kisses. "These are for you." He handed her a bouquet of wild flowers.

"Have a seat, and I'll go put these in water." She passed Darius on the way to the kitchen, signaling him with her eyes. Her father had forgotten she was allergic to flowers—another sign of their strained relationship—but he'd made the effort. This might not be as bad as she'd worried. While in the kitchen, she checked the food, happy everything was ready and they wouldn't have to sit around making meaningless small talk.

They were already into dinner when Cassidy's mother asked, "When are we going to meet our granddaughter?"

"She's sleeping. I thought I'd wake her after dessert if she hasn't woken by then."

"Is it proper for her to sleep this late?" Her

mother's English accent only bothered Cassidy when she was criticizing.

"I didn't want her to be cranky."

"Cranky?" her mother asked as if she didn't know the meaning of the word. "Is it a recurring problem?" The question sounded as if she was asking about contagious side effects of some disease.

"Mom," Darius warned.

"My twins," she countered. "Always sticking up for one another."

"Has it been hard?" Dad asked, genuinely concerned.

"It was hard at first," Cassidy admitted. "I have more respect for what you went through raising us, Mom."

Her mother nodded curtly, concentrating on her dinner.

"I think I have a handle on everything now. Courtney and I have a schedule that works well for us. Darius helps out a lot."

"But don't you see, dear," her mother piped in. "It isn't Darius's responsibility to raise your child. This is the reason it is so important to be married before you have children."

"I don't mind helping Cassidy. Even if she were married, I would help out with my niece."

His mother cut him a look that said she didn't want him to interfere, or defend Cassidy.

"You do understand. dear." Her mother leaned forward, her hand outstretched on the tabletop. "I only want what's best for you. I want what's best for my grandchild. Life is hard. A mother has to step in when she sees her child making it harder for herself."

Cassidy placed herself in her mother's position,

imagining what her response would have been if Courtney had come home talking about having a baby with a sperm donor and becoming a single mother. Her response would have been explosive, to put it mildly. Her mother had popped a gasket, but in looking back, her reaction hadn't been that severe. Cassidy laughed at the absurdity of it all.

"What's funny?" Darius asked, already beginning to laugh himself. They did that sometimes, shared emotions.

"I had a baby by a sperm donor." She doubled over now, resting her forehead on top of the table.

"You always were different," Dad observed.

"*Special,*" Darius added. "As in special education."

Mom pressed her hand to her chest. "Do you know how bizarre this is?"

"It does sound ridiculous," Cassidy choked out between laughs.

"But Courtney is beautiful," Darius said, sobering them all.

"I want to meet my grandbaby," Mom announced, pushing her chair away from the table.

Courtney played the perfect hostess to her grandparents. Adorably dressed in soft shades of yellow, she crawled from one to the other offering them a toothless grin. Since things seemed to be going smoothly, Darius said his good-byes and made a quick exit, wanting to get home to his own family. Dad drifted off to sleep in the recliner as he was prone to do after consuming a large meal. Cassidy and her mother shared the sofa, whispering in hushed tones.

"She is adorable," Mom admitted, cradling Courtney in her lap while she played with her favorite doll.

"I'm really happy, Mom. We're really happy."

"This is so unusual. What should I tell the family? Our friends?"

"Don't tell them anything. All they need to know is I'm a mother now. The intimate details of how it happened aren't important."

"What do you plan on telling her? When she's old enough to ask about her father?"

"I've decided to tell her the truth. I don't want unnecessary secrets to come back and haunt her."

"You don't think finding out she's a test tube baby won't haunt her?"

Cassidy swallowed the insult and remained cordial. "It depends on how I explain it to her. If I focus on the fact I wanted her so badly I couldn't wait for a daddy to come along, she'll feel more loved. I'll make sure she feels loved. If I focus on the procedure that brought her to me, she'll feel awkward. I don't want her to feel anything but loved."

"Children will tease her."

"This should stay within the immediate family. Children won't know anything about it."

Her mother's accent thickened, signaling the start of an argument. "Information leaks out."

"I've never asked you the circumstances around Darius and I being conceived."

Her mother gasped.

"Now you're understanding how absurd your argument is. I don't share the details of my sex life with anyone—Courtney especially."

"You're being trite."

"Trite?" Cassidy breathed deeply, calming herself. She smiled pleasantly. "Maybe I'll be married when this becomes an issue for Courtney and kids won't question her about her father."

"Now you want to get married." Her mother raised her voice, rolling her eyes.

"Mom, enough with the insults. I know you don't approve of what I did and how I did it, but you have to admit it turned out okay."

Her father stirred.

"It hasn't turned out well. It will be years before you know the effects of what you've done."

"What I've done? What have I done?"

"Ladies," Dad interjected.

"You have brought this baby in the world, condemning her to a poor quality of life."

She stood up. "Now you're saying I can't provide a good life for my child just because I'm not married?"

"You and Darius had a father at home. You still have a father at home. Children need the stability of a good home, and a good home has two parents in it."

"I can't believe you."

"Ladies, please."

She ignored her father's plea. "I can't believe you're accusing me of not being a good mother. I care for Courtney. She doesn't want for anything—material or emotional."

Dad stood, patting her on the arm. "Your mother didn't say that, Cassidy. We brought you and Darius up with certain values. It's hard for us to see you going outside those values. We see the problems ahead, that's all."

She looked between her parents, open-mouthed. She tried to blink away the tears threatening to fall. "You don't think I'm capable of caring for my child." She took Courtney out of her mother's arms.

"Don't get hysterical, darling. We came to talk. You knew how we felt about this before we came. We were clear when you came up with this crazy idea."

A hot tear ran down Cassidy's cheek. She hugged Courtney closer for added strength. "I knew you didn't approve of me having a baby the way I did, but I never knew you felt I would be a bad parent."

Together, her mother and father tried to defend their position. Their words were clumsy, jumbling their message into one repetitive thought: *You are an unfit mother.*

"We should go," Dad said as Cassidy came close to disintegrating into tears. Mom agreed. They left hastily, not taking time to put on their jackets or say goodbye to Courtney.

Courtney reached up and captured one of Cassidy's tears. She stuck her fingers in her mouth, sucking away the salty taste.

"Do you think I'm a bad mother?"

Courtney answered by throwing her arms around her mother's neck.


Cassidy was still staring up at the ceiling above her bed when she heard a soft knock at her bedroom window. She glanced at the clock. She'd been trying to put her parents' words out of her head and fall asleep for four hours. She waited for the knock at her window again before she climbed out of bed, afraid her imagination and sleep deprivation were playing tricks on her.

"Kirkland." She immediately felt lighter. Her problems became more manageable. She raised the window, pressing her hand to the screen. "Why didn't you come to the door?"

"It's late. I didn't want to wake up Courtney. Or you, if you were sleeping."

She didn't ask him why he didn't just call. He had never called her since they'd met. She found it a little quirky, but endearing, when she remembered his explanation of needing to see her when he talked with her.

He pressed his hand against hers. "How did it go with your parents?"

"Terrible," she answered in a rush of tears.

"Open the door." He sounded desperate to get to her. "Go, open the door." He jetted away from the window.

Cassidy wiped her tears away, trying to put herself together before she reached the front door. She didn't want to go to pieces in front of her boyfriend. Especially when he looked so weary and defeated himself.

He rushed inside the door, grabbing her up in his arms. He kissed her forehead and stroked her back, moving her to the sofa with him. "Tell me what happened. Every word. From the beginning."

She huddled against him in the darkened living room, giving him every detail of the dinner. She told him how well it had started out and how relieved she was they were getting along. And then she told him about how quickly it had deteriorated. She let him soothe her. She rested in his arms, inhaling a mixture of the cologne on his body and hard alcohol on his breath. His body was hard and muscular, but soft and yielding at the same time.

"You are not a bad mother," he declared. "Put that

out of your mind right now. It makes me mad your parents would even play that head game with you."

"Are they right?" She looked up at him, trying to make out the outline of his face in the shadows. "Did I do the wrong thing not waiting until I could give Courtney a stable home with a father?" She waved off his argument before he could make it. "I know it sounds strange to ask when there are so many single parent households. I'm not naive. I know lesbian and gay couples are having babies. But is it morally right? Every day you see how our society is falling apart. Families are endangered. Did I do the best I could by having Courtney out of wedlock? Did I give her the best life possible? Or was I being selfish and a little desperate because it was my last chance to have a baby?"

Kirkland studied her in the darkness. "Are you finished?" he asked after a short pause.

Cassidy settled against him again.

"Cassidy, listen to me. *You are a good mother.* No, Courtney's life isn't the same as it would be if you were married before you had her. Does that make it worse? There are a lot of two-parent homes with messed-up kids. You provide for Courtney and give her all the love she needs. What's she missing?"

"A father." She wished she could take the words back as soon as she said them. "Kirkland, you have been great with Courtney, but you're not her father. I don't know what the future holds for us, and what happens between us affects your relationship with Courtney."

"I can't predict the future either." His voice sounded funny, sad, and reflective. "I can tell you this. When I held Courtney after you delivered her, I knew right then and there I would always be in her life. Regardless of what happens between us. It doesn't matter if you go off and marry someone else. I will always be there for Courtney." He held her tightly, kissing the top of her head. "I will be there for you as long as you let me, Cassidy."

He sounded so sad she wanted to comfort him. There was extra meaning behind his words she couldn't read. Whatever was happening, it was hurting him deeply.

"You've been drinking."

"Chevy and I went to dinner and had a few drinks. I assure you I'm sober. I mean every word I'm saying."

"I don't doubt you." She wrapped her arms around the indentation of his waist. "I depend on you to keep every promise you make me."

"I will." He kissed her head again.

"You seem different—preoccupied and sad. Is something going on?"

It took him a while to answer. "There is, but I don't want to talk about it right now."

"What can I do?"

"Do you know what I would really like?"

She looked up at him.

"I would like to get into bed like an old married couple."

She giggled. "And what's that like?"

"Let's crawl into bed, snuggle, and watch television until we fall asleep in each other's arms."

They moved to Courtney's bedroom and stood next to her crib, holding each other for a long time. A sliver of light escaped Cassidy's room, shining on Courtney's fat cheeks.

"You do right by her," he whispered. "Don't let your parents make you doubt it."

As she watched her baby sleep, and held him near, she fell in love with both of them all over again. "Do you want kids?" she asked.

He nodded. "Kids are cool."

"You get along well with Courtney and Sierra."

He tried to hide his smile. "Kids are cool," he whispered again, a look coming over his face telling how much he cared for both the girls.

They left Courtney's room, and he took a shower while she climbed into bed. As she listened to the water beat off the bathroom tiles, she allowed herself to imagine the three of them as a family. As much as she didn't want to admit it, having two parents would be best for Courtney, and she wanted to give her child the best possible life. She asked herself hard questions, including whether or not she wanted a long-term relationship with Kirkland because he would make a good father, or because she loved him that much. He walked into the room with a white towel tied around his waist, the color a strong contrast to the red tones in his skin. He was drying his sandy-brown curls with another towel, oblivious to the sensuality he carried into the room. His essence was so thick she couldn't breathe.

"What?" he chuckled.

She blinked away the lust and reached for the remote.

"Tell me what you were thinking."

She watched as he slipped into his boxers and crawled into bed beside her, immediately taking her in the protective fold of his arms.

"Tell me." He tickled her side.

"I was thinking cuddling with you is going to be a lot of fun."

# Chapter 20

Half the town turned out for the Ballantyne's anniversary celebration. In a small town like Hannaford, parties were rare-but-welcomed events. Everyone was curious to see the white octagon gazebo Jack Ballantyne and his boys had built as his gift to Marybeth. Of course, Marybeth had used her green thumb to surround the gazebo with her prizewinning rose bushes. The town had been unkind when Jack moved there with his pregnant wife many years ago. Today, they would make amends for their unfairness and intolerance. This would be Marybeth's happiest anniversary. All her boys were home, she still loved and respected her husband, and the town had finally embraced her as one of their own. The music played into the night and the food kept on coming. The gifts were elaborate, but heartfelt. The Ballantynes couldn't ask for a better day for their family.

"Quiet down, everybody." Greyson used the microphone on the karaoke machine to get everyone's attention. "My brothers and I want to give our parents their anniversary gift."

Someone shouted: "You built them a house when you came back home. What's next?"

The crowd laughed, but couldn't mask their curiosity. They were as anxious as Jack and Marybeth to find out what the boys had done now.

Kirkland and Chevy flanked Greyson. Their parents moved through the crowd in the backyard until they were in the front, the center of attention.

"Mama, Pop, this was Kirkland's idea, so I'm going to let him take the mike."

Kirkland took the mike from Greyson, searching the crowd by instinct to find Cassidy and Courtney. They were near the gazebo sitting with Sutton and Sierra. Cassidy's eyes were glued to him, intensely watching as if he were getting ready to make a presidential acceptance speech. He greeted the crowd, and Courtney turned in the direction of his voice, seeking him out. His heart burst at the reception his girls gave him. He felt taller when they were around; more responsible and needed. He was building another wing of his family.

He checked his pocket before beginning. "We want to thank everyone for coming out to celebrate our parents' anniversary." He waited until the applause died before going on. "I'm not as good a speaker as my big brother, so I'll keep this short and sweet. Those of you who know my parents know they have devoted their entire lives to making us successful." He gestured to Greyson and Chevy. "They were born and raised about fifty miles from here and have never left the state of West Virginia. Mama, Pop." His gaze narrowed in on his parents as he pushed the overwhelming emotions away. He didn't want to start crying in front of all these people, no matter how much he loved his parents.

"Greyson, Chevy, and I are giving you a ten-day cruise to Alaska for your anniversary."

Mama Ballantyne's hands flew up to her mouth. She swayed, but her husband steadied her in his arms. Those standing near clapped Jack on his back and congratulated them both on raising such fine boys. A chant of "Speech! Speech!" rose from the crowd. Reluctantly, Pop Ballantyne stepped to the front and took the microphone. He gave each of his boys hugs before he spoke. "My boys know I don't like them spendin' their hard-earned money on us, but they never listen." His voice softened and cracked. "I cain't thank them enough for this."

Mama joined him, hugging him tight and shielding his face from the crowd by drowning him in kisses. Jack Ballantyne did not consider it proper for a man to openly show his emotions. He would not want the crowd to know how choked up he was over this gift. Greyson understood this, too. He reclaimed the mike. "Play some music, DJ. Everybody back to the party. It's still early and there's plenty of food."

The scene emotionally overwhelmed Kirkland. He wanted this. A loving wife and adoring kids. His eyes found Cassidy again. She was laughing with Sutton. She was the most beautiful person he had ever met, both inside and out. A sobering thought hit him. How could he have this when he was deceiving the town, and his family, and Cassidy? Without a second thought, he told his brothers he needed to speak to them in private.

"Now?" Greyson asked, wanting to rejoin the party.

"It's important."

Greyson and Chevy shared an inquisitive look before turning to follow him inside. They closed themselves up in the family room.

"What's going on, Kirkland?" Chevy asked.

Kirkland dropped down on the sofa, but Greyson and Chevy remained standing. He hadn't realized how much of an emotional burden his secret was until that moment.

"It must be pretty bad," Greyson told Chevy.

"It can't be. Kirkland is the good one," Chevy added sarcastically.

He looked between them, not sharing their laugh. At this inopportune moment, memories of Alex pummeled him. The mischief they always found themselves in, the fun they had on their weekend trips to Jamaica, meeting for dinner when one or the other was in town—these were the small things that solidified their friendship. He wished he could talk to Alex right now. He'd ask what he should do with the land. He'd tell him not to get into his car on a rainy night with a woman who wasn't his wife. Like so many times before, his chest tightened over the loss of his best friend.

"What's going on?" Greyson asked.

"This stays between us for now," Kirkland started.

Greyson and Chevy shared another look.

Chevy dropped down next to him on the sofa. "You in some kind of trouble?"

He braced himself for their reaction. "The land deal the town's upset about . . . I know what the proposed project is and I know where it's going to be built."

"How do you know?" Greyson asked.

"What is it?" Chevy asked at the same time.

A sharp pain ripped through his stomach. He pressed his palm into his abdomen, forced himself to ignore the pain, and continued. "I'll start with where." He paused to capture their expressions. They would drastically change in a minute, and he feared that more than anything—losing the respect of his brothers.

Greyson and Chevy asked together, "Where?"

"The old Galloway land."

Greyson's face dropped. "You own the old Galloway land."

Chevy looked confused. He probably didn't know the specifics of the boundaries of the property Alex had willed him. But Greyson, undoubtedly, had spent many nights listening to Sutton go on about the foul deal.

"You own it?" Chevy clarified. "You're the mysterious developer?"

Greyson and Chevy simultaneously converged on him. They were firing questions and accusations too fast for him to answer. They were angry, and didn't try to hide it. They shamed him as only brothers can, making him feel lower than he already did. They wouldn't allow him to finish a sentence, but he managed. "I need your help."

"Our help?" Chevy asked, appalled. "To do what?"

"Do you remember what I told you a year ago?" Greyson asked, quieting the commotion. "I told you to get yourself together, Kirkland. Don't live in Alex's shadow anymore. Take responsibility for your own actions. I told you to stop acting like a victim. Is this how you've done it? By lying to everyone and plotting to destroy Hannaford Valley?"

"I can't believe you would do this, Kirkland," Chevy added. "This isn't just about business, or destroying the land. It's about family and commitment and honor. Right now, I don't think you have any honor, and you don't know the meaning of family and commitment." He left the room.

Greyson added the fatal blow before following Chevy out. "He's right, and that makes me afraid for Cassidy and Courtney."

# Chapter 21

"Cassidy, don't take what Mom and Dad said to heart." Darius slipped on his suit jacket in a rush to get out the door.

"How can I just ignore it?"

"I understand." He kissed her forehead. "I have to run. I'm a little late. We'll talk tonight? If it's still okay for me to crash here?"

"Of course. You don't have to ask." She followed him out onto her front porch. "Where are you rushing off to?"

"I have a meeting scheduled with your boyfriend's brothers. Greyson knows of a detective who can find out all the information about the developer. Once we know whom we're fighting, we can put a face to the corporation and make them answer to the people of Hannaford Valley. It'll make our fight much easier."

"Good luck."

"See you tonight." He jogged down the steps. "We'll talk."

Cassidy went inside and completed her morning routine. Once she had Courtney settled in the middle of her studio with a bunch of toys, she began to sketch a cover for her latest project. *The romance novel business must be booming*, she thought. She had received several new projects over the past few weeks, providing her with a steady income. Once she had established herself in the industry, it became a lucrative profession. By no means was she wealthy, but she made a good living and was building a nice savings. Courtney's college would be paid for long before she graduated. Cassidy owned a modest car, and was working toward paying off her mortgage.

By midday, she had completed several sketches and was hashing out ideas for another. Courtney had been extremely cooperative, not whining once. She played until she was tired and then crawled onto a pallet near Cassidy to take her nap. Courtney was being wonderful, but the weather was a distraction. By lunchtime Cassidy decided to pack a picnic lunch and take Courtney out for a few hours. She was ahead of schedule and could afford to knock off early. If the mood hit her, she'd come back to the studio later. Besides, being outside would motivate her with fresh, new ideas.

*Honk! Honk!* "Where are you ladies going?"

She looked over to see Kirkland trailing them down the street in his car. "I don't talk to strangers, Mister." She added sass to the rock of her hips.

"Why, Ma'am, I'm not a stranger."

"Ma'am? Did you call me Ma'am?"

"No disrespect intended. Can you stop walking for a minute so I can talk to you?"

She did.

"Where are you going, and can I come along?"

"We're going on a picnic."

"Great. I know the perfect place."

The perfect place engulfed them in lush greens

and sprinkled them with sunshine. They spread the blanket under a huge tree and ate the lunch Cassidy had prepared. Afterward, Kirkland held Courtney's hands above her head and helped her to take her first steps. Cassidy held outstretched arms, coaxing her baby to toddle over to her. Courtney would take one unsteady step, but she wasn't ready to walk yet. Just when Kirkland was consoling Cassidy, Courtney did the greatest thing.

"Ma—Ma—Ma—Ma."

"Did you hear that?" Kirkland asked.

Cassidy was too overjoyed to speak. "She said her first words."

"Ma," Kirkland repeated. He knelt next to Courtney and encouraged her to repeat it. Her attention had already gone to her toys.

"She didn't walk, but she said 'Ma'."

"If she had walked and said her first word, I would have had to call the national news—she hasn't turned one yet." Cassidy clutched her chest. "Wow. This is . . . spectacular."

"You're all lit up—glowing." He left Courtney to play, and joined Cassidy on the blanket beneath the tree.

"You can't imagine how good I feel. I'm happy. Really happy." She searched his face, sending him a silent signal. "I've never been this happy in all my life. I have Courtney and I have you. My work is booming. I know things aren't great between my parents and me, but you know what? I've decided I'm going to patch things up with them, or at least I'm going to give it my best try." She took his hand into her lap, tracing the outline of thick, ropy veins. "I want everything to be right in my life. You're responsible for making me feel this way."

"How so?"

She shrugged. "I don't know if it's one specific thing. I just know I like the feeling of serenity I get when I'm with you, and I want that feeling to carry over to all parts of my life. Aren't you going to eat anything?"

Kirkland shook his head. His hand instinctively went to his stomach. "I have an upset stomach—too much restaurant food lately."

"Your appetite hasn't been good for a couple of weeks now. Should you see a doctor?"

"Are you worried about me?" He leaned over and gave her a kiss.

"Yes, I'm worried."

"It's nothing. Really." He watched Courtney play in reflective silence. "Do you have any baggage?"

"Baggage, no. You would know by now if I did."

"Do you have any fears?"

She didn't understand the nature of his questions, but she answered him with humor. "I have a fear of falling from high places."

He didn't laugh.

"Most of my nightmares are about falling out of the window of a skyscraper, or being trapped somewhere and having to jump in order to save my life."

He stopped her rambling with the serious set of his jaw. "Cassidy, where do you see this going? Us— where do you see us going?"

She was nervous, and a little shy about confessing the depths of her feelings for him. He seemed to need to hear it, so she wouldn't deny him. He had been distracted lately, and she knew something was bothering him, although he hadn't shared the details with her.

"Kirkland, I honestly don't know where we're going, and I can't decide alone. We have to make that decision together." She stroked his palm. "I can tell you I consider you more than a temporary relationship. When I think of you, I dream about having a future with you. I picture you sitting next to me at Courtney's graduation."

He pulled his hand away.

"I've scared you." He was so mature, she often forgot about the differences in their ages. Talk of commitment and raising a child together were enough to frighten anyone his age. "You asked me. I answered honestly. Don't worry. I'm not going to push you or give you ultimatums. I understand you're younger than I am and your priorities are much different."

He watched her intently. "You love me," he said after a few minutes. "You love me for who I am, even though I'm not perfect."

"We're all flawed. Don't be so hard on yourself."

"Our priorities aren't far apart. I love you and I would be happy to sit next to you at Courtney's graduation—high school and college." He took her hand in his lap as she had done, and stroked her palm.

They watched Courtney play.

"Cassidy," Kirkland said, his eyes glued on Courtney. "I need to tell you something."

The sadness in his eyes gave her a clue to what it might be. He was seeing someone else. He wasn't ready to take on a ready-made family. Things were moving too fast. It could be any number of things, but Cassidy panicked because she knew whatever it was, he was going to end their relationship. "No," she whispered. "Don't tell me now."

He looked at her strangely. Once he saw her stricken expression, his look turned to concern.

"Not here," she said. "I don't want to fall apart here. In front of Courtney. In public."

"What do you mean, 'fall apart'?"

She fought tears to look at him. "When you break it off, I'm going to fall apart. I want to go with my dignity."

"Baby." He pulled her in his arms, kissing away his mistake. "I don't want to break up with you."

She exhaled hard, relieving some of her emotional burden, but she still felt uneasy. "What's going on? You've been acting strange the past few days. What do you have to tell me?"

After he was sure she was calm, he pulled away to see her face clearly. "I'm the developer who's going to industrialize the town."

She listened in shocked silence as he told her how he acquired the land, and why he had decided to prove his manhood by pulling off the largest industrial project by an individual company in West Virginia. She remained nonjudgmental as he explained why he had changed his mind, and how Pete Frawley wouldn't let him out of the deal without consequences. She let him hold her as he described his remorse about almost destroying her home and Courtney's future.

"Cassidy, I love you and I don't want to lose you," he said. "But I'll understand if you don't want to see me anymore. My own brothers won't talk to me."

"Kirkland." She pulled him into her arms. As she comforted him, she found comfort for herself in twisting his curls around her finger.

"Is it over between us?"

"You made a mistake. You're trying to fix it. I won't leave you if you mess up. I'll leave you if you cheat on me, or hurt Courtney."

He looked at her with disbelief. "Everyone else in this town hates me."

"No, they don't, and you have time to correct this before it gets out of hand. Greyson was right. You have to take responsibility for what you did and make it right."

"I will. I am. I just need to know you're going to stand by me."

"I will support you, Kirkland, but I won't endanger Courtney."

"Courtney? I'd never hurt her."

"I know you wouldn't, but you told me Pete as good as threatened you."

His gaze lingered on her, then transferred to Courtney. "I won't let anything happen to you or to Courtney. I'd walk away from you first."

They were sitting in her living room when they continued the conversation. Courtney was tucked in for the night, and Kirkland was about to leave to drive home to the capital.

"Do you have any more secrets you're keeping from me?" Cassidy asked.

"There's more, but they aren't mine. Alex made me the keeper of his secrets."

"Will they affect our relationship?"

He contemplated his answer. "They will affect your friendship with Sutton."

"My friendship with Sutton is important to me. She's a friend and part of your family. Sierra and

Courtney are spending a lot of time together. You should tell me."

When Kirkland gathered her tightly in his arms, she knew the secrets would be bad. It was worse than she could have imagined.

# Chapter 22

"Hey," Darius said as he entered Cassidy's house.

"How'd your meeting go?" She shut off the television.

Darius loosened his tie, discarded his jacket, and dropped into a chair. "We didn't get anything done. The Ballantyne brothers were strangely elusive. Chevy has been so passionate about saving the land—Greyson, too—but today they're tight-lipped. They reminded me of witnesses after a mafia boss has threatened them."

"How did you leave it?"

"They were apologetic and said we'd get together soon." At her silent reply, Darius lifted his head. "You know what's going on, don't you? Your boyfriend gave you the inside scoop?"

She knew he could read her and would know if she lied to him. "They're probably protecting Kirkland."

He sprang forward in his seat. "What do you mean, 'protecting' him?"

She told him what she knew about Kirkland's involvement in the land deal.

He watched her unblinkingly. "Did he tell you what kind of construction he's planning?"

"It was going to be an industrial park—office complexes, small businesses, rental space for large companies to have remote offices. But here's the thing, Darius. He's changed his mind. He realizes how it would damage the town, and he wants to cancel the construction."

"Is that what he told you? He just changed his mind."

"It's a little more complicated than just a change of mind, but the bottom line is he doesn't want to go through with it."

Darius sat back against his seat. "Why do you keep phrasing it like that?"

"What do you mean?"

"You're not saying he cancelled or scrapped the project. You keep saying he doesn't *want* to go through with it."

"Well—"

"He's still going to build the industrial complex."

"I don't know all the details, but the people he's working with won't let him out of the deal. He went to Greyson and Chevy for help, but they were so angry, they refused."

Darius bolted out of his seat. "They should have. Cass, please tell me you aren't falling for his I-don't-know-how-to-get-out-of-this-so-I'm-going-to-have-to-go-through-with-it-after-all routine."

"It's the truth. He *is* trying to find a way out."

"You believe what you want. There's no use in me arguing with you about it. Let me tell you, I'm going to fight him all the way. I don't care if he is your boyfriend."

She stood, rushing to him. "You can't repeat the

information I just gave you. He told me in confidence."

"He told *you* in confidence. I don't have an alliance with him."

"Darius, you can't—"

"I can do anything and everything I can to help save Hannaford. Not just because I've been hired to do it, but because it's the right thing to do for people who live here. I won't turn my back on them because they can't fight for themselves."

"If you do this, you'll hurt me—and Courtney."

"Don't try to guilt me."

"You may not believe it, but Kirkland is trying to fix this. If you truly want to save the town, wouldn't it be better to have him on your side? If you can work from the inside without pitting the town against itself, why not?" She desperately tried to appeal to his decency. "You'll hurt so many innocent people if you go public with this. Mr. and Mrs. Ballantyne have just begun to be accepted by the town. What will happen to them? Greyson and Chevy are on your side. They could lose the paper mill, and then their families will suffer. You know how judgmental Hannaford can be—think about how Courtney and I will be treated."

Darius's anger began to diminish. "I said don't guilt me."

"But I do it so well." She tried to inject humor into the situation.

Darius exhaled loudly.

"And you love me. I'm your favorite sister."

"You're my only sister."

"I could talk to Mom and Dad about changing that."

He rolled his eyes, softening. "All right. I'll talk to Kirkland. Maybe we can work together to cancel the land deal. If he's open to it. If I sense he's hiding anything I go to the city council."

"That's all I ask. Give him a chance to prove he's changed."

Darius flopped down in the chair again. "Fine. Now let's talk about your parents."

"Maddie, stop looking at your watch," Sutton scolded.

"I don't want to leave my father for too long."

Cassidy walked shoulder to shoulder between Sutton and Maddie at the mall as the conversation volleyed back and forth.

"The nurse is with your father. She has my cell number, and she promised to call if there's a problem. He'll be fine. You're supposed to relax and enjoy a ladies' day at the mall."

"I don't come to the capital much because it's so far from home."

"I can get you home in less than a hour if I have to," Sutton promised.

"Your father's sick?" Cassidy asked.

Maddie nodded. "He had a stroke not long after my mother passed away. I've been taking care of him ever since."

Sutton added, "She had to care for her mother, too."

"Don't make it sound like it was a burden."

"I'm only saying you've had to sacrifice a lot of your life to take care of your parents. Your birthday is this weekend. Cassidy and I want you to think

about your happiness, have some fun for once."
Sutton transitioned into matchmaker mode. "You
should let me invite you and Chevy to dinner this
weekend. I won't say anything to him. We'll let it
happen naturally."

"You promised me you wouldn't say anything to
him."

"I haven't. What do you think, Cassidy?" Sutton
asked.

She looked from one to the other. "You have to
do what Maddie wants."

"Listen to her," Maddie gloated.

"Okay, fine."

After visiting several more department stores,
they found a restaurant that anchored the mall to
a mega bookstore.

"Every time we get together, we end up eating,"
Cassidy said as she dipped into the appetizer plate.

"We should start jogging," Maddie suggested.

"Jogging?" Sutton made a face. "I hate exercis-
ing."

"Look at your figure. You don't have to exercise.
Although I don't know how you stay so thin when
you eat like a Sumo wrestler." Cassidy turned to
Maddie. "Maybe we can meet in the mornings, or
on your lunch break."

"The high school isn't far from the library. We
could use their track."

"We'll start tomorrow." It felt good to offer Maddie an outlet from caring for her father.

"Cassidy, any idea why the boys are fighting?" Sutton piled hot wings on her plate.

"'The boys'?" Maddie asked.

Sutton spooned ranch dressing onto her wings. "Greyson, Chevy, and Kirkland."

All eyes turned to Cassidy. She busied herself by sampling from the appetizer plate, but Sutton and Maddie waited patiently for an answer. "I have an idea, but I don't think I should say anything."

Sutton sat forward, ready to pounce.

"Why don't you ask Greyson?" Cassidy asked.

"Because my husband has been stomping around the house like a mean grizzly bear. Whenever I try to find out what's going on, he says nothing and stomps away."

"Whatever it is, it can't be good," Maddie said

"Thanks, Maddie." Cassidy threw her a look. Kirkland had confided in her about the land deal, and she felt it was okay to talk to Darius about it, because he hadn't told her otherwise. When Darius called to set up a meeting with Kirkland, he hadn't been upset, but did ask her not to mention it to anyone else until the business was settled. The land deal was one thing, the other things he confided in her were definitely not her business to repeat. Even if he had given her permission to repeat it, she wouldn't because too many people stood to be hurt. "I really can't say, Sutton. But I want to say this. What happens between Greyson, Chevy, and Kirkland is between them. I don't want our friendship mixed up with their business."

"Agreed." Sutton sank back against her seat. "I was right. It has something to do with Kirkland."

# Chapter 23

"Hey, Pop. Do you have a minute?"

"C'mon in." Pop turned off the television and discarded the remote on the sofa beside him. "What's goin' on?"

"I need to talk to you about something." Kirkland entered the den and closed the door behind him. He'd already talked with his mother, giving her all the details about the land deal he was mixed up in. He'd also told her about the secrets Alex had died and left him with. After the initial shock, she'd demanded he do the right thing by Sutton and Sierra.

"You in trouble?" Pop asked, gauging the seriousness of his tone.

"Nothing illegal, but I've gotten in over my head with some business I've been trying to do." He sat next to his father on the sofa and told him about the land deal and how he couldn't get out of it with Pete Frawley.

"I raised you better," Pop said, shaking his head. "Money, business, prestige—none of those things make a man. A *man* knows how to handle his money, his business, and his prestige in the community."

"I realize that now."

"Why now?" Pop fired back.

"It has a lot to do with Cassidy and Courtney. Being with them has helped me realize what's really important in life. I want to make this right. I want to give Cassidy and Courtney a good life. I want them to be proud of me."

"How you gonna get out of it?"

"I'm not sure."

"What did your brothers say about all of this? I'm a simple man—Greyson's a lawyer, he can help you. And Chevy knows all about the environmental stuff. Your brothers are the best ones to go to about findin' a solution for this."

Kirkland sat forward, resting his elbows on his knees. "Greyson and Chevy are pretty mad at me about it."

"So! Greyson and Chevy are your family. Don't matter if they're mad or not. If you need help in this family, we step in and help each other."

He wished Pop's words were true, but his brothers were too angry to even discuss it with him. "Unfortunately, they don't feel the same way."

"You mean to tell me you went to your brothers and they wouldn't help you get out of this? They wouldn't help you find a way to keep Hannaford Valley the way it should be?"

"They're pretty mad."

"I'll go talk to—"

"No, Pop. I need to handle this myself. I can't let you or Mama fight my fights."

"Why'd you come to me?"

"I wanted you to hear about it from me. I want you to know everything."

"There's more?" Pop raised a suspicious brow.

"Yeah, there's more." He settled in to tell his father

everything he had shared with his mother. Pop's reaction wasn't as dramatic, and he hadn't expected it to be.

When he finished, Pop leveled a long look at him. "I'm proud of you, son. You made a mistake or two, but you're taking credit for it and trying to straighten it out. I really 'preciate what you're doing. Being a man is about taking responsibility, and you're doing that. I respect you more for it."

Kirkland stood and encouraged Pop to stand by offering him a hug. Pop didn't like men to outwardly show their affection, but he complied. They shared a long embrace and he realized how much he missed moments like these growing up. His mother had always been affectionate, kissing and hugging her boys until they were old enough to shame her about embarrassing them in front of their friends. He never tired of her hugs. He was an affectionate man. He liked it when Cassidy showed her adoration by kissing, holding, and caressing him. Some of their best times together were spent holding each other in silence while watching television together.

"What you gonna do now?" Pop asked, breaking their embrace.

"I'm going to talk to Greyson and Chevy and make them help me fix this mess."

Cassidy took a long, deep breath before she rang her parents' doorbell. It was a beautiful day for a drive into the capital. She hoped the sunny weather would have a positive effect on her parents. She was determined to mend her relationship with them. Even if they didn't accept her decision to have a child out of wedlock, they could be grandparents to Courtney and have an amicable relationship with her. Their poor opinion of her parenting skills still hurt, but Darius had helped her see she would have to be the one to bend. He encouraged her to work to salvage their relationship. She was the child, after all. And Courtney would need her grandparents, since her paternal grandparents wouldn't be in her life. Her parents had the right to voice their opinion, but it didn't mean she had to believe it.

She could hear her father moving to the door. He was talking to her mother, probably asking if she was expecting company. The latch clicked and the door swung open.

"Cassidy, is something wrong?"

"No, Dad."

"Come inside. Where's the baby?"

She made small talk with her father while waiting for her mother to join them. They watched her suspiciously, waiting for the argument to begin. There would be no arguing today. She'd come in peace, ready to put their differences aside and build a solid relationship with her mother and father. Darius and her parents seemed to get along so well, whereas there had always been tension with her. Even as they grew up, Darius had always had to be the buffer between them.

"Courtney's first birthday is about a month away," she started.

Her mom and dad shared a blank look.

"Mom, can you help me plan a birthday party?"

"Me?" She pressed her palm against her chest. "You want me to help plan the baby's birthday party?"

"I know you don't approve of what I've done—

having Courtney before I was married—but there's nothing you can do to change it now. Courtney is a beautiful baby. If you get to know her, you'll love her. I want her to have a good relationship with you, so I'm here trying to encourage you to look past your disapproval of my decisions and spend time with her."

Her parents silently communicated. They had been together so long they were able to speak volumes with a glance passed between them. It brought Courtney's secret language with Kirkland to mind. The bond had been formed when he delivered her, and was growing stronger every day.

"Well, Mom?" Cassidy asked after a long moment.

"We know it took a lot for you to come here like this—"

Dad interrupted. "But we don't think it's a good idea for your mother to get involved in the party planning."

"Why not?" She felt as if she had been sucker-punched and her chest was caving inward.

"I would love to—" Mom began.

"But," Dad threw her mother a sideways glance quieting her, "we're not sure it would be productive to build a relationship with Courtney, or repair the one we have with you."

"Mom, is this how you feel?" She didn't like the way her father kept cutting her mother off. All this time she had been upset with her mother when it was actually her father who was the obstinate one.

Her mother squirmed. She didn't agree with the decision being made on her behalf. She tried to smile. "Your father's right."

"Can you tell me why?" Cassidy felt everything slipping away. Suddenly, she realized how important having a good relationship with her parents meant to building a good relationship with her own daughter. If she couldn't fix this, how would she handle Courtney's teenage years? How would she explain the absence of grandparents and a father to Courtney?

Seeing her growing distress, her father answered carefully. "Cassidy, we just don't believe this is the way to repair our relationship. Dinner was a good start." He offered a false smile. "Let's just take it slowly."

"Or maybe you'd prefer to keep it this way." Cassidy couldn't control her growing anger. "Are you this ashamed of me? Ashamed enough to deny Courtney her grandparents?"

"We didn't say all that." Dad shut down her escalating temper.

Mom intervened, her accent thick with emotion. "We'd love an invitation to Courtney's party."

Dad abruptly shifted the conversation. "Tell us about the young man you've been seeing." She quickly understood why her dad had taken the lead in this battle.

"Kirkland? He's a good man. He's been there for me since Courtney was born." She went on to tell her parents about his job, education, and family—all the things parents would want to know.

"How old is this young man?"

"What does it matter?" Her defensive armor shrouded her heart. Her father would make this a him-or-us contest, and she wasn't sure her parents would win. Either way, if she was forced to choose, she'd lose someone she loved very much.

"It matters because we're worried about your judgment," her father answered.

"There's nothing wrong with my judgment, Dad."

"The choices you've been making . . ." Mom stated.

Cassidy shot a look at her mother, who wisely let the thought trail off. But the sentiment was in the air now, exposed for all parties to see. "Kirkland chose to be a part of Courtney's life when her own grandparents choose not to be. In my book, it makes him a good person to invest my heart in."

"Darius says this guy is nine years younger than you are," her father said. "He might enjoy playing house with you right now, but he'll leave when the fun is over and he realizes you expect him to be a father to that baby."

Mom touched his arm. "We're worried about you and Courtney. We don't want to see either one of you get hurt."

Cassidy spoke slowly, sifting the anger out of her words so as not to provoke a huge fight with her parents. Subconsciously she knew this was a relationship she still wanted to save—even if she didn't agree with their viewpoints on anything. "Mom. Dad." She nodded at each one in turn. "I love you and I want you to be a large part of me and Courtney's life. A *large* part. Not just occasional visits or dinners. I had hoped involving you in the planning of Courtney's first birthday party would be a nice way to show you how much we need you. Even though you've refused, I hope you'll come celebrate Courtney's birthday with her family and friends." She jumped up before they could comment, and bolted from the house.


Kirkland sat in the middle of the paper mill's department head meeting, not hearing a word as Greyson spoke. Until recently, he'd been lax about attending the meetings. The inconvenience of the drive from the capital coupled with other work obligations had made it hard for him to be involved with much of the management of the mill. After meeting Cassidy, he had begun to spend more time in Hannaford, but his attention was so divided that he still hadn't become very involved in the day-to-day management of the mill. But today he had come to the departmental meeting because he needed to speak to his brothers. They'd been avoiding him, still upset about his involvement in the land deal. Greyson and Chevy couldn't ignore him forever. He understood the burden was on him to make it right between them, and he planned to do just that immediately after the meeting.

As he rehearsed how he would approach his older brothers, he considered how much to tell them—about the land deal, and about Alex's secrets. He would give full disclosure about the land deal. He'd been dishonest enough and would have to work hard to win their respect. He was torn between his loyalty to his friend and his commitment to his family.

*Alex had come to him in a panic that day. When he stepped into his penthouse after work, he found Alex pacing the floor, his clothing disheveled. Dark circles sagged beneath his eyes. A bottle of cognac sat uncapped on the coffee table with a significant portion missing.*

*He knew before he asked that whatever was bothering Alex would not be good. "What's up? I didn't know you were in town."*

*"I'm in trouble, Kirk."*

*Kirkland tossed his keys on the telephone table. "You're always into something." Hungry, he went into the kitchen.*

*Alex followed with a glass of cognac in his hands. "It's bad this time."*

*Kirkland pulled a ham from the refrigerator and began making a sandwich. "What did you do?"*

*Alex started pacing again. "I'm going to lose Sutton for sure this time."*

*There was a hitch in his voice that got Kirkland's attention. He turned away from what he was doing and focused on his friend.*

*"I picked her up in a damn bar." Alex's anger exploded and he threw his glass against the wall, shattering it.*

*"Who?"*

*"I was under pressure to bump up my numbers at work. Sutton was on my back about not spending enough time with her and Sierra. My mother went out and bought that house, which she expects me to pay for, without discussing it with me first. Everything was on my shoulders."*

*"You said you were going to leave the women alone and work on your marriage."*

*"I know what I said," Alex snapped.*

*"Then what's with the excuses? You met a woman in a bar and slept with her. What happened? Did Sutton find out?"*

*Alex froze suddenly. He turned to his friend, and the sullen look he gave Kirkland told him there was much more than he ever wanted to know. "She's pregnant."*

*Stunned, he couldn't speak. As much as Alex fooled around, they both knew it was bound to happen if he didn't stop, but it didn't dull the reality of it coming to fruition. "Didn't you go through this before? I thought the last pregnancy scare was enough to make you get your act together."*

*"I know. It was. It did. But everything was coming at me from every direction. I was in Chicago for a week. I needed—"*

*"You needed to go home to Sutton if you were lonely. How could you do this?"*

*"Don't you come down on me. You're supposed to be my friend. Help me fix this."*

*Kirkland dropped down at the kitchen table. Alex pulled out a chair and straddled it, resting his chin on the back.*

*Kirkland asked the logical first question. "Is the baby yours?"*

*"She says it is. I can't be sure until after it's born." Alex ran a hand over his face. "What am I going to do, Kirkland? I don't know how I'm going to hold it together until the baby comes and I find out if I'm the father. How long am I going to be able to keep a baby from Sutton? You know how long it took her to convince me to have Sierra. What is she going to do when she finds out I have a baby from a one-night stand with a woman in Chicago? I'm going to lose her for sure." Darkness fell over his features. "What will Sierra think of me when she gets old enough to understand?"*

"Where are you?" Chevy stood over Kirkland. Greyson flanked his other side with a worried expression.

"I need to talk to you," Kirkland said.

His brothers pulled chairs up to the conference table on both sides of him. "What's going on, Kirkland?" Greyson asked.

"I know you guys are mad at me, but I need your help."

"You've made certain choices, Kirkland," Greyson said. "You have to live with them."

"When you went after Sutton in Chicago, you dragged Chevy and me along without asking us how we felt about it." He swiveled toward Chevy. "And how many times have I defended you to the prejudiced people in Hannaford? Now I need you two to help me. You're my brothers. You're supposed to be here for me when I need you."

# Chapter 24

To anyone who didn't know about the quiet, gentle nature of the Ballantyne brothers, they appeared large and intimidating. Tall and broad shouldered, fiercely educated and stubbornly determined, it didn't pay to match wits with them. Their opponents lost each and every time they attempted to challenge them directly. When Pete Frawley stepped into the office at the paper mill, his face dropped—he was in big trouble. Kirkland loomed large behind his desk. Chevy sat perched on the corner, arms crossed over his chest wearing a dangerous scowl. Greyson sat quietly, angrily watching Pete squirm as he sat in the only available chair.

"What's this?" Pete asked, already looking uncomfortable.

"Mr. Frawley, these are my brothers Greyson and Chevy."

Pete nodded, still unsure about the situation he had walked into.

"Mr. Frawley—" Kirkland started.

"Why so formal?"

"Mr. Frawley," he continued undaunted. "I have

solicited the help of my brothers concerning the pending land deal."

Greyson stood and approached Pete. "I've looked over the paperwork. My brother never signed a contract with you. If he wants out of the deal, he only has to tell you he wants out."

"We had a verbal contract."

"A verbal contract is not as binding as a written contract. The paperwork you signed when Kirkland accepted your bid over the others clearly has a clause stating he can cancel the deal at any time for any reason."

"Greyson's an attorney," Kirkland clarified.

"I'll sue you if you try to back out of this, Ballantyne." Pete's face blushed red.

"Feel free to try," Greyson answered. "I enjoy a good courtroom battle."

Chevy stood up. "And I'd be happy to testify. I'll have so many environmental groups picketing outside the courthouse, no judge in this county will uphold your claim."

"Do you think I'm afraid of a bunch of tree-huggers?" Pete spat.

"You should be," Chevy snapped. "I'm a 'tree-hugger' and I've gathered enough reports and land surveys to tie this case up in court for years. Do you have the resources to fight this case year after year?"

"You have another problem, Pete," Greyson added, handing over a document from Kirkland's desk. "There may be a dispute over who is the rightful owner of the old Galloway land. My wife and our daughter have a lawful claim to the property."

Kirkland interjected. "I have no intentions of challenging them for the land. As soon as possible,

I'll sign the land over to my sister-in-law and my niece."

Pete grumbled several curse words. "You think you can run over me because you're rich. Well, we had a deal, Ballantyne, and where I come from a deal is a deal. There are people involved who want that land. They have the resources to fight you in court for as long as you want to fight. And while you're fighting, they'll be watching you."

"Are you threatening me or my family?" Kirkland slowly rose from behind his desk. He moved around his desk until he was standing in front of Pete. He pulled the man up by his collar, lifting him off his feet. "You don't threaten my family."

Greyson and Chevy pried his hands off Pete. Chevy stepped in, one foot in front of Kirkland, shielding Pete from the full blast of Kirkland's anger.

"My dealings were with you," Kirkland said. "I don't have anything to do with any side deals you were putting together. You have to answer to your people for what you've done. If you think you've got trouble with them, wait until you have to see me for threatening my family. If anyone comes looking for me—if I get so much as a phone call—I'm coming looking for you."

Pete took a wobbly step backward. "I'm not afraid of you."

"Then be afraid of me," Greyson said, stepping up.

"Or me." Chevy moved closer too.

Pete began backing out of the office.

"Don't mess with me, Pete," Kirkland called after him.

"Or any of the Ballantyne brothers," Chevy added.

"You hardly ate a thing at dinner," Cassidy whispered. She enjoyed snuggling into the protective strength of Kirkland's arms in the darkened movie theater. Even though there were other people in the room, she felt as if she were inside a cocoon and nothing negative could penetrate its walls.

"I ate a big lunch with my brothers." He concentrated on the movie screen.

"For some reason I don't believe you. Are you feeling okay?"

He nodded once. "I have a lot on my mind."

"What? You said Greyson and Chevy helped you deal with Pete Frawley."

He looked down at her, and it hit her how young he was. Feeling like all the troubles of the world were on his shoulder, he appeared vulnerable and inexperienced with the miseries of being an adult. She'd spent so much time allowing him to support her, she'd forgotten how much support he needed. He still hadn't gotten over the death of his best friend, and now he had to deal with the consequences of his mistakes in making a bad land deal.

"Let's go." She gathered her purse.

"The movie's not even halfway over."

"I don't care. I want to go." She moved down the aisle and he followed.

She turned to him in the parking lot. "Do you mind if I drive?"

He handed her his keys. "Do you mind if I ask why you wanted to leave in the middle of the movie?" He helped her into the driver's seat, rounded the front of his car, and got into the passenger's seat. "Cassidy?"

"You don't need a movie right now, Kirkland. You need me."

He turned to the side window, trying to hide his amused smile. "Where are we going?"

"You ask too many questions." She started out of the lot. "Can't you just sit back and wait to see where we end up? A person who asks so many questions is doing it because they don't like to relinquish control."

"I like being in charge." He answered too heartily. "I *am* the man in this relationship."

She tossed him a frown. "Not funny."

He turned to hide his smile again. He liked the challenge he received when he ruffled her.

"Tonight you don't get to be in charge."

"Hmmm," he hummed. "I might like the sound of that if I had more details."

She smacked her lips. "Why have you been solemn and quiet all night, but when I want you to be quiet you're giving me a hard time?"

He reached over and squeezed her thigh, making everything all right again. He knew just how to stroke her, and how to make her feel reassured. He'd taken the time to learn what she needed, when, and how to give it to her. She'd been neglectful and hadn't done the same. When she thought about the times they spent together, she realized he seemed happiest when they were alone, at home, enjoying each other's company. She could see him not getting many moments like these growing up with two testosterone-driven older brothers.

Little sisters and girlfriends provided tender moments—not a best friend who messed around on his wife.

She stopped the car at the park where they'd had their picnic. "Do you want to get out and walk?"

"Sure." He would oblige her anything. They walked hand in hand, stopping beneath the tree where they had eaten lunch. It was quickly becoming one of her favorite places to go with him, because it held so many memories of the good times they shared.

"This is where Courtney said her first word," Kirkland reflected.

She smiled at the memory. "Do you think she'll walk before her first birthday?"

He shrugged. "Does it matter?"

"I guess not."

He wrapped his arms around her waist from behind, resting his back against the huge tree trunk. "We should plant a rose bush here—the place Courtney said her first word. I'll ask Chevy about what we have to do to get permission for it."

"That's really sweet."

"Wait until you see what I'll do when she graduates high school."

She twisted her face up to him. With his height, she could only see his chin. "You've thought that far ahead?"

"Much further—college graduation, her wedding."

"And you plan on being in her life that long?"

He met her gaze and the vulnerable little boy disappeared. "I plan on being in both of your lives that long."

She worked her body into his. "You want to tell me what's on your mind? It isn't like you to be so serious and so quiet."

"Actually, I don't want to tell you. Is that a problem?"

"Depends on why you don't want to tell me."

He dipped his head, whispering into her ear. "I don't want to tell you because it's something I have to work out on my own. You know about the land deal. You know about the mess Alex left me to take care of."

"It has something to do with those things? The reason you're so distracted?"

"Yes." He rested his chin on top of her head, pulling her closer from behind. "Are you okay?"

"Yes." She could feel the intimate definition of each of his muscles. He had the perfect body of an exercise fanatic, yet she had never seen him lift a free weight, walk on the treadmill, or drink a protein shake. He widened his stance and she wiggled into the V of his thighs.

"What are you doing, Cassidy?" His voice had dropped an octave.

"Nothing," she answered innocently. She rocked her hips.

"How did it go with your parents? Is your mother going to help with Courtney's party?"

"It did not go well with my parents."

"Baby." His arms tightened around her waist. "I should have asked earlier. I'm sorry."

"It's okay. I don't want to talk about my parents any more than you want to talk about what's bothering you."

"What do we talk about then?" he asked, trying to

sound worriless. "Look at the sky. It's so clear, you can see a hundred stars."

"I have a very nice view of the moon back at my place."

He must have remembered the night he pulled her bed underneath the bedroom window, because his body responded, growing hard and long against the swell of her behind.

"The best place to see it is from my bed." She turned in the circle of his arms. "I have this giant bed—the mattress is long enough to keep your feet from hanging off the bottom of it. And it's so soft—but firm at the same time, you know?"

He grinned. "I know."

"The pillows are great too. Just right for resting a weary head."

"Sounds interesting."

"Unbelievable things happen in my bed. Troubles disappear. People fall in love."

"I'd like to see this magical bed."

Cassidy peeled away Kirkland's shirt and marveled at the light splattering of sandy-brown hair covering his pecks. She traced her fingers over his wide shoulders, down his long arms, intertwining her fingers with his. His hands were large and she lost herself in his grip. She stood on tiptoe, but it wasn't enough, and he had to lean down to consume her mouth. He helped her keep her balance by holding her hands. She unfolded around him, allowing him to delve deep into her mouth.

She pulled away when she felt his control slipping. She watched his rum-colored eyes for emotion as she unsnapped his pants and slipped them down two miles of sun-kissed thighs and calves. She perched on her knees, helping him step out of the last of his clothes. Without warning, she gripped the hard mounds of his behind. Her tongue lapped at the birthmark on his inner thigh.

She glanced up. His head was tilted back. His hands squeezed her shoulders, encouraging her to go a step further. He moaned and she liked the control she had over his body. She teased his other thigh. His step faltered, but he recovered, spreading his feet farther apart on the carpet. The wisps of hair at the base of his manhood matched the other sandy-brown hair of his body. With long, concentrated strokes, she measured him from base to tip. He jumped, his body becoming more tension-filled with the quantifying assessment of her tongue.

She weighed the twin sacks between his thighs in her palms—separately and then together to achieve an accurate accounting of the hefty weight. His leg twitched with impatience, but slipping the tip of him between her lips quieted the movement.

"Hmmm." His fingers cascaded through her hair. He liked this. His words were unintelligible, but she could tell by his body's response. Her body fed off his response to her manipulation. Her nipples hardened while other parts became more pliable. She took him deeper into her mouth, pulling him in by the grip on his behind. Her movements intensified in speed as the scene became more erotic. Her hands traveled over his abdomen, up his chest. He began a slow thrust, fueled by her wandering tongue. He steadied her, demonstrating by rocking his hips what he liked best. She gave him what he wanted and added more of what he didn't realize he needed. His legs buckled and he toppled down on the bed, quickly reaching for her and dragging her on top of him.

He rolled over, trapping her beneath his body. She felt safe there. She wished she could remain this way forever—protected by the sheer masculinity of his body. But she had pushed him over the edge of erotic patience. He tore away her clothes, lifted her under her arms, and positioned her at the head of the bed.

"Look at the moon," he said, opening the condom wrapper and sheathing himself. "Tell me what you see." He plunged deep.

She gasped as he entered her in one harsh motion.

"Describe what you see, Cassidy." He pummeled her with piston precision while his voice sounded calm and in control. She couldn't talk. She couldn't concentrate. She could do nothing but fall into the rhythm of their bodies. The moon—the world—nothing was as important as what he did to her body. He came to her for a kiss, kissing her deeply, but ending it too quickly. "What do you see?"

"Nothing," she panted. "Can't talk."

He became relentless, chuckling at his expertise in ruling her body. "Close your eyes and tell me what colors you see."

She yielded to his requests—he was in a talkative mood tonight. She closed her eyes and stepped out of her body for a brief moment. Only long enough to separate her from him. "Blues, and greens."

His stroke slowed, grew more thorough. He moved into her body with finesse. He pulled out to the tip—a kiss away from separation—before he moved back into her heat with a slow, sure, torturous push of his hips.

"Reds and yellows," she told him. "All swirling around my head."

"Open your eyes and tell me about the moon, Cassidy. I want to see how you see the world when I make love to you." His tongue danced across her collarbone as he moved in and out.

She opened her eyes, tilted her head back and saw the moon for the first time in her life. This was no ordinary moon. This was the moon she'd read about in fairy-tale books. "The moon," she panted. "This moon—our moon—is—"

He began kissing her neck, moving deeper and deeper still.

She placed her lips against the shell of his ear and told him, using explicit words, why the moon was similar to what he was doing to her body. His control slipped away by degrees and he consumed her body the way he consumed her mouth until they tensed and exploded together.

Cassidy awoke when Courtney climbed onto her belly, pushing the air out of her lungs.

"Tell your mom good morning, Courtney."

"Ma—Ma—Ma," Courtney laughed.

Kirkland leaned down and placed a kiss on Cassidy's lips. "Good morning."

She ruffled his hair. "Good morning." She sat up, taking Courtney into her lap. "Why do I always oversleep when you stay over?"

He lifted a mischievous eyebrow.

"How long have you been up?"

"Long enough to get Courtney breakfast." He climbed back into bed and Courtney crawled into his arms. They communicated in their secret language. Cassidy could make out a word or two. They were evolving together and one day they'd sit together and have long, candid talks.

"This is nice. Being together."

"It is." He lifted Courtney high into the air and she squealed with laugher.

"You want to have kids." She remembered them discussing this at the art gallery.

He looked over at her, suspending Courtney in the air. "Only if it were possible to have them with you."

"But it's not."

"No, it's not." He brought Courtney in for a kiss.

"It could be a deal-breaker. You're so good with Courtney. If you told me you couldn't commit to being with me long term because you wanted your own family, I would understand."

He sat Courtney between them and turned to her with blazing eyes. A dark memory crossed his features. "Would you? Would you let me walk away so easily?"

She watched him closely and decided on telling the truth. "No. I wouldn't."

"Would you like to do this every morning? Be together as a family?"

"This is nice."

"So you've said. I'm asking if you could be a family with me? Would you allow me to be Courtney's father?"

Courtney gave her gurgle of approval.

"You're not emotionally ready to make such an important life decision."

"You sound like a shrink," he ground out.

"Don't be offended. I'm not ready either. How can I plan my future when I can't resolve the problems I have with my parents?"

He watched her for a long moment, struggling with how to respond. "We're emotional cripples unable to plan our future?" Courtney urged him to lift her. He raised her above his head with gentle playfulness, a direct contrast to the mood between them. "What are we doing here, Cassidy? Where are we going?"

She remembered this conversation from the park. They were crisscrossing over the important issues in their relationship. "What are you really asking me?"

His cell phone rang as he brought Courtney in for a kiss. He shot her a meaningful look, telling her the conversation was far from over. She took Courtney while he retrieved his phone. A few short words and he hung up, scrambling from the bed.

"What's wrong?" she asked, leaving the bed too.

"That was Chevy. There's been a bomb threat at the paper mill."

# Chapter 25

Kirkland stood in a closed circle with his brothers, away from the mill employees. A heavy rain beat down on him, but he never noticed his drenched clothing. His anger made the rain turn to steam as it hit his shoulders.

"Three bomb threats in a week," Greyson said.

Chevy adjusted his wide-brimmed hat. "Is there any doubt Pete Frawley is behind this?"

"He's trying to ruin me," Kirkland said.

"But he's taking us all on," Greyson interjected.

"We might as well send the employees home," Chevy said. "We know the drill. By the time the bomb squad clears the building, most of the day will be over. Besides, the police want us to come down to the station. They're suspicious, too."

"I'm sorry about all this," Kirkland apologized. "If it wasn't for me getting involved with Pete, none of this would be happening. We're losing thousands each day he pulls one of these stunts."

"This isn't your fault, Kirkland," Greyson assured him. "Pete is the one doing this."

"What are we going to do about it?" Chevy asked, shaking his head to remove the water pooling in the brim of his hat.

"I'll go down to the police station," Kirkland announced. "I'll tell them about calling off the land deal and Pete's threats. If they put surveillance on him, they'll get all the evidence they need to prove he's the one calling in the bomb threats."

Greyson shook his head. "It doesn't work that way. The police can't put surveillance on a man without enough evidence to justify it. The police do take bomb threats seriously—especially with the threat of another terrorist attack—but they still need evidence."

"What about the private detective you used to help Sutton?"

"She doesn't need as much evidence. But her services are not cheap."

"Look how much we're losing." Kirkland waved his hand at the employees huddled together under umbrellas. "It's my fault. I'll foot the bill. Can you put me in touch with her?"

Greyson nodded.

"How about giving everyone two weeks off until I can get this straightened out?"

"Might as well," Chevy jumped in. "Pete isn't going to let us get any work done. I'll go make the announcement."

Greyson flipped through his wallet.

"Grey?" Kirkland asked.

"Yeah?" Greyson pulled out a business card and handed it to Chevy.

"I need to talk to you."

"The last time you needed to talk to us, the news wasn't good."

"It's even worse this time."

"I'm soaked. Walk to my car."

Kirkland waited until they were inside Greyson's Volvo wagon before he shared Alex's secret. Greyson stared out the window for a long time. He watched the employees scatter, running to their cars. The parking lot was clear and only a few emergency vehicles lingered when he finally turned to Kirkland. "Alex has caused more trouble for me from the grave than he did when he was alive."

A stabbing **pain** ricocheted between Kirkland's heart and his **stom**ach. The acid in his belly began to burn. The pain rarely left him anymore. Even when he was with Cassidy and Courtney, the slow fizzle never let him forget his troubles.

"How in the hell could you have been friends with him?" Greyson shouted. "He got off on ruining everyone's life. He was selfish and conniving. I tell you one thing, he sure isn't in heaven looking down on us."

"You don't understand why Alex was my friend, but he was, and I don't appreciate you talking about him like this when he's dead."

"I don't appreciate you dropping his problems in my lap. He didn't handle his finances so he had to hide all his assets in his mistresses' names. Then he dies and leaves my future wife and her child penniless. Years later, we find out he used my brother to hide his land. Sutton and I got past all that, but the secrets just keep on coming. You expect me to respect your friendship with a man like this? Forget it! I love you and I forgive you for your part in it all because you're my brother. I won't forgive him for threatening my marriage from his place in hell." He turned the key, starting the ignition.

"I'm going to get the PI on Pete, then I'm going to have a conversation with Sutton," Kirkland said.

"Not without me there."

"Fair enough." Kirkland stepped out of the car and Greyson sped off, spraying him with red mud.

Kirkland buckled Courtney into her stroller before interrupting Cassidy at work. Her latest paintings were bursting with vibrant colors. The women wore determined, lustful expressions, and the men had taken on a certain chiseled-chin rogue appearance. He often teased her about the materialization of her fantasies through her work. He was proud of her skill as an artist. She'd been commissioned to complete four paintings—one would hang in the home of a gallery owner. This news had really excited her. She rambled on that evening, giddy with the possibility of turning something she loved into a lucrative career.

"I'm going to take Courtney for a walk," he announced, entering her studio.

"Let me get cleaned up and I'll come with you."

"No. Keep working."

"It'll only take a minute."

He wrapped his arm around her waist. He wished he could live in the softness of her body forever. Loving her night and day. Giving her everything she needed to be happy. He should be her lifeline. Her world should revolve around him as his did around her. "I'd like to spend time with Courtney alone."

She hugged his neck, careful not to mark him with paint. "Are you two sharing secrets?"

"You're the keeper of my secrets."

She kissed his lips, his cheek, and his lips again. "Hurry back."

"You still don't think I can handle her?"

"I know she's in safe hands. I want you to hurry back and *handle* me."

Sitting in Cassidy's living room, he'd been perfectly content watching television while she worked. He stared at the screen, not absorbing one thing he watched. Alex was heavy on his mind. Partly because the PI in Chicago still hadn't found any concrete evidence about Pete's involvement in the bomb scares at the mill. Mostly because he knew he was about to dredge up old pain for Sutton.

He needed the fresh innocence and unconditional love Courtney offered. Not that Cassidy didn't offer unconditional love. She hadn't condemned him once for his involvement in the land deal. She'd never spoken an unkind word, no matter what dirty secrets he'd shared with her. He appreciated her most of all for allowing him to express his pain over losing his best friend. She soothed him and encouraged him to talk about Alex. He could never repay her for her understanding.

But today he needed the innocence of a child to help him deal with his sins. Courtney's bubbly laughter as he flew her through the air, mimicking an airplane was just the thing to direct his conscience. He placed her on the ground, coaxing her to take her first steps to make her mother happy. What a wonderful birthday present it would be for Cassidy if Courtney walked up and gave her a kiss, thanking her for the trouble she'd gone to, to make the first birthday a memorable one. He stretched out a blanket beneath *their* tree and held Courtney on his chest until they both dozed off. Waves of laughter aroused them some time later. They watched a group of girls jumping rope until Courtney whined, signaling dinnertime. He placed her back into the stroller and started home amid a group of curious mothers, whispering and wondering about his connection to Courtney—and Cassidy.

Cassidy had revisited a curious question the other morning: "Do you want to have kids?" Of course he wanted a child if the child they were referring to was Courtney. She had asked if her not being able to have a baby was a "deal-breaker." Hadn't she learned yet he would not leave her? Not because of children. Not because she was older. Not for any reason. She had shown him love without negotiation. She made love to him when she wanted him to know how much she cared, and when she wanted to use his body for her pleasure. She opened her door, she opened her heart, and she opened her life, inviting him in to take what he needed. And never once had she placed conditions on their relationship. She didn't try to push him into marriage because they had been dating more than six months. She didn't count how many times he took her out. She never complained about him not calling. Cassidy accepted him as he was, flaws and all, and nothing would keep him from doing the same.

But he couldn't come to her the way he wanted to, with unclean hands. He had to correct his mistakes. He had to make things right with the people

who were hurt by his actions. The list was long—
Greyson, Sutton, the employees of the mill, and the
townspeople. There was much to do before he
could go to Cassidy and offer her a stable future.
After he made amends, he had to prove to her he
was stable and accountable. He demanded she feel
safe with him. With Cassidy, everything needed to
be *right*. He would be her husband. He would be
Courtney's father. As he was now, he could not take
on those roles until he considered himself an honorable man. As much as he needed Cassidy's love,
he also needed her adoration and respect.

Cassidy was sitting on her front porch when he
rounded the corner, trying not to look concerned.
She still had a hard time being separated from
Courtney. Her face lit up when she saw him. Her
smile was a beacon—the bull's-eye. Everything he
did was aimed at winning her heart. He wanted her
happy.

Her parents saddened him. So far, she'd kept
him outside of the perimeter. Things were touchy.
The relationship she was trying to build between
her parents and Courtney was too fragile to introduce him into the mix. It made him edgy. Made
him feel as if she wasn't planning to make him a
permanent part of her life so it wasn't necessary to
upset her parents by introducing them.

"How'd it go?" Cassidy asked as they rolled up the
walk.

"We had a good time." He lifted the stroller onto
the porch. Cassidy went ahead and held the door
open.

"Are you hungry?" She lifted Courtney out of
the stroller, checking her diaper as she did. He

knew she would check. He'd changed Courtney after their nap. She glanced at him, pleasantly surprised a *man* had thought about more than just playing and having a good time. He winked, and she grinned.

"Are you staying for dinner?"

"No. I have work to do."

She shifted Courtney to her other hip so she could lean in for a kiss. "You've been working so much lately."

"My family would say it's about time."

She pressed her palm against his chest. He liked the way she seemed not to be able to be near him without touching him.

"I'd like to meet your parents."

She tried to hide her unpleasant surprise at his request, but he knew her too well.

"Problem?"

"Why do you want to meet them now?"

"I've wanted to meet them for a long time, but I didn't want to interfere."

"But now it's okay to interfere?"

He followed her into the kitchen. She'd been cooking. The aromas would have made his mouth water if his stomach wasn't bubbling with hot acid. "Is it a problem?" He should have let it drop, but he felt confrontational about it. "I don't like being hidden."

"Hidden?" Her mouth dropped. "I'm not hiding you, Kirkland."

"Then it's a go."

She watched him for a long moment. "I invited them to Courtney's party. If they show, you'll meet them."

"In a very discrete way. I want them to know I'm your man, Cassidy." And he wouldn't settle for the "friend" label.

The corner of her mouth quirked upward.

"What's funny?" He helped her fit Courtney into her high chair.

"I don't know what happened at the park, but you're awfully . . ."

"What?" His tone softened.

"Commanding. Demanding. Domineering." She wrapped her fingers in his shirt and pulled him to her for a kiss. "My parents will know you're *my man*."

He ran his fingers through the softness of her hair. "Thank you."

"You're welcome." She moved to the stove to prepare Courtney's dinner. "Sutton called while you were gone. I asked her to help me plan Courtney's party. She seemed excited about it. She wants to have lunch tomorrow."

"What did you tell her?"

Cassidy turned to him, reading the distress on his face. "When are you going to talk to her about Alex?"

"I thought I'd clear up the trouble at the mill first."

"You shouldn't wait one more day."

# Chapter 26

Kirkland's stomach wound in a tight knot as he stepped across the threshold of Greyson's home. This was reminiscent of his visit a little over a year ago, when he had to tell his sister-in-law he owned land rightfully belonging to her. His body had come to react when he thought of Alex—chest tightening; or the land deal—a knotting gut; and his betrayal of Sutton—the acidic burning and bubbling of his stomach. He wanted to be anywhere but there. He thought of Cassidy sending him telepathic moral support. Knowing he could go to her afterward would get him through this.

He followed Greyson into the study, doubting his sanity in coming. His brother was angry. Greyson tried to hide it. Tried to hold on to his love for his little brother and use it to hide how badly he wanted to pummel him into the ground. Since Alex's death, Kirkland had been privileged to receive all the hate Greyson had for Alex, but was unable to direct to the principal subject. The realization struck him as they stepped into Greyson's study and Greyson perched on the corner of his desk, peering at him with narrowed eyes. They had never been as close as they should have been, because of the differences in their ages. Even as they began to bond as adults, there was always something between them—a wedge keeping Greyson from getting as close to him as Greyson was to Chevy.

"Sutton's taking Sierra to her parents' house for the night." His gaze shifted then flipped back. "I didn't know how she would take it. I didn't want Sierra to witness any . . . *hysterics*."

Kirkland answered with a brisk nod.

"She should be back in a minute."

Kirkland crossed the room, looking out the window. He wished she'd hurry so he could get it over with. He wished she'd change her plans and not come back home today. He shoved his hands in his pockets and turned to his brother. "How mad are you at me?"

"Pretty mad." Greyson was the cerebral brother. He articulated himself with finesse. And was paid top dollar to do so. He could be stewing with anger inside but not a drop of it would make it outside his body. He controlled his emotions like any great attorney would. He internalized it and used it to fuel his resolve, always winning the fair fight like the knight in shining armor he was. The only time Kirkland had seen him lose his cool was when it came to Sutton or Sierra. His anger would explode into raw energy when there was a threat to his family, which made Kirkland being here today more dangerous than an outsider would perceive.

"You've been mad at me since Alex died."

"What are you talking about?" Greyson folded his arms over his chest—a protective stance.

"You blamed me for his dying before you could settle the score with him. Somehow, my friendship with him made it my fault he died in that car crash."

"You're not making any sense," Greyson mumbled.

"It doesn't make sense, but it's true."

"My problems with Alex had nothing to do with you. If they did, I would've stopped you from hanging out with him when we were kids."

"You tried!"

"Not hard enough, apparently." He moved behind his desk, taking his place on the throne. Greyson flaunting his superiority made Kirkland's anger flare.

"You were jealous of Alex."

"Jealous?!"

"Jealous of how close we were. Jealous he had the guts to go after Sutton when you were afraid to."

"You're talking about things you know nothing about, Kirkland." He rose slowly, menacingly, from his seat.

Kirkland was not daunted. "Tell me, big brother. Tell me why you've had such a problem with my friendship with Alex since we were kids?"

"He used you. Look at the mess he's stuck you with. You were running around thinking you're best buddies, and all the while he was using you to do his dirty work."

"I'm not all that innocent, Greyson. I've done my share of wrong, too."

"Really?" Greyson raised a thick eyebrow.

"Really." A confession he had not planned to make.

"Like what, little brother? Tell me what messes

Alex had to get you out of, that equalize what he's done to you?"

The tightening in Kirkland's chest halted his words. He used the opportunity to push away the emotional grip on his heart to formulate his words. "If it weren't for Alex, I wouldn't have finished college."

Greyson threw his hands up. "So, your college education justifies destroying his wife and kid."

"Alex was my brother when you and Chevy were off living your lives."

"Chevy and I were always a phone call away."

"*Away*. You were away from this place. I've never been further than the capital. And even then I had to spend every free minute of every day here with Mama."

Something Greyson could latch on to, to prove his argument. He grabbed it with the tenacity of a pitbull, not knowing he was the one about to be on the losing end of the fight. "You've been running and telling Mama and Pop every little thing Chevy and I did since we were kids. You could've left here whenever you wanted. Nobody was holding you hostage."

"I couldn't leave Mama." His arm pressed into his stomach, pushing away the pain.

The way he said it caught Greyson's attention. Greyson rounded the desk to stand in front of him. He lowered his voice, phrasing his question carefully. "Why couldn't you leave Mama? Mama had Pop."

Kirkland leveled a steady look at his brother. "No. Mama did not have Pop."

Greyson's eyes narrowed. After a moment, he asked, "Where was Pop?"

"Rumor has it Eileen Putnam took her husband's passing pretty hard." He sounded so countrified, forgetting to pronounce his words just so as emotion clogged his throat.

"Rumor?"

"Saw it with my own eyes. Saw him carrying on with Eileen Putnam, pretending her family was his family. Watched Mama fall apart little by little while she pretended it wasn't happening. I held Mama together. And Alex helped me do it."

"I'll kill the bastard," Greyson mumbled. He dropped down on the corner of his desk.

"Pop doesn't know Mama found out. I was going to confront him, but Mama wouldn't let me."

"She's ashamed."

Kirkland nodded.

"What did Alex do?"

"Kept me from killing Pop. Had a nice talk with Eileen Putnam and three days later she moved out of Hannaford."

Greyson watched him disbelievingly. "I had no idea . . ."

"What's going on?" Sutton bounced into the office. Greyson reached for her, greeting her with a kiss and tossing Kirkland a look over her shoulder.

Kirkland's eyes locked on the swinging pendulum on Greyson's desk. Sutton had come when the tension in the room was beginning to dissipate, but her arrival escalated it to new levels.

"Have a seat, honey." Greyson directed her to the sofa, but she perched next to him instead. "Kirkland needs to talk to you."

"Whenever Kirkland needs to talk to me, it isn't good."

The pain in Kirkland's stomach forced him to sit on the sofa, one hand pressed into his abdomen while the other moved rhythmically up and down the crease of his pants.

"What's going on?" Sutton looked between them, readily reading the tension in the room.

Where to start? "I'm the one behind the industrial development project here in Hannaford Valley," Kirkland said. A simple confession, not drawing much of a response from her.

"I know," she answered smugly. She gripped the edge of the desk. "Did you think I wouldn't discover the owner during my environmental law project?"

"You never said anything," Greyson said.

"I wanted Kirkland to admit it on his own."

Kirkland shared a look with Greyson. "Greyson has drawn up papers giving you and Sierra your fair shares. I kept one fourth, but if you have a problem with it, I'll give it up."

"No problem. I only want my fair share of Alex's estate."

Kirkland moved away from that emotionally charged subject. What he had to tell her was hard enough without reliving the fact that Alex had given away all their possessions to his mistresses before he died.

"There's more," Greyson said quietly. He placed his hand atop hers.

"What?" She looked between them. "What else is there?" Mild panic coated her words.

"Alex loved you," Kirkland started, using the delay to tamp down the queasiness of his stomach.

"Don't stall," Greyson warned.

"You know what it is?" Sutton asked her husband.

"Alex had a baby a year before he died." There. Everything was out in the open. Kirkland should have felt relieved, and to some extent he was, but the horrified look on Sutton's face drowned him in newfound guilt.

"My husband had a baby with another woman?" He nodded.

"And you've known—" she did the math—"for three years?"

"I didn't know if I should tell you."

"A baby?" She looked at Greyson who nodded, confirming what she'd heard. She turned her hateful gaze to Kirkland a second before she jumped off the desk, shot across the room, and slapped his face—twice. Greyson was there in a flash, pulling her off of him. The rest happened too fast to know what order everything occurred. Sutton swinging at Kirkland, cursing him; Greyson accidentally getting pummeled by her small fists as he tried to pull her off his brother; things flying across the room in Kirkland's direction . . .

"Get out!" Sutton screamed. Tears rolled down her face and sobs choked her words. "Get out of my house and never come back!"

"Sutton," Greyson panted, breathing hard after the workout she'd just given him. "Kirkland is my brother, and my brother—"

"Is always welcome in my house. I know the drill, Greyson. Don't forget this is *my* home, too. Mine and Sierra's. Now *you* have a choice." She jabbed a finger in his direction. "Choose between your brother and your family. Because if he shows his face in this house again, *Sierra and I* will never come back here!"

The writing was so plainly on the wall. Greyson's face twisted in anguish. He was being forced to make a decision no man should ever have to make.

"What are you going to do, Greyson?" Sutton pressed. "Whom are you going to choose?"

Greyson watched her unblinkingly. Suddenly, he looked ten years older than his true age. But Greyson had loved Sutton all his life. He loved Sierra like she was his flesh and blood daughter. He turned to Kirkland, sadness etched into his mouth. "Kirkland—"

The pain was unbearable. He grabbed his stomach, sinking to his knees. Acid poured past his lips, stained with bright red blood.

"Kirkland?" Greyson dropped down next to him on the floor.

"My chest," Kirkland managed, struggling to catch his breath.

"Call an ambulance."

Sutton was already dialing.

# Chapter 27

Cassidy stood at Kirkland's bedside, gripping the rails with white knuckles, when he opened his eyes. The pain medication had hit him hard, and it took a few minutes to focus on her fear. She blinked rapidly, warding off the huge tears welling in her eyes. He'd told Greyson in the ambulance not to worry his parents until they knew what was going on—had Greyson done as he asked?

"Kirkland?" Cassidy ran her fingers through his hair.

"Who's keeping Courtney?" His voice was raspy and sore from vomiting.

Greyson appeared on the other side of his bed. "How do you feel?"

"Drugged."

Cassidy tried to smile. She kept stroking his hair. It felt so good to have her touching him. "You scared me half to death."

"Where's Courtney?" he asked again.

She glanced at Greyson. "Sutton's keeping her."

"How's she doing?"

"She's fine, Kirkland. We're worried about you."

Greyson watched their interaction with curious eyes. "The doctor wants to keep you overnight."

"I'm going home." A macho statement with little merit, because when he tried to sit forward the tube in his nose yanked him back onto the pillow.

"You have a bleeding ulcer, Kirkland," Greyson told him. "You can't mess around with something like this."

"I have things to do. I can't waste a day lying in bed."

"Getting treatment," Cassidy corrected, "is the only thing you have to do."

"I can take pills at home."

Greyson shrugged, speaking to Cassidy. "I don't think we can make him stay if he wants to leave."

"Think again." She turned to Kirkland. "You're not leaving here until the doctor discharges you. Settle back and relax."

"I'm not—"

"*Settle* back . . . and relax."

Kirkland avoided Greyson's shocked expression and settled against the flat pillows.

"I have to call Mama." Greyson moved to the phone.

"Tell her I'm okay and not to come. I'll stop by when I'm released."

"Like I could keep her away." Greyson dialed, turning his back and speaking with a low voice.

Cassidy touched his cheek. "Sutton didn't take the news well."

His hands went to his face. "Do you have a mirror?" He hadn't noticed the damage to his face until Cassidy's caring touch brought attention to it. Such a contradiction—Sutton's infliction of pain, and Cassidy's loving caress.

"The nurse left a jar of cream next to your bed."

She retrieved the cream and carefully dabbed it over the scratches. His masculine side wanted him to turn away, but her touch felt too good. Relief in the middle of the war.

"Mama said she wants to see you tomorrow. If you get out, come to her. If not, she'll come to you." Greyson's nose wrinkled as he watched Cassidy tending to his wounds. "I'm out of here."

"Cassidy, can you give us a minute?" Kirkland asked.

"Sure." She left carrying the jar of cream. It reassured him to see she left her purse next to him on the bed. She wouldn't go far.

"I'm sorry about all of this," Kirkland started. "I'm going to make it right with Sutton."

"Well, I've been thinking about what you said earlier. I have been holding Alex's sins against you. It isn't your place to make it right with Sutton. You weren't her husband. You didn't sleep around on her and get another woman pregnant. *I'll* take care of Sutton."

A quiet moment of understanding passed between them. "One more thing," Kirkland said.

"Yeah?"

"What I told you about Mama and Pop and Eileen . . ."

"I can't wait to get to Pop—"

"Here's the thing. Mama doesn't want him to know she found out about Eileen."

Greyson mumbled several curse words. "Why not?"

"It's the way she wants it. Even while it was all going down, she wouldn't let me say anything.

She'd be upset if she found out I told you. I think it's a matter of pride."

"Pride?"

"Mama's not going to leave him. Not after all these years of marriage. She wants things to remain the same between them. I don't think she could handle his guilt."

"I don't understand."

"Me either, but it's what she wants. She'll kill me if she finds out I told you. This is why Alex stepped up. He handled the problem without letting Pop know Mama had found out what was going on."

Greyson mumbled more curse words. "I don't know what's going on in Hannaford. Everybody's living a hidden life."

Kirkland didn't know what to say.

"And you're the keeper of everyone's dirty secrets."

True.

"And keeping so many secrets has landed you in a hospital bed with a bleeding ulcer."

Kirkland's eyes dropped to the dull green blanket.

"I'd better go. I don't want to leave Sutton too long." Greyson leaned over the side rails and gave Kirkland a brotherly hug before leaving. "I'll send Cassidy back in. I don't think she's finished with you." He grinned. "She got you straight real quick."

"I wouldn't talk if my wife was at home waiting with a mean right hook."

Greyson looked relieved they could laugh about it. He lifted his hand in a wave as he left the room.

Dark jeans hugged Cassidy's thick thighs. The sight made Kirkland coax her to sit on the bed with him so he could touch her in scandalous places. She wore a multicolored tunic with a deep opening in front. Her breasts were on display, taunting him in his weakened condition. She had tied a matching scarf around her head—kind of a 70s ultra funky thing. Her eyes were painted, too. Unusual for her because she wore very little makeup. The blue eye shadow brought out the dark brown of her eyes.

"You look so cute," he said. "You make a sick man want to get well—quick."

"Okay, sick man. You just concentrate on getting better. I don't ever want to be called to the hospital to see you again."

"Hey, some of my favorite memories of you involve hospitals."

She smiled, remembering.

"I think I fell in love with you in this hospital. One look at you in the puke-green hospital gown and I was gone."

"You're such a charmer."

"Climb up here next to me."

She obliged, not giving him an argument. She snuggled next to him, oblivious to the nasty tube coming from his nose draining liquid the color of coffee grounds into a wall container.

He placed a firm hand on her thigh. "I wish I could kiss you, Cassidy."

"How do you feel? And don't try to be macho with me."

"Lousy."

"Why didn't you tell me you weren't feeling good? I kept asking about your appetite."

"I've been having these pains since Alex died."

"And you thought you were coping."

He flipped the channels on the television suspended above his bed.

"I was really scared when Sutton called." Her voice was soft, small, and vulnerable. "I can't lose you, Kirkland."

"You're not going to lose me, Cassidy."

She rested her head on his shoulder. "Really scared."

"I didn't mean to scare you. I'm sorry."

A warm tear soaked through his gown. "I'm staying with you tonight."

"I don't know if the nurse will let you."

"I already asked. I'm staying."

"Good."


Cassidy awoke to Kirkland's harsh whispering. She stretched out the kinks from sleeping in the lounger next to his hospital bed. She wasn't surprised to find him on the telephone discussing business. "What are you doing?"

He placed his hand over the receiver. "The PI in Chicago has a lead on who has been calling in the bomb threats at the mill."

"Didn't the doctor tell you to relax?"

He offered a lopsided grin. "Getting the jump on whoever's trying to ruin the paper mill is very relaxing."

"You have five minutes," she said sternly. She held up her hand and ticked off five fingers, reiterating his time limit. He offered a sheepish grin, half-rolled his eyes, and went back to his phone conversation. She left him to his devices while she used the pay phone to check on Courtney.

Sutton remained pleasant, overtly avoiding inquiring about Kirkland's health. "Greyson's with the girls in the backyard. We can keep her as long as you need."

"Kirkland should be discharged later today. We're waiting for the doctor to make his rounds."

"Maybe one more overnight then. Sierra loves having her over."

Cassidy missed Courtney when they were separated, but Courtney needed to develop her own identity. Cassidy couldn't hold on too tightly. "I'll come for her tomorrow afternoon, then—if it's okay. I need to do some shopping for her birthday party."

"No problem. About the party, Cassidy, I'm not going to be able to help with the planning. We won't be able to make it, either."

"Sutton," she breathed. She understood Sutton's pain, but Courtney was being shortchanged because of everyone else's mistakes. "Is it because of Kirkland?"

"He's told you?"

"Everything."

Sutton's voice lifted in heightened exasperation. "And you're still seeing him?"

"I love him, Sutton. He's done things he's not proud of, but I'm not perfect either."

"Please don't say you think he's changed."

Cassidy treaded carefully, trying to preserve her friendship with Sutton, but not backing down about her feelings for Kirkland. "Kirkland and I have a friendship with our relationship. He shares things with me I can't repeat, but I will tell you this. Alex's death has been harder on him—harder than he's let anyone know. It's one of the reasons he's in the hospital now. He's struggled with how to make things right for everyone Alex destroyed, while remaining loyal to his friend. I'm not sure it's fair to expect him to be perfect. Alex was responsible for Alex. Kirkland can't undo what Alex has done." She anxiously waited for Sutton's counter argument.

"Cassidy, I know what you're saying is true, but . . ." When Sutton began speaking again her voice was strained. She tried to hide her misery and pain, but it poured over the phone line, drowning Cassidy in sorrow. "But he's opened these wounds. I thought I had worked through Alex's transgressions. Now I find out my husband started another family."

"Is it right to hold it against Kirkland?" Cassidy asked gently.

Sutton sighed. "I don't know what's right. I just know how I feel."

"I can't imagine what you're going through, Sutton, but I'm your friend. If you want to talk, I'm here. If there's something I can do, let me know. Before you back out of Courtney's party, talk to Greyson. Let some time pass before you make a decision. This isn't about a child's birthday party—this is about pulling away from your family and friends."

"I can't promise anything."

"Just think about it."

Since becoming involved with Kirkland, family and friendships were very important to Cassidy. He'd shown her they were by forming a strong foundation for Courtney. It was time to heal all these fractured relationships around her. How could Kirkland and Cassidy build a strong relationship when their relationships with their families were so bad? They couldn't live in a cocoon. And they couldn't live in a house of cards, waiting for one incident to destroy what they were building.

"What's the look for? Did you speak to my doctor?" Kirkland asked when Cassidy returned.

"Sutton." She lowered herself next to him.

He placed his hand on her thigh. "I'm going to fix it."

"How? You can't fix everything, Kirkland. Some things are the way they are. If you keep trying to fix Alex's messes, how will you live your own life?"

His face contorted into a strange expression. Understanding, maybe? He didn't share his feelings with her. He clicked on the television and sank deep into thought, coated with a heavy silence.

She would remember the aura of their short conversation for the rest of her life. She made concrete decisions about the direction she wanted her life to go in. She set forth goals for Courtney. Kirkland's fingers massaged her thighs as he worked through issues in his life he had been struggling with for years. He would never tell her the specifics, but from time to time he would repeat the conversation and tell her how it had caused him to reflect in a way he had never done before.

# Chapter 28

Kirkland hated Chicago. The city was too big, too noisy, and too busy. He had only visited Greyson once when he lived there—and that had been prompted by a "favor" Alex needed him to do. But that was another time, for other purposes. His purpose in coming was to meet with the PI investigating the bomb threats. He could've had her Fed Ex the file and spoken to her on the telephone, but he needed to get away from Hannaford. He had to clear his head and decide what direction his life would take. Cassidy and Courtney were a positive influence on his thinking, but he needed to be certain the decisions he was making were his own—not influenced by what might be, or what could be.

Clearing up the land deal was only the beginning. His life was a scramble of activity, none of it showing any commitment to anything. He lived in Charleston, but spent most of his time in Hannaford Valley. He held onto his job at the construction company in Charleston, was part owner of the paper mill in Hannaford, and had jumped into land development with the old Galloway land. He needed to figure out what was most important to him and pursue it to the fullest. Where did he want to live—Charleston or Hannaford? A fairly simple question. He wanted to live as close to Cassidy as possible. But where in Hannaford would he live?

He had to make peace with Sutton. It would tear his family apart if he didn't. He loved Sutton. She was the sister they'd never had. She was his best friend's widow. He wanted her to be happy. So far, he had been a huge part of her misery. He had to change that fact.

And then there were Cassidy and Courtney. He smiled, wondering what they were up to at that very moment. He loved them both and wanted to make them his family. Cassidy had issues with her parents—parents he hadn't met yet—that only she could resolve. But would those issues keep her from making their relationship a permanent one? Because he did want their relationship to become permanent. After entering her world, no other woman would ever do. Courtney needed a father. Would Cassidy allow him to assume the role? Or would she not think him good enough? The thought confounded him. Was he good enough to be Courtney's father? What could he give her? Could he teach her? Cassidy's hesitation would definitely be justified.

Pondering it all, he realized there were too many questions and not enough answers. He wouldn't return to Hannaford until he had answers to them all. And the first step was to meet with the PI and find out what she had learned about Pete Frawley and the bomb threats.

Stacy Taro's one-room office was cluttered with electronic gadgets. Five-feet tall on a good day, she sat behind her desk squawking into the phone, buried behind mounds of files. The seeming disarray of the office made him doubt her competence, but Greyson had guaranteed she was the best. Stacy's skin was a golden mocha and her eyes slanted upward with distinct Asian flare. According to Greyson, her mother was African and her father Japanese. She was innocently exotic with an underlying lethality. She cursed and slammed the phone down.

"Incompetent—" Her head snapped up as if seeing him for the first time. "Well, well, well. How many more of you are there at home?"

Greyson had also warned him of her flirtatious nature.

"How's the mountain man doing?" She started digging through the files littering her desk.

"Greyson is good."

She smacked her lips. "Gave everything up for a woman. Who's not me!" She dropped out of her chair onto the floor, searching the files there. "Tell the mountain man to come visit me, will you?"

"I will."

She disappeared behind the desk. "The only time I hear from him is when he needs work done. When he was living here we used to go to dinner all the time. Catch a movie here and there. I miss him."

"I'll tell him."

"Here it is." Her head popped up from behind the desk. "I knew I had your file buried here somewhere." She returned to her seat and flipped it open. She slid an envelope of pictures across the desk to him. "Here's your culprit. So, what's his wife like?" she asked as he peeled open the manila envelope.

"She's in law school."

"Hmmm."

He removed the photos. "This isn't a surprise. I told you I suspected Pete Frawley. We need proof."

"Oh, I have proof—and a whole lot more." She reared back in her chair, placing her feet on top of the desk. "The surprises just keep on coming out of Hannaford Valley, West Virginia. What are you people doing down there?"

"What do you mean?" He replaced the photos and focused on the Japanese-African dynamo.

"You're the brother who was friends with Alex Galloway, right?"

He nodded, bracing himself for the tightening in his chest.

"What is it with your families? I've heard about situations like these where two families intersect, and no matter what, their paths keep crossing throughout life."

"What are you talking about?" His patience with Stacy's roundabout disclosure wasn't as good as Greyson's.

She tossed him a cassette tape. "Here's your proof Frawley made the phone calls to the emergency operator. With it and the transcripts, you'll have enough to convince the police Pete's the caller." She placed her feet on the ground, leaning toward him in the chair. "I testify at trials for an extra fee."

"So you've told me. You mentioned finding a surprise in your investigation?"

"I was curious about why this guy wanted to shut

down the mountain man's paper mill. Didn't make sense to me—the mill is bringing jobs, which keeps the town afloat, which makes investors want to pay more for the land. Am I right?"

"You're right."

She smiled. "I don't know a thing about running a corporation." She paused, giving him a full appraisal. "You're cute with that big-city look and country accent."

"Thank you." He squirmed. "You were telling me what else you found."

She gave him one last going over before continuing. "Couldn't really find a connection between Pete and Greyson—couldn't find one between you and Pete, either."

"I'm the one who hired him."

She shook her head emphatically. "Doesn't fly. So what that you want to cancel the land deal with him. He moves on and gets another deal. I kept asking myself why he wanted to ruin the mill. It's not so much the mill. It's the town. He wants to destroy Hannaford. Now I have to ask why anyone would want to destroy a whole town. This isn't *Dynasty* or *Dallas*." She flipped pages of his file. "So I began to dissect Mr. Pete Frawley's life." She licked her finger and flipped more pages.

"What did you find?" He moved to the edge of his seat, wanting to snatch the file away and see for himself.

"The strangest thing jumped out at me. When Greyson had me doing the investigation for his then-girlfriend, it led me to a small town called Belva. You know it?"

"Hannaford is between Charleston and Belva.

Small town." He shrugged. "Nothing notable comes to mind."

"I pulled my notes from the investigation I did for your brother, and sure enough, I came across Belva. A little digging and I had the answer to why Pete would hold a grudge about the Galloway land." Stacy stopped digging through the piles of paper on her desk and looked up with a large, satisfied smile. "Pete Frawley might be a little vengeful since he's been looked over his entire life. He might want what he feels he's entitled to . . . his land."

"What?" He rounded the desk, leaning over the back of Stacy's chair to read the file along with her. He was shocked by the document she was perusing. "Pete is Mr. Galloway's son?"

"Seems like the 'only child.' Alex has two half brothers. Eddie by his mother, and Pete on his father's side."

"No. Someone would have known—"

"Everybody knows! Mrs. Galloway ran off and had an affair when she found out about her husband's indiscretions. She became pregnant, had Eddie, and left him behind for his father to raise while she repaired her marriage with her husband. I encountered a woman in Belva with the last investigation who made the hairs on the back of my neck stand up. She was *so* in love with Mr. Galloway, even though he dumped her to go back to his wife. Any other woman would have hated his guts for doing that. She still loved him." She shook her head. "It didn't sit right with me. When I found out Pete was born in Belva—it being such a small town and the Galloway land being the focus of this fight—I searched for a connection between him and the Galloways. Mr. Galloway ran like hell when he found out about Pete, but he did live up to his responsibility to the tune of a monthly check."

"Does Mother Galloway know about Pete?"

"Hard to know. If everything falls into place, I would suspect so. She left her husband once the heart attack left him incapacitated. Why would she do this?"

"Her husband was having an affair—many affairs."

Stacy shook her head vehemently. "No. She knew about the affairs when she reconciled with him. Hell, she had a baby from an affair. Why wait so many years to leave him? She wouldn't have come back to him at all. No. I think she found out about Pete—maybe she traced the checks. When you want the truth, trace the money trail."

Kirkland stood stunned, trying to process it all. No way Alex knew he had two half-brothers. He hated being an only child. He would have found his brothers and started a relationship with them. What did this mean in the big picture? It didn't excuse what Pete was doing, but Kirkland could understand his anger.

Stacy bent her head back to look up at him. "How'd you get those scratches?"

They were fading, but not quickly enough. With one innocent question, Stacy had reminded him how complicated his life had become.

"You must enjoy some hellacious sex play." Maybe her question wasn't so innocent after all. "How long are you going to be in town? And what are your plans for tonight?" The smile definitely wasn't innocent.

The Paynes lived in an obsessively neat home nestled in a picture-book Charleston neighborhood. This would be the family everyone envied, not knowing the people inside had their problems too. All the kids would gather here to play with the twins, Cassidy and Darius. Kirkland imagined it all as he stood on the doorstep waiting for someone to answer his knock.

In Hannaford, his home had been the gathering place for Alex and Sutton. Other kids tried to penetrate their tight-knit circle, but soon gave up. The Ballantyne brothers, Alex, and Sutton were inseparable. They played together, went to school together, and grew up together. Looking back on it now, he wondered if their closeness had actually been dysfunctional. Greyson and Alex's rivalry wasn't good for anyone. Two years after Alex's death, they were still fighting over Sutton. Chevy hadn't discovered the secret to having a meaningful relationship with a woman, although he wanted one desperately. His inability to relate to others outside of their circle could be the cause. Sutton was still a spoiled brat, and they all still catered to her . . . And Kirkland was a mess of emotional contradiction.

"Can I help you?" Mr. Payne was a man of average height and average build. He would not be noticed in a crowd.

"Mr. Payne, I'm Kirkland Ballantyne."

His nose wrinkled in recognition. "The boy Cassidy is seeing?"

He brushed off his offense at being called boy. One thing he learned in Chicago, he had to pick his battles. "Cassidy and I are dating, yes."

"Well, she's not *here*."

"Actually, I came to speak to you—you and your wife."

Mr. Payne assessed him from the doorway before inviting him in. "Have a seat. I'll get Cassidy's mother."

*This might've been a big mistake.* He was debating whether or not to sneak out the front door and deny ever having shown up on the Payne's doorstep, when Cassidy's mother rounded the corner. The striking resemblance between Cassidy and her mother shocked him. Except for the dark chocolate color of Mrs. Payne's skin, Cassidy could be her clone. Her rich darkness surprised him, knowing she was from England. Even before she spoke, he knew she would be a woman of propriety who had worked hard to raise a proper maiden. She sat with her husband in twin chairs, immediately crossing her legs and taking her husband's hand.

"Does Cassidy know you're here?" Mr. Payne asked.

"She would be quite upset if she knew I was here."

"Why did you come?" The English accent seemed out of place coming from a woman who looked like an African queen.

"You can consider me the advance team. I asked Cassidy to introduce us at Courtney's party. I came to find out if you plan on coming."

Mr. Payne answered. "We haven't decided yet."

"Is there anything I can do to persuade you to

come? If I tell you how much Cassidy is hurting because of the distance between you, would that do it? How about if I described Courtney's efforts to learn to walk? Would any of those things entice you to get to know your granddaughter? Whatever it is, I'll do it, because I love Cassidy and Courtney and I want them to be happy. And from what Cassidy's telling me, she won't be happy without her parents in her life."

"I don't like your tone," Mr. Payne scolded.

"I'm sorry, but I'm not sorry about coming here or saying what I've said."

"What did you plan to accomplish by coming here, Kirkland?" Mrs. Payne wanted to know.

The visit wasn't selfish. He had come on Cassidy's behalf. As far as he was concerned, his family was loving enough to take Cassidy and Courtney within their circle. Cassidy wanted her daughter to know her parents and he didn't feel it was an unreasonable request. "I want you to make my girlfriend happy by coming to her daughter's birthday party."

"I want Cassidy to have a good life." Mrs. Payne released her husband's hand and leaned toward him, assessing his reaction to her words. "I want her to marry and have a family. I want her to have a good career. Cassidy has backed into this in a very untraditional way. How do you fit into her life? I can see you're much younger than my daughter—"

"Nine years."

"Are you settled in your career? Or are you still trying to find yourself? Are you prepared to be a part of a single mother's life? Are you ready to be the only father figure Courtney has ever known?"

Mr. Payne piped in. "Instead of trying to tell us how to handle our daughter, you should be trying to figure out what kind of future you can offer her."

"I respect your concerns," he answered smoothly. "I have spent a good amount of time thinking about what I want for Cassidy and Courtney. Mrs. Payne, I'm college educated and have a stable job. My financial future is very secure. Courtney stole my heart the day she was born. No matter what goes on between Cassidy and I, I'll make sure Courtney is financially secure. As far as Cassidy, I love her too much. Just knowing her has made me want to be a better person. I'm working to deserve her. I'm almost there. I don't know if Cassidy wants me in her life forever, but I plan on marrying her."

Cassidy's parents silently communicated. He wished he knew what either of them was thinking. They gave him no clue.

"Are you going to tell my daughter you came here today?" Mrs. Payne wanted to know.

"Probably not."

Another nondescript look passed between the couple.

Mr. Payne stood. "We'll think about everything you said."

Kirkland took his cue and stood also. He extended his hand and offered a firm shake. "Will you be at the party?"

"We'll consider it."


Greyson and Chevy stared at Kirkland in utter disbelief. Chevy was the first to regain the ability to speak. "You're making this all up."

Kirkland tossed his copy of Stacy's investigation onto the middle of the conference table. It slid across the polished top until Chevy stopped it with a swat of his hand. He leafed through the photos, handing them to Greyson one at a time. While they reviewed the contents, Kirkland played the cassette tape of Pete's phone calls to the emergency operator. "By the way, *mountain man*, Stacy wants you to come for lunch."

"What's that about?" Chevy asked Greyson.

"You have to know Stacy," Greyson answered with a coy smile. "So Pete Frawley is Mr. Galloway's son. Does he know about Alex or Eddie?"

Kirkland pulled back a chair and took a seat. "Not as far as Stacy could find."

"What happens when Eddie and Pete find out about each other?" Chevy tossed out the question that silenced the room. The three brothers looked at one another.

"How far does the deception in the Galloway family go?" Greyson asked.

"More importantly," Kirkland added, "how tangled up in it is our family?"

"It seems we get more and more involved with every passing year," Chevy answered.

"So now what?" Greyson asked. "Pete can't hold us responsible for what the Galloways have done."

"He wants his fair share." Chevy flicked the corner of one of the surveillance photos. "And you know what? I don't blame him."

Kirkland and Greyson didn't disagree.

"This sucks," Greyson said.

"'*This sucks*'? From the attorney in the family?

The only thing you can think of to say is '*this sucks*'? Of course it sucks, Greyson."

"Don't start with me, Chevy."

Their conversation escalated into playful banter.

"Okay, guys," Kirkland reeled them back in. "I have an idea I think will get Pete Frawley off my back and out of our business. Let me run it by you."

Maddie lived in a modest home within walking distance of the library. The living room had been transformed into a sick ward for her father. A hospital bed and respirator consumed most of the room. Medical supply boxes were stacked high in every corner. Machines beeped and blinked and buzzed. A nurse was at her father's bedside, performing range of motion exercises with his legs. The only personal items in the room were photos of her mother. Tons of family photos cluttered any spaces vacant of medical equipment.

Cassidy watched, engulfed in the solemn mood of the home, as Maddie greeted her father hello. She doubted the elderly man was alert enough to recognize her, but Maddie spoke to him with love and tenderness. "This way." Maddie waved for her to follow into the next room. The third bedroom had been remodeled to provide her with a small den. The thirty-six-inch television monopolized the room. They sat together on the love seat and Maddie pulled the sofa table up close so they could use it to fan out the brochures they had gathered on their trip into town.

"I envy you," Maddie said, completely off the

subject of the cake designs Cassidy had come to discuss.

"Me? Why?"

"You have a fabulous life. Courtney and your career. You're in love with one of the best-looking, wealthiest men in Hannaford Valley. You've traveled to New York!"

"I'm grateful for what I have, but don't judge your life by mine. I have no relationship with my parents for the very reasons you say I'm living a charmed life. Your father may be ill, but I've watched you interact with him. Something transpired between you when you walked into the house."

"I love my dad, and it's going to tear me apart to lose him. My parents were over forty when they had me. They'd tried many times to have children, but it never worked out. Once my mother had me, it was too late to try for more, so I'm an only child. They gave me a good life. I have some very good childhood memories." Her mood shifted to palpable sadness. "The problem with waiting too long to have children is they become the caregiver too quickly. I started helping to care for my mother when I was in high school—ninth grade. When she died, my father became sickly. I've never really been able to live my own life."

"What would you be doing if you didn't have to care for your father?"

Maddie's eyes lit up. "Traveling."

"Where to?"

"Anywhere! Everywhere!"

"We should plan a trip to Charleston. You and me and Sutton. We could stay overnight at an expensive hotel none of us can afford and pamper ourselves."

Maddie's smile slowly faded. "I couldn't leave my father overnight."

Cassidy wanted to suggest having the nurse provide overnight care for one weekend, but she didn't know what all went into caring for a terminally ill person. "You need a break. You can't take good care of your father if you're not in good physical and mental shape."

"True. There is respite care . . ." Her eyes glazed over as if she were calculating a way to take a weekend for herself. "Maybe one day."

"I'll hold you to it."

Maddie shuffled through the brochures. "You don't have a good relationship with your folks?"

Cassidy shrugged one shoulder. "I'm a twin. My brother, Darius, gets along well with them. He can do no wrong, whereas I can do no right. They didn't approve of me having Courtney before I got married."

"Ouch."

"Yeah."

"Nothing you can do about it now. It's not like you can give her back. They don't want you to do something drastic like adoption, do they?"

"No. They don't approve of anything in my life right now—including Kirkland. He's too young for me."

"Ouch again."

Cassidy handed Maddie a brochure for her approval.

"I like this cake," Maddie said. "It works well with the circus theme. This is going to be some party."

"I'm hoping it'll be an occasion for the adults as much as for the kids."

"Sutton and Kirkland?"

"And my parents. Maybe some healing will take place."

They completed the menu before Maddie asked, "Do you think Chevy will be there?"

"I invited the entire Ballantyne family. I thought it'd be a good opportunity to spend more time with them."

Maddie tried to hide her smile.

"You're crazy about Kirkland, aren't you?"

"Crazy is one way to put it."

When Cassidy returned home, Darius was sitting in her kitchen, crunching numbers. He tried to jerk off his reading glasses before she could see them, but wasn't quite quick enough. After ribbing him about the downfalls of being the oldest twin, she joined him at the table to eat her dinner.

"Is everything set for Cinderella's coming-out party?"

"I haven't gone overboard."

"Really?"

"Any word from *your* parents? Are they coming to the party?"

He shrugged. "Don't know. I've done my part and told them how pigheaded they are being."

Cassidy swallowed hard. She'd made every effort. They would have to come around on their own. She wouldn't let her failed relationship with her parents ruin Courtney's first birthday. "Are you still working on the project for the city council?"

"Wrapping it up. Have you heard from Kirkland? Is he deliberately avoiding me?"

"He's trying to straighten this mess out."

"The mess he made."

"He admits what he's done wasn't in the best interest of Hannaford."

"It wasn't in the best interest of anyone—except himself."

She waved away the comment. "Don't start, Darius. Kirkland is a good person. He's going to take care of this."

"I hope so," he mumbled. "I'll talk to him at the party."

"Do that, but don't cause a scene."

"I won't. I just want to know how he's going to get out of this land deal."

Days later, everything had been decided on for Courtney's birthday party, and Kirkland still hadn't called. Cassidy tossed and turned through the night and couldn't concentrate on her work. Hard to paint romantic book covers when your heart is twisted into a tight knot. The health scare had really spooked Kirkland. Before he left for Chicago, he talked about correcting life mistakes and becoming a man everyone could be proud of. He was much too hard on himself. Sure, he had made some mistakes, and his judgment hadn't been right every single time he needed to make a decision, but he wasn't perfect. He needed to stop trying to be. She didn't tell him this, though. *Let a man be a man.* He had to work it out in his head the best way he knew how. She would support him through the process. She just missed him so much she felt lost, and a little bit vulnerable.

Unable to sleep, she slid into her slippers and robe and ventured into the backyard. She checked

Courtney first. Courtney lay on her back with her tiny fists balled tight as she snored lightly. Cassidy envied her daughter for being able to sleep so hard.

"What are you doing out here?"

She whirled toward the voice, clutching her chest. "Kirkland! You scared me half to death."

He greeted her with a tender kiss. "What are you doing outside so late? In your pajamas?"

"Couldn't sleep. What are you doing here?"

He wove his arm around her waist protectively. "Working on Courtney's birthday present."

"What?" She craned her neck around, but Kirkland blocked her vision by offering his kiss.

"You're too curious," he scolded.

She fought to clear her head of the dizzying kiss. "I've missed you. How did it go in Chicago?"

His brow furrowed. "Enlightening."

"Doesn't sound too good."

He pulled her tight against his body. "You want to hear about it?"

"You want to tell me about it?" Part of her letting Kirkland be his own man included knowing when not to press him for information. When faced with a dilemma, he tended to pull back and work the problem out on his own. From what she had heard from Sutton, this was a good sign. He didn't rely on others to solve his problems.

He took her hand and led her to the back porch. They sat together while he told her an incredible story of lies and betrayal.

"What are you going to do with this information?" She kneaded his hands between hers, offering comfort.

"I did a lot of thinking while I was in Chicago." He straightened his back, sitting tall. "I've made some major life decisions. I'm going to make drastic changes to my life."

Her heart fluttered. "Do any of these changes have anything to do with me?"

He pulled her into the muscled protection of his body. "Everything I do has your name written on it somewhere."

"Are you going to tell me what these drastic changes are going to be?"

He nodded. His expression didn't give a clue. "I'll tell you everything soon enough. The first thing I have to do is face Sutton."

They shared a comfortable silence.

"I hope my parents show for Courtney's party. Darius saw them, but he said he couldn't get a good read on them."

He kissed her forehead. "It'll all work out."

"If they come, we're just going to have a good time. No arguing, or big emotional talks. We're going to enjoy Courtney as a family. I don't want her party ruined."

"It's going to be a blast."

She lightened the mood. "Is Chevy coming?"

He shrugged. "I haven't asked. Why?"

She smiled, anxious to play matchmaker. "Maddie is wild over him."

He pushed away to clearly see her face. "Chevy?"

"Don't sound so surprised. Chevy is handsome, kind, intelligent—"

He stopped her diatribe with a heated kiss. "Hey. You're going to make me jealous."

"With kisses like this? You don't have anything to worry about."

They shared several more kisses before he pulled away, bringing her to stand with him. "I have to go."

"Go?" The abbreviated make-out session left her wanting more.

"I have to catch up since I've been away. I stopped by, hoping your light would be on."

"Stay."

"I can't. I'm being responsible now, remember?" She poked out her bottom lip.

"Stop." His thumb caressed her lip. "I'll tuck you in."

A large smile bloomed. "If you put it that way."

# Chapter 29

"Why did you call me here, Kirkland?" Sutton's anger had not dissipated since the last time he saw her. Of course, she hadn't jumped across his desk and scratched up his face, so maybe she wasn't as angry as before.

"I thought this would be a better place for us to talk." Kirkland gestured for her to have a seat in front of his desk.

"Where's Greyson?"

"I didn't invite him. I wanted to talk to you alone."

Her expression changed. Suspicion showed in her eyes. "Are you sure that's smart?"

"We've been friends since we were kids. Your first husband was my best friend. Your current husband is my brother. If that isn't enough history between us to allow a civil conversation, I don't know if Greyson being here would help."

This seemed to deflate her anger some. She loosened up, dropping her purse to the floor beside her. "What do you want to talk to me about?"

He chanced coming around his desk and sitting in the chair next to her. "First of all, I want to apologize to you. I shouldn't have gone along with Alex when I knew what he was doing was wrong. I won't make excuses for it anymore. I felt obligated to him because he was my best friend. I should have felt the same obligation to you. I'm sorry."

She shifted in the seat. Her scowl softened, but she wasn't ready to verbally acknowledge his apology. He forged on. "My part in it all also hurt Sierra. You have to know I love her and would never hurt her on purpose. I'm going to spend the rest of my life making it up to her." His words were passionate—real, very real. He pushed away the chest tightening that choked him when he thought of Alex.

Sutton shifted again. "I haven't been treating you as fairly as I should," she admitted. "I can't hold you responsible for everything Alex did." Her anger slipped away, giving way to the painful suffering she had endured over the years. "Your part in it all—I was so hurt by it." She turned away from him, collecting herself before facing him again. "I can't give you what you want right now."

"What do you think I want?"

"You want me to forgive you."

He wanted to hug her and tell her everything would be all right. He wanted to assure her their relationship was reparable and they would become even closer than they had been as kids. He had learned from his past experiences that things don't always work out the way you want them to. Sutton might never be able to forgive him. He was the symbol of her husband's sins—and now his indiscretions were being tossed back in her face in the form of an illegitimate child. She might never get beyond the hurt and betrayal.

"Sutton." He tried to convey his emotions through his tone. "I do want you to forgive me for what I've done, but I know it'll take time—if it happens at all. I know I have to prove to you I've changed. I'm not the spoiled youngest Ballantyne brother anymore. I'm living my life, taking responsibility for my wrongs, and trying to make good to the ones I love." He almost reached for her hand, but caught himself, not wanting to force too much on her at once. "All I ask, Sutton, is that you give me a chance to prove I would never do anything to hurt you again."

"You have to give me time. Don't push me."

"Fair enough."

She searched his face for sincerity. "Okay, then." She reached for her purse, but he stopped her. She listened unblinkingly as he told her Pete Frawley's story. Her reaction, like his brothers', was expected. The Galloway and Ballantyne families were destined to live interwoven lives.

"I want to make it right for him," Kirkland told her.

"How are you going to do that?"

"I want to give him the land Alex left me, but I couldn't make the offer without talking to you first. You and Sierra own three-fourths of the land, which will make you neighbors. I don't know how good of a neighbor Pete will be. Once he gets the land, he might go away and leave us all alone. Or he might not like having only a portion and fight for more. I don't know."

"You should definitely make him the offer. Speaking as someone who didn't receive her fair share, I wouldn't do it to another person. Sierra and I will deal with him if it becomes necessary."

"I'll talk to Pete and let you know how it goes."

"The only thing . . . It's not right you walk away with nothing. Alex wouldn't have wanted it that way—you were his best friend."

"I'll be fine."

"No," Sutton said sternly. "Sierra and I are fine. We needed this property two years ago. Now Greyson has provided us with a good life. I'm in law school, so I'll be financially secure soon. Alex leaving us penniless taught me a good lesson. I want you to split the land fifty-fifty with Pete Frawley."

"No. Alex would want me to give it to you."

"Frankly, it doesn't matter what Alex would want when it comes to me. He left us with nothing. What's important to me is my new family. Greyson hasn't said anything, but I know him. The land— the baby—this is eating him up. He is the provider for our family—not Alex. I'll rely on him to take care of us." She stood, shoving her purse onto her shoulder. "Split the land with Pete."

He watched her walk away a much more confident person than she had been a few years ago. He hoped he could make such a drastic change in his own life. She stopped at the door, gripping the doorknob. "I'm glad we talked." She left before he could tell her he was happy things had gone civilly between them.

Pete's in-your-face posturing reminded Kirkland of Alex's business demeanor. With more confidence, Pete would resemble Alex—eerily so.

Kirkland didn't know how he had missed the resemblance. You could see the stressful life Pete had led in his tight facial features, but soften the lines and add a teasing smile and you had Alex's face. The resemblance brought memories of Alex crashing in on him. Instinctively, he pressed his hand into his abdomen. He faithfully took his medications every morning, but today he needed a double dose.

"You had the nerve to come on my territory without your back up?" Pete scowled, taking the offensive. "Or are your brothers waiting for you to lure me outside?"

"I came to make you an offer." Kirkland followed Pete around the warehouse. Employees in hard hats glanced up, nodded, and went back to their repetitive jobs on the assembly line.

Pete waited until they were inside his office with the door closed before he asked, "What kind of offer?" He hung his hard hat next to the door and sat behind his desk.

Kirkland sat in the wobbly metal chair. "I know you've been calling in bomb threats against the paper mill." He rushed on, stopping Pete's denial. "I also know you're Mr. Galloway's son."

It took a minute for Pete to recover. "How'd you find out?"

"It's not important. I'm glad you're not going to deny it. It makes things much easier for us both."

"How's that, Ballantyne?"

"I'm prepared to offer you half of the Galloway land."

"Half?" A million questions flashed in his eyes. He asked suspiciously, "What's the catch?"

"The only catch is you not use the land for industrial development—ever."

"And the land's mine? Free and clear?"

He nodded, understanding Pete's suspicion. "Why?"

"If I'm right, you only want what should be rightfully yours. You don't want to destroy the mill, or Hannaford Valley. You have a right to be angry. I talked with Sutton, and she agrees. You're entitled to a portion of the land."

His suspicion remained. "You and Sutton are keeping the other part? To make sure I do what you want me to do with it?"

"I'm holding onto the other half, yes. I already know how I'm going to develop it. You're welcome to come in on the deal if it suits you."

"And that's it? No strings?"

"You'll have to sign a contract agreeing not to sell it to commercial developers, or do any industrial building yourself. Other than those terms, it's all yours."

"Why are you doing this? After what I did—"

"Because it's the right thing to do." Kirkland stood and offered his hand. "I hope we can forget the past and learn to be good neighbors."

Pete rose slowly, but accepted his offer of civility. "Tell me what you have in mind for your acreage."

The best thing about having Cassidy was the way she responded when Kirkland came around. There was always a smile waiting for him. It didn't matter if it had been an hour or a week since he'd seen her; she welcomed him home as if he were returning from a long trip. This evening was no different. When he showed up at her place unannounced, she pulled him inside, into her arms for a hug and sensuous kiss.

"Have you had dinner?" He greeted Courtney by lifting her in the air and spinning around in an elaborate circle. She had inherited the happy demeanor of her mother.

"I was about to sit down. I'm glad you're here to provide some adult conversation."

They shared a laugh because before she could finish the compliment, he was conversing with Courtney in the secret language only they could understand. Cassidy had told him to cut it out, afraid Courtney wouldn't develop her speaking skills if he encouraged her unintelligible babbling. She withdrew her request when he explained the language he shared with Courtney was taken from the French he'd learned in college. She had been highly impressed to find out her child would be bilingual by the time she could form complete sentences. He hadn't shared that he read an article in a parenting magazine encouraging parents to raise bilingual children to work in a global community.

"Can I persuade you to have dinner with me tonight?" he asked. "I have reservations at the Charleston Inn."

She whistled. "The Charleston Inn. What's the occasion?"

"Does there have to be an occasion for me to take you out to dinner?"

"No, but the Charleston Inn is pretty swank."

He checked the time. "I'll pack Courtney a bag while you dress."

She crossed her arms over her chest in mocked defiance. "And exactly where is my child going?"

"Greyson and Sutton agreed to keep her."

A thousand questions were asked in the knitting of her eyebrows. She left them unsaid. "Give me fifteen minutes."

He took Courtney into her room while he packed her diaper bag. He kept her entertained while he packed the essentials. Caring for her had become second nature. He knew just what she would need. He didn't forget to pack her favorite toys. After assembling her bag, he changed her out of her pajamas into something to protect her from the cool evening.

"I could do this for the rest of your life," he told her. "Would you let me?"

Courtney cooed. "Hi" and "Mama" were the extent of her recognizable vocabulary.

"I wonder what you'll be like when you're fifteen?" He slipped her arms into a soft green sweater. "Cassidy is going to be the strict parent. I was so wild when I was fifteen, I think I'll identify with you better."

Her arms shot out for him, wanting to be lifted into his arms. He happily obliged.

"Although," he laughed, "knowing how boys are at that age, I might be the one you have to worry about." He brought her close and she wrapped her arms around his neck. "I should ask your permission before I go making plans for the rest of your life. Do you want me to be your daddy?"

"Da—da—da—da."

His heart flip-flopped. He craned his neck across the hall, wanting Cassidy to be a witness to Courtney's declaration. Between the two of them, it had been decided. He was inevitably entwined in their future.

He kissed Courtney's cheek. "I love you." Emotion welled in his eyes. He hadn't felt so overwhelmed with raw emotion since learning about Alex's death. What he felt for Courtney tilted the spectrum the other way. These feelings were good, warm, and ever-lasting. Regardless of how Cassidy received his wishes for their future, Courtney would love him like a father. And he would be a good father to her. He would mold his actions after his own father. Pop might not have been perfect, but he was close. He didn't openly display his emotions, but there was never a doubt he loved his family and would sacrifice anything for them. Kirkland didn't understand the indiscretion with Eileen, but if his mother could forgive it, he had no choice but to honor her decision.

"What do you think?" Cassidy stood in the door-way, arms spread wide, awaiting his approval.

He whistled long and low. "You're the prettiest woman in Hannaford Valley."

Cassidy twirled around in a lazy circle, watching him watch her. The slinky dress matched the red silk tie accenting his black suit. Backless, the mate-rial of the dress reappeared just above her full be-hind. Thick curls floated above her almond shoulders. She blinked her heavy lashes at him as she completed her circle. Her sly smile told him she was happy with the response she elicited from him. He put Courtney into her crib and placed his hands on the cradle of Cassidy's rounded hips. He guided her close, pressing his body firmly against hers. "You like doing this to me." He punctuated his meaning with the flex of his hips.

"Love it."

"And I thought you were innocent when I first met you." He lifted a chunky curl and brought it to his nose. He inhaled jasmine. "You fooled me."

"How so?"

He placed his chin atop her head. He liked her height—great for cuddling and perfect for dancing. Tonight, he would keep her in his arms on the dance floor until she begged him to make love to her. "You're a devil in red." He pressed a kiss against her temple. "Do you want to skip dinner?"

"The offer is very appealing, but I've never been to the Charleston Inn."

He clucked his tongue in mock annoyance. "Do you have a jacket?"


Cassidy sighed when they stepped into the amazing six-story atrium of the Charleston Inn. The contemporary décor of the restaurant was highlighted by an art-filled atrium constructed of windows and mirrors. The mountains and the river below filled most of the 360-degree view. "There's our moon," she said, pointing up above.

They would have a skylight in their bedroom above their bed.

The Charleston Inn was composed of five handsomely decorated private dining rooms, each jam-packed with elite business owners and celebrities seeking asylum from adoring fans. The banquet and private rooms were filled, easily reaching the 1,000-person capacity on a Friday night. Well-suited men and sophisticated women swarmed the bar and lounge area. Men nodded, letting their eyes linger on Cassidy too long for Kirkland's liking as they moved in and out of the Cigar Room. There was a wait for counter seating, so many patrons sipped from their cocktails, making small talk. Kirkland and Cassidy passed the full bar and entered the nonsmoking area off the outdoor patio where they would have dinner. He had requested the table specifically, knowing they would spend most of their evening dancing on the patio, taking in the view of the mountains. His hand guided Cassidy to follow the maître d' as he showed them to their table. Kirkland couldn't help sticking out his chest a little. He had gone to great pains to plan this special night for her. Many promises had been made and a very large advance tip had been given. Their relationship had grown from the newness of getting to know each other to handling life problems. Tonight, he wanted to give Cassidy a bit of magic. He wanted her to feel special and know she was loved.

"Look at the view!" Cassidy exclaimed as he pulled out her chair.

"Sir," the maître d' asked, "would the lady prefer a table on the patio? The weather tonight is perfect for outdoor dining."

Cassidy peered up at him, her eyes as big as saucers.

"A table on the patio would be great." Already he was digging in his pocket for another tip.

With prompting, Cassidy took their waiter's suggestion and ordered seared Maine diver sea scallops with lobster and teardrop tomato salsa, lemon risotto, and basil froth. Kirkland found his adventure with a watercress salad mixed with Maytag blue cheese, shaved radishes, Vidalia onions, and pepper bacon. A traditional grilled steak would be his main course. They sampled the basket of the house breads, rolls, and muffins—sourdough and focaccia with rosemary and olive flavorings added to give a gourmet flair.

The waiter appeared as they completed their main course. "Dessert?" The dessert platter was brought to their table, but they couldn't decide what to have so Kirkland ordered everything. They fed each other white chocolate ravioli with hazelnut crème anglaise, fresh fruits sprinkled with confections, and house-made vanilla ice cream and raspberry sorbet.

Cassidy wrapped her arms around his waist on the dance floor as he kissed away the last droplets of raspberry sorbet. "What did I do to deserve this night?" she asked.

"You love me."

"It's so easy to do."

"You're such a loving person you don't realize how wrong you are."

"I wasn't so easy to convince at first."

He laughed, remembering his first shunned attempt at seducing her. "No, you weren't, but I'm persistent."

"Good thing." She laid her head against his shoulder as they moved to the music. "Can we stay here forever?"

"If I could make it happen, I would." He meant his words. "What would you take home with you if you could?"

"The view. The food." She stopped abruptly, locking her eyes with his. "Scratch what I just said. This evening is so special because of the way I feel about you. If I could take anything home with me, it would be your love. I'd want to bottle your love and keep it with me forever."

"Forever?" *Finally.* He realized her mind was contemplating their future.

"Forever." She smiled. "I sound like the romance novels I illustrate, don't I?"

He held up two fingers, measuring. "A pinch." He kissed the corner of her mouth. "And I love it."

They swayed in loving silence while the band played two more romantic tunes.

"Guess what Courtney did tonight?" He watched her expression closely, knowing his revelation could swing either way, evoking a positive or negative reaction. "She called me Dada."

"Did she? Really?" She gave no clue as to how she felt about it.

"Please don't tell me I've been spending too much time with her if she sees me as a father figure."

"You aren't her father. Does it bother you to have it forced on you?"

"I have never been as happy as I was when Courtney called me Da."

They rocked side-to-side, body contact being more important than dancing.

"I visited a support group today," he announced boldly.

"A support group? What kind of support group? Why?" Concern consumed her face.

"I need to find a better way to handle Alex's

death. The grief is making me physically sick." The hospital admission for the bleeding ulcer had been a harsh call to reality. "How do you feel about it?"

"I am proud of you. Alex was like a brother to you. It takes time to get over losing someone so close. You need to talk with other people who are going through the same thing."

"It doesn't change your feelings about me? You don't think I'm weak if I'm a man who needs a support group to handle a friend's death?"

"I think you have to be pretty strong to ignore the stereotypes and seek the help you need. You have my respect for what you've decided to do."

"Taking control of my life has wonderful fringe benefits."

# Chapter 30

The house was quiet, except for Courtney's light snoring. Cassidy looked up at Kirkland and they burst into laughter.

"She must be really tired," he said.

"Sierra is a handful."

"Greyson will have his hands full when she becomes a teenager."

Feeling unequally undressed as she stood before him in her nightgown, she began to loosen his tie. "Sierra and Courtney are well on their way to forming an unbreakable bond, which means you'll have your hands full too, Mr. Ballantyne."

He smiled, completely satisfied with the challenge.

Her fingers moved to the buttons of his soft, black shirt. The tuft of sandy-brown hair on his chest peeked out at her, encouraging her to reveal more of his body. He watched her with raw intensity, as she removed layer after layer of his clothing. Caught up in the glory of a young, lean, splendid body, she moved around him with the sleekness of a predatory feline. He did something to her, and she let him know. "You excite me."

"Good."

She slipped her arms around his waist from behind, and unbuckled his belt. Hurriedly, she opened
his pants and pushed them down sinewy legs that
seemed to never end.

"Help yourself," he whispered and she thought
she would melt into a puddle at his feet. When had
he taken complete control of her mind and body?

He turned to face her. She expected him to say
something funny, flip, or seductive to spur on her
aggressiveness. He placed his hands on her shoulders. "I love you, Cassidy. I want to spend the rest of
my life with you."

"What you're doing to me now . . ." Her eyes
roamed his body, fixating on his erection. "Let's see
if I can survive *this* moment."

Only someone who knew Kirkland as well as she
did would have noticed the subtle change in his expression. She'd said something wrong, but she
didn't know what it could have been. Her mind
wasn't in the analytical mood—not with him standing nude in her bedroom. She licked the tip of her
finger and used it to trace the birthmark on his
inner thigh. He moved suddenly, scooping her up
and pulling her, hard, into his body. He crushed
her in his arms, kissing her neck and collarbone.

"Lift me."

His maddening kisses stopped. His hazel eyes
darkened with emotion. "Can I make love to you?
Are you ready for me?"

She smiled in recognition of their first time.
"Thought I was, but I was wrong." Her breath came
in short puffs. "Couldn't have imagined how you
were going to change my world."

"I'm not done yet." He lowered his head, taking

control of her emotions through his kiss. "I've only just begun to change your world, Cassidy."

"I've never been this—"

"In love?"

"In love, and—"

"And?"

"Crazy, excited—happy in my life." She had no control over her hands as they traveled over the hard planes of his body. "Lift me," she panted.

He gathered the hem of her gown and lifted it over her head. Tossing the gown across the room, he dropped to the floor. He filled his hands with her bottom as he tasted the back of her knees. She dropped to the carpet with him and he hurriedly arranged her beneath him. She lifted her hips, anxious to have him inside her. Tonight he controlled every crevice of her heart and mind; now she offered her body, sacrificing sanity for the pleasure he offered. He pressed her wrists into the carpet, stilling her as his tongue journeyed over the curves of her body.

"I want *you* inside *me*," he whispered against her hip. His hands slipped beneath her, lifting her hips off the floor. Her thighs fell apart and his head disappeared into the opening. He drank from her, tasted her, and consumed her until she began to shudder from the pleasure. She begged him to stop. He ignored her pleas. He devoured her gift until she submitted, falling under his spell in utter capitulation.

She lay on the carpet, breathing hard and needing time to recover before she could speak. He did not allow it. He stood, lifting her into his arms and carried her to the bed. They fell down together and he entered her quickly. He joined with her in a rush, but his hips thrust languidly as he made love to her. He awoke her passion with the painful look of desperation on his face. His eyes were squeezed tightly closed, and perspiration covered his forehead.

She ran comforting fingers through his tight curls. "What's wrong?" she whispered.

His eyes flipped open, unaware his emotions were so visually telling. "What?" he panted, losing his rhythm.

"You look like you're . . . desperate."

"I am." No hint of his joking personality.

"Why?"

"I'm desperate to keep you in my life."

She cradled his face. "I'm not going anywhere."

"I've been trying to get you to discuss our future for weeks. You keep avoiding it."

She tried to recall the conversations he referred to. Things had been so hectic in their lives lately, she had been too distracted, missing his need for assurance.

"I'm not going anywhere, Kirkland," she promised.

His nose brushed the shell of her ear. "I want to come home, Cass." He placed a finger beneath her chin.

"Then come home, Kirkland. You're welcomed here."

It seemed enough for him. He began to rotate his hips again, watching her, looking through her into her soul.

"Really. I'm not going anywhere," she whispered, bringing his mouth to hers. She kissed him deeply, making a thousand promises in one wordless exchange. He toppled quickly, gyrating his hips with heightened intensity. He kissed her wildly, finding the release he needed in the safety of her body.

# Chapter 31

Cassidy's backyard was transformed into a child's wonderland. A giant tent consumed the small yard. The circus theme promised fun for everyone at the party. She had hired a clown and there would be plenty of snow cones, cotton candy, and popcorn. Hamburgers and hot dogs with plenty of vegetable sticks would keep the kids full. Adults would have the luxury of barbecued chicken and steak. She had gone overboard and over budget with the party, but at one year old, Courtney's birthday party would be a celebration of Cassidy's greatest achievement. She'd used the funds from two commissioned paintings to cover the costs, refusing to let Kirkland contribute one penny. He had offered, but she would not allow it. She loved him for much more than his financial worth. He had to know that. Sutton had imparted upon her the importance of maintaining financial independence and this small gesture was a way of keeping it. It would be too easy to be blinded by Kirkland's overwhelming perfection and let him do everything for her financially, emotionally, and physically, but she had to be smart and in love. Anything else could leave her devastated.

As Cassidy checked the last-minute preparations

for the party, she hoped her parents would realize their importance in Courtney's life and share in the celebration.

"People should start arriving in thirty minutes," Maddie said.

"I should get dressed." Cassidy headed inside. "Did I tell you Chevy told Kirkland he would be here?"

"Cassidy!"

"What?" she giggled.

"No, you *forgot* to mention it."

"Well, don't freak out on me. I need you to help me run this circus." A play on words only a librarian could appreciate.

"Look at the way I'm dressed!"

"You're the hostess. You should be dressed like a clown. You're adorable."

"I'm a clown!" Maddie marched her into the house. "If I'm dressed up like a clown, *you're* dressing up like a clown."

The guests loved the two clowns who greeted them at the entrance of the circus tent. Courtney squealed and giggled when she discovered the clown with red apple cheeks was her mother. Mr. and Mrs. Ballantyne were among the first to arrive, along with Chevy. With a little prompting, Cassidy managed to get Maddie and Chevy in the same place, at the same time. Nature would have to step in and do the rest.

"What I said upset you; I apologize." Cassidy swung around, surprised to find Mrs. Ballantyne had joined her in the kitchen. She stepped to the sink and washed her hands, preparing to help Cassidy replenish the snack platters. "I love all my boys equally, but

Kirkland has always been special to me, because I'm special to him. Maybe it's because he's the youngest. I don't know." Mrs. Ballantyne pulled the plastic covering off a vegetable platter and began to add dipping sauce. "Whatever it is, we've always been very close and I'm not ashamed to admit I was a little jealous of his relationship with you."

"I'm not using him. I love him."

"I understand now."

They completed the platters, making small talk. Cassidy viewed it as a beginning. Sutton was complimentary of Mama Ballantyne and Cassidy hoped to develop a close relationship with Kirkland's mother too. Today, they put bad blood behind them and began to get to know each other.

Sutton tried to make a quiet, discrete entrance, but Sierra's squeals of delight wouldn't allow it. Sutton wore a smile, but those who knew her realized there was much effort behind it. Cassidy managed to steal a few minutes alone with her. "How are you doing?"

"Emotionally whipped. I'm trying to find a way to come to terms with everything. Greyson wants me to push it away as part of the past, but it's not in the past for me." She shook her head in defeat. "Alex hid so many secrets from me and they're still haunting me."

"Greyson is a good man. He'll do whatever's necessary to help you get through it."

"And right now his solution to everything is having a baby." She scanned the crowd for her husband. "He is a good man."

Cassidy hugged her shoulders. "You're made for each other."

"Hey, enough about me. I promise you there

won't be any fireworks today." Sutton craned her neck. "Where is Kirkland?"

"He hasn't arrived yet."

"I thought he would be greeting people at the door. You know he acts like Courtney is his."

"Courtney encourages it."

Greyson waved to Sutton from across the yard.

"Go have fun. We should get together for lunch next week with Maddie." Cassidy nodded in Maddie's direction. She was in an isolated corner with Chevy. "I think she might have something to tell us."

Cassidy mingled with the crowd, making light conversation and checking the food supplies. She hadn't been able to keep Courtney in her arms for more than five minutes since the party began. Courtney was crawling around with the other kids at the party, or perched on someone's hip as they cooed about how much she had grown in a year.

"Look who I found." Kirkland's warm hand brushed her waist, turning her into his kiss.

"I thought I'd have to send Greyson and Chevy after you."

Kirkland stepped back, and her parents came into view. There was a moment of awkwardness where she reminded herself there would be no arguing and no big emotional scenes at her daughter's birthday party.

"Where's the birthday girl?" Dad asked.

"I saw her with the other kids in the tent," Kirkland volunteered.

"Congratulations." Mom kissed Cassidy's cheek, handing off Courtney's brightly wrapped birthday present. "Let's go see our granddaughter."

Kirkland held Cassidy from behind as she watched her parents head toward the tent. "They came," she whispered. She tilted her head back to see him. "What do you think this means?"

"I think they love their daughter and want to get to know their granddaughter."

Like most parties, after a time the men and women separated into two groups. Kirkland took on the responsibility of hosting the men, boldly asserting his place in Cassidy's home. Darius had been avoiding him for most of the party, so he took the first opportunity to approach him. Family was as important to Cassidy as it was to him, and he needed everyone to approve of his future with her.

"I was skeptical about you when I found out you were dating my sister," Darius admitted. "The land deal didn't make it any better. But your brothers explained everything to me."

"What I did was wrong. I don't make any excuses about it. I love Cassidy and I love Courtney. I would never do anything to hurt them."

"My father was impressed with you coming by to try to repair their relationship with Cassidy." He drained his drink. "I am too."

They shook hands before Kirkland left to stand with Greyson and Chevy as Cassidy helped Courtney rip through her presents.

"I'm going to need a beer after this," Greyson said.

"You love kids, and you know it," Chevy chastised. "Nobody told you to roll around on the ground with all those babies."

Greyson hid his smile behind his fist. "You want to get a drink after, or not?"

"I'm in," Chevy answered.

"Count me out." Kirkland's eyes never left Cassidy's smile.

"Have you told her yet?" Chevy wanted to know.

"Told who, what?" Greyson went ignored.

"I gave her the bank papers for Courtney's college fund a little while ago."

"Nice gift," Greyson said.

"No matter what, her college will be paid for in full." He valued education—Alex had showed him the importance of holding an advanced degree. He had watched so many of his peers being forced out of college because of financial issues. He never wanted Courtney to be faced with those problems.

"What about the other stuff?" Chevy asked.

"What other stuff? You two never tell me anything," Greyson said.

"Because you tell Sutton everything and Sutton will tell Cassidy," Kirkland explained.

"What's going on?" Greyson pressed.

"You'll have to wait." Kirkland weaved through the crowd, leaving Greyson confused. Kirkland stood on the fringes, watching the joy in Cassidy's eyes. When Courtney spotted him, her arms shot out to him. He proudly stepped forward, lifting her for a kiss. She squirmed, wanting to be put down. He sat her on the ground and she crawled to her feet using his pants leg for leverage. She took two wobbly steps toward her mother. Tears ran down Cassidy's face as she cuddled Courtney. "She did it."

He joined them, giving each a kiss.

\* \* \*

The party ended at dusk. Parents tossed their exhausted children over their shoulders like potato sacks, carrying them home. Kirkland proudly cradled a sleeping Courtney in his arms as he stood with Cassidy seeing everyone off. The smile never faded from her face. Everything had come together nicely, and the party had served to heal many wounds.

"I'm beat," Cassidy said as they went inside. "Maddie and Sutton are going to help me clean up the backyard tomorrow."

"The cleaning service will take care of it." He stopped her before she could argue. "I've already scheduled everything. The bill has been paid in full. If you make me cancel, they'll still get paid."

She wouldn't let him throw away good money. "Thank you," she conceded. "I'm going to wash away this clown makeup. What's left of it anyway." The powder-white face and cherry-red cheeks had begun to fade.

He carried Courtney to bed. He was careful not to disturb her sleep as he undressed her. He covered her with a light blanket, kissed her cheek, and rejoined Cassidy in the living room.

She flopped down beside him on the sofa. "Courtney had a good time."

"Courtney had a great time."

She laid her head on his shoulder. "Will you stay?"

"Of course I'll stay. I want to take you and Courtney to breakfast in the morning."

She yawned. "I need a shower. Join me?"

"You're tired. How about a bath instead?"

She purred.

He drew her a hot bath with too many bubbles. He carried her weary body from the living room to the bathroom and peeled off her clothes. She relaxed in the tub while he lined the sink with vanilla-scented tea candles. While she bathed, he prepared his surprise. After slipping out of his clothes, he helped Cassidy from the tub. They laughed together as he dried her and applied cream to her back. Quiet, stolen moments like these made him love her much more.

"What's all this?" Cassidy asked when she entered her bedroom.

He took her hand, leading her to the bed. "These are the preliminary plans for Ballantyne Wilderness Lodge."

"Ballantyne Wilderness Lodge," she repeated in a whisper.

"Yes. I've found a way to develop my land without destroying Hannaford Valley. It's a twenty-seven-acre vacation resort. See how it backs up to the forest." He pointed out the detail on the blueprint and then the artist's sketches. "Chevy designed the rustic homes. Each has five private suites with wet bar, private balcony, fireplace, and Jacuzzi tub. Each home will have its own library, TV room with satellite and videos, a great room with a large river rock fireplace, and an outdoor hot tub."

Cassidy climbed onto the bed to take a closer look at the drawings.

"I'd like to commission you for the artwork."

She batted her big brown eyes at him in disbelief.

"I'm planning snowmobiling, skiing, hiking, fishing, eagle watching, golfing, tennis, boating, and bicycling. Chevy has agreed to oversee the activities. He wants to keep a close eye on things—make sure we don't destroy the wildlife."

"Kirkland, this is breathtaking."

"Darius has agreed to meet with me about crunching the numbers—calculate the number of employees that'll be needed, forecast the revenue potential for Hannaford, that sort of thing."

"This is great." She held out her arms for him. He fell into her embrace and was greeted with a heated kiss. "You did it."

"Pete's going to use a portion of his land to build cabins to accommodate weddings, retreats, and meetings."

"I love you." The look in her eyes confirmed it. "I'm so proud of you for doing this."

He pulled her close. "I'm moving back to Hannaford . . . to be close to you and Courtney."

She pulled back just enough to see his face. "You're giving up the penthouse in Charleston?"

He nodded. "I quit my job there, too. I've decided to be a silent partner at the paper mill. I'm going to concentrate all my time on building Ballantyne Wilderness Lodge . . . and making you and Courtney happy."

"Are you sure you want to do this? Will you be happy?"

"Will I be happy making you and Courtney happy? Hell, yeah. I've taken a lot of time to think about this. I've talked it over with my parents and my brothers. Now I'm talking it over with you. This is what I want to do—make a good life for you and Courtney. Will you let me?"

She answered him with her kiss.

"Tomorrow, after breakfast, I want to take you to my parents' old house. I've been doing some work there—modernizing it. I'll stay there until the lodge is completed."

"You really have been busy."

"You asked me, now I want to know. Will spending more time with me make you happy?"

"Ecstatic."

# Chapter 32

"Hello."

"Kirkland? Has something happened? Are you okay?"

"I'm fine, Cassidy."

"You've never called me on the phone . . ."

"Did you like the work I've done on my parents' old house?"

"It's great."

"What do you think about giving up your mortgage and moving in with me?"

"Moving in . . . as in living together?"

"As in, will you marry me?"

The phone thudded across the carpet.

"Cassidy?" He laughed. "Cassidy? Pick up the phone, baby."

"Who is this?"

"Will you marry me?"

"This is a cruel joke, whoever you are."

"It's me, Kirkland Douglas Ballantyne. And this is no joke. Will you marry me?"

A pause—much too long.

"I love you. Will you marry me, Cassidy?"

"Yes."

"Really? I couldn't hear you."

"Yes!"

A sharp intake of breath. "Let me speak to Court-ney. I need to ask her if I can be her daddy."

Cassidy giggled.

"While I'm discussing it with Courtney, pick up the package on the front porch."

Cassidy dropped the receiver and flung the front door open. Kirkland stood on the top step hold-ing a ring box wrapped in gold foil.